A John Garrison Mystery

A RUDE RECEPTION

John Layne

First Edition 2024

eBook ISBN: 978-1-956856-49-1
Paperback ISBN: 978-1-956856-40-7

Library of Congress Control No.: 2024907686

Published by thewordverve (www.thewordverve.com)
Canton, GA

Cover and print interior design by Robin Krauss
www.bookformatters.com

eBook design by thewordverve

For Christine Baker
Colleague, Mentor, Friend

CHAPTER 1

THURSDAY

A dense layer of gray clouds shrouded the post-midnight moon, casting a shadowy canvas over the Kutseena County Administration Building. Built two years earlier north of Bison, Texas, its low-bid security features included a single lamp illumining the front entrance and an alarm system containing two weak dual-tone sirens affixed to opposite corners of the building's exterior. With no video cameras present, there would be no video evidence of the dark figure approaching the building's lone rear window.

The burglar, clad in a black hooded shirt with gloves to match, crouched under the window as his bolt cutters sliced through the padlock on the alarm system's control box. A quick snip of wires rendered the system irrelevant.

The rear window was the standard tempered glass, double-glazed slider with two rotating levers that fraudulently passed as locks. The burglar placed a strip of electrical tape over the glass in front of the latch, then placed a tape-covered flathead screwdriver at the bottom edge of the glass, directly in front of the first latch. A firm strike with the palm of his hand pushed the tip through both layers of glass, producing a small hole with barely a sound. After repeating the procedure on the second latch, the burglar slid the window up and slithered through its gaping mouth.

He switched on a small flashlight, then swiftly passed the costly electronic devices adorning each desk and targeted the filing cabinets at the back of the room. Discovering the metal drawers were unlocked, the burglar cracked a gaping grin, exposing two rows of rotted teeth.

After rummaging through numerous folders, the burglar located the prized file. He quickly replaced the genuine documents with counterfeit copies provided by his employer.

After checking that everything was in order, he slipped out the window.

The thought of getting $10,000 for such an easy job danced around in his mind. The random phone calls from a nameless voice, blocked numbers, and the long trip from El Paso were damn worth it. The first $5,000 up front, and the other five when the courier received the stolen documents at an abandoned gas station south of Bison.

The burglar peeled the tape off the window, collected the few glass fragments not captured by the sticky tape, and closed the window. He slipped a wire loop through the holes and closed the latches, covering the tiny openings in the glass, then reconnected the severed wires of the alarm before securing the box with a new padlock and disappearing into the black abyss of the night.

The burglar found the feeble chain used to secure the boarded-up front door of the abandoned gas station had been cut. Once inside, he found a small lantern, sleeping bag, food, and two bottles of vodka in the corner of the room near a cobweb-covered cash register.

He twisted the top off a plastic vodka bottle and took a long swig of the fiery fluid. The distilled spirit soothed his parched throat and calmed his trembling hands. He set the bottle down on the dusty counter and stripped off his sweat-soaked black clothing, then dressed in the clothes hidden inside the sleeping bag. He found a metal stool and sat, then took a few more gulps from the plastic bottle. He waited for the other $5,000 to be delivered. In fact, it would take three more days . . .

The old gas station's feeble walls creaked and screeched like a rusted hinge under the late-night assault of gale-force winds. The corroded screws and nails held on as the whipping wind did its West Texas best to rip them from their grasps. Long past its prime, the corrugated tin roof shuddered from the thirty-degree temperature drop that preceded what tomorrow's meteorologists would call a "West Texas haboob." Eyewitness reports of a twister or two would surely follow.

The burglar sat atop a rusty stool, seething at the fact he'd spent the last three days and nights in the trash-laden building. A nest of armadillos scurried about in the far corner of the room at the outer rim of the lantern's light ring. The lengthy stay in the rickety building included three hours spent huddled down in a dank hole passing as a storm shelter beneath the ramshackle wooden floor. He'd been forced to stay hidden while a group of idiot teenagers smoked weed and drank cheap beer the night before.

A glance at his watch confirmed eleven o'clock straight up. The howling wind pummeled the old building in every direction, generating the sound of a thundering locomotive. The mind-numbing clamor muffled the sound of the vehicle approaching from the adjacent dirt road.

The SUV's massive tires crept along the dirt road, crushing scrub and loose clumps of terrain recently tilled from nearby farmland. The wind whistled through the doorframe seams and rocked the vehicle like a ship on rough seas.

The courier killed the headlights as it neared the old gas station. Despite the pitch-black darkness, there was no threat of crashing into anything substantial since the land was flat as far as the eye could see. He parked directly behind the old station, slowly opened the driver's door, and stepped out into the unrelenting bombardment of the West Texas plains. Hanging onto the vehicle, the courier eased around the front end and dipped his head as low as he could before rushing around the building to the front door. After three attempts, and against the wind's objection, he finally opened the flimsy door. He stepped inside, breathing heavily. The battened door slammed shut behind him, causing four armadillo pups to scatter, their claws scrapping across the floor's warped surface.

The stench was overwhelming, causing him to grimace. He scanned the small space, finding the burglar staring at him across the dimly lit room. Cloaked in a long black coat and hood pulled up over his head and face, the courier stepped forward and pulled the hood back. The burglar's face immediately registered confusion.

"Who . . . who the hell are you?" the burglar exclaimed, backing up a step.

"I thought I'd come by and put you out of your misery," the courier announced.

"Put me out of my—"

Boom! The explosion of the semi-automatic pistol sent shockwaves into every crevice of the old building. The armadillo pups scattered, and a giant rat squealed in fear as it bolted across the room. The jacketed hollow-point bullet punctured the center of the burglar's forehead with a near-perfect sphere, the heated powder following right behind, burning a neat circle around the bullet's entry wound. The bullet found little resistance as it raced through brain matter before exiting the back of the skull, taking a half-dollar-sized jagged piece of bone with it.

Blood, bone, and brain matter splattered a mosaic pattern on the wall behind the burglar, whose body dropped to the floor with a thud. The courier slid the pistol into an ankle holster and secured it around the burglar's ankle. After removing a leather billfold from the burglar's right rear pants pocket, the courier flipped the wallet open and found three one-dollar bills, an expired Texas driver's license, and an old appointment card to one of those plasma donation facilities in El Paso. After slipping the wallet into his other coat pocket, the courier removed the burglar's watch and stepped around the old cash counter to pick up the file containing the prized documents. He then rolled up the sleeping bag and, after ensuring there were no other personal or identifying items left behind, took it with him as he coolly exited the building.

The front door slammed against its frame, causing one of the plywood sections to break free and crash to the ground. After another battle against the relentless wind, the courier fell into the driver's seat of the SUV and slammed the door shut. When he reached the dirt road, he flicked the headlights on, ensuring there were no unexpected obstacles in his path. Seeing none other than uprooted sage and thicket, he hit the gas, forging his way through the thick dust, dirt, and grit swirling into cone-like shapes.

The courier pulled off the road about a mile from the old gas station and abandoned the SUV. He had effectively eliminated any concerns about the police connecting the vehicle to him. It had been stolen from the Mexico side and retagged several times with new plates and registration, none of which led to an actual vehicle. The interior was clear of trace evidence that would identify the courier. The law would be at it for countless hours and days. Giving the police something to play with—something that would bring them absolutely no joy at all—brought the courier a mild sense of delight.

Nickel-size hail began to plummet like pellets from an icy shotgun blast, smashing into everything in its path.

The courier left the doors unlocked, hunkered down into his hooded coat, and quietly disappeared into the black abyss of the storm tunnel's gaping mouth.

CHAPTER 2

MONDAY

The constant hum of the air conditioner—a flimsy metal box bolted to the wall beneath the window—was intermittently interrupted by the clanging sound of two hammers banging together. The continuous clatter prevented any resemblance of a good night's sleep. The Houston Police Department's latest retiree lay on top of questionably hygienic linens, watching a giant black spider slowly crawl across the textured ceiling directly above his head. The ceiling, once covered by a fresh coat of white paint, now possessed a dull yellow hue, courtesy of years of cigarette smoke the room had endured. The man had declined the offer of a pleasing ranch-house room on a 200-acre cattle spread north of town, choosing the more politically correct decision to stay in town at the local motel. His fitful night of sleep proved again that politically correct decisions weren't always the best ones.

John Garrison wouldn't make that mistake again. After all, being politically correct wasn't his primary concern anyway.

At least he was working with a city-government schedule, meaning he didn't have to wake in the middle of the night for a ridiculously early-morning meeting. According to the mayor, this adventure would allegedly begin at 9:00 AM sharp. The cell phone buzzed, alerting the room's only occupant that 7:00 AM had finally arrived. The spider had made it clear across the room and was now working its way down the far wall, eventually disappearing behind what passed as a flat-screen television perched atop one of those do-it-yourself media stands made of particle board.

The faucet handle shrieked like a rusted hinge begging for oil, and the pipes shuddered inside the paper-thin wall. Finally, the water burst through the showerhead, pounding the tub floor like torrential rain. The water looked clean and was mainly odorless. The folks back in Houston had told Garrison to beware of the water in Bison, since the town sat on top of one of the country's largest oil and gas deposits—thus the immediate belief the water was contaminated.

After an unexpectedly refreshing shower, he slid the room's lone window curtain aside, allowing the morning's bright sunshine to penetrate the cave-like atmosphere. The sky was clear and blue as far as the eye could see. The West Texas sunrise didn't disappoint. The bright orange sphere looked like part of a blazing inferno that was already delivering punishing heat through the dirty window.

A quick check of the room for lingering belongings was followed by a hasty getaway past the front desk and out the door. Having paid in advance, there was no reason to stop and chitchat with the clerk. The pimple-faced kid might have set a world record for the most words spoken during a motel check-in the afternoon before.

Fifteen minutes later, the dark red Ford F-150 FX4 sat on the rise facing west toward the distant Guadalupe Mountain range that mostly called New Mexico home but whose majestic vistas were enjoyed by the residents of at least three bordering states. Notes about Bison and its history littered the front seat and dashboard, allowing for a final review before what was sure to be a thorough examination by the town's council members. Knowing the council meeting wouldn't begin until 9:30 AM at the earliest, the mayor had instructed him to meet in the town hall lobby at nine for a final briefing before passing through the chamber's door. After all, the session couldn't begin until the mayor arrived anyway.

The west Texas town of Bison, population 2,519, had begun as a trading post in the middle of Comanche territory in 1871. After the native tribes relocated, Bison grew into a cattle and settler stop before becoming an organized town ten years later when its big brother to the east, Odessa, had hit the map as a water stop and cattle shipping point on the Texas and Pacific Railway. The subsequent oil and gas deposits discovered under the Permian Basin pushed the further development of both Odessa and Bison to their current status on the Texas landscape. The recent retirement of Bison's police chief had made Garrison's impending appearance before the town council possible—that, and the fact that the current mayor of Bison was himself a retired Houston police captain.

The Bison *town hall*—folks didn't like the term "*city hall*—was" a quaint, old, red-brick building with two white pillars framing the front door. The pillars looked somewhat out of place since the building was only one story tall, but they gave the impression this was the place of official business. The mayor was waiting at the front desk, occupied by a petite woman in her thirties with long, dark hair, framed eyeglasses, and lips perfectly painted with bright-red lipstick.

"Good morning, John. I trust you spent a comfortable night here in town?" the mayor asked with a wry grin.

"Oh, it was fine. Nice place over there," he lied to his prospective boss.

"Good. This is Connie Maxwell, our city secretary. She runs the town hall and basically the town," the mayor said, replacing the wry grin with a bright, wide smile. "Connie, meet John Garrison, our candidate for police chief."

Connie Maxwell stood and greeted Garrison with a smile and soft handshake, the kind ladies do when they aren't comfortable touching a man. Garrison noticed her impeccably manicured fingernails, polished bright red, complementing her lipstick, and the small yet sparkling diamond wedding ring on her left hand. She was short with an attractive figure and face to match.

"Very nice to meet you, ma'am. May I call you Connie?" Garrison asked, maintaining a firm yet delicate grasp of her hand.

"Please do," she replied before stepping back, accommodating the release of her hand.

"Come on into my office. None of the council members have arrived yet," the mayor advised.

Mayor Dan Barber was a tall, well-built man of sixty. His years of dedication in the gym paid dividends, although it couldn't hide the full head of gray hair he possessed. Cut high and tight, military style, and combed straight back, it was the perfect complement to his hardened good looks and square jaw. Like most former cops who'd shaved every day for twenty-five-plus years, he sported a short, neatly trimmed goatee that sat nicely beneath his steel-blue eyes and tan Stetson cowboy hat.

A native Houstonian, he'd retired as a captain after thirty years of service with the police department, picking up a master's degree in public administration at the University of Houston. As commander of the Detective Bureau, he'd watched John Garrison be promoted to sergeant-detective, then lieutenant and leader of the Robbery and Homicide units for the last ten years of his HPD career. One of the best cops and investigators he'd ever seen, Garrison was the natural choice to offer the vacant police chief's job. More importantly, he possessed the intestinal fortitude necessary to ward off the impending pressure of being an outsider running the highest-profile department in town.

"Okay, you can be honest in here. How was the motel?" Barber asked after taking a seat in his oversized calfskin-leather chair, adorned with the seal of the state of Texas branded into its headrest.

"It was horrible. The TV didn't work, the AC sounded like a Monday morning at the mine, and I didn't sleep more than a couple of hours tops. But on the plus side, the water was clean and didn't stink," Garrison reported with a chuckle.

"Contrary to popular belief, the water here is just fine," Barber assured with a laugh of his own. "My offer still stands if you'd prefer to use our guestroom at the ranch."

"I'm not foolish enough to turn that offer down twice."

A soft tap on the thick wooden door interrupted the jocularity between the two friends.

"Come in!" Barber called.

The polished oak slab opened slightly to a thin crack along the frame.

"Council is seated, your honor," Connie whispered as though she was front and center in a darkened theater.

"Well, you ready, candidate Garrison?' Barber asked, standing to stretch his six-four frame.

Garrison stood, straightened his silver bolo tie, and ran his thumbs across the front of his waist inside his belt, smoothing out his crisp, white dress shirt.

"As ready as I'll ever be, your honor," he replied.

CHAPTER 3

MONDAY

The mayor led Garrison through the double oak doors into the council chamber, followed by Connie, who quietly closed it behind them. Garrison was the only entry on the day's agenda. The Bison town council met every other Tuesday except for emergencies or special requests of the mayor. Dan Barber had called this special session for this first Monday in June due to his formal recommendation of Garrison for the position of police chief. Connie directed Garrison to a chair at a table set directly in front of the long table the council took their positions behind. Garrison noted two men and one woman had joined the mayor, all looking casual and omnipresent. The councilmen were dressed in Western-style shirts, one brown, the other white and blue paisley, with yoked fronts and denim jeans, while the councilwoman looked sharp in a navy-blue blouse, khaki knee-length skirt, and navy-blue heels that'd make a runway model jealous. They all appeared to be in their early- to mid-forties and carried an aura of being legacy residents of the town. Garrison looked around the small room, also occupied by more than a dozen townsfolk who were curious about the goings-on.

Dan Barber took a sip of water, then called the meeting to order. "Good morning, everyone. This special session is officially called to order. Mrs. Maxwell, would you announce the first order, which I guess is the only order for this morning's meeting?"

"Yes, your honor. The Town of Bison council calls for the review and approval vote on the mayor's recommendation of candidate John G. Garrison to fill the vacant position of chief of police," Connie formally announced.

"Very well. Members of the council, you have Mr. Garrison's resume, letter of application, and my summary report of Mr. Garrison's qualifications, all of which exceed this communities' requirements for a police chief. I'll now open the floor for questions or comments," Barber explained for the record.

After a moment's pause, the councilwoman spoke up. "Mr. Garrison, good morning and welcome to Bison. I'm Natalie Hollingsworth. I've read Mayor Barber's summary and viewed your resume. While it's quite impressive, I can't help but wonder how a big-city police official will be successful in a small-town setting such as ours. What, if anything, have you done to prepare for such a dramatic change in your career?"

Before Garrison could respond, both councilmen added their names to the question, announcing their curiosity about Garrison's desire to accept such a moderate salary in a small country town. Garrison had assumed this to be one of the first, if not the first, questions he would address. Therefore, he'd prepared and thought over his answer numerous times during his restless night.

Garrison assured the council members that after thirty-five years of big city policing, he welcomed the benefits and challenges a small-town police chief would bring. He also leaned heavily on his love of horses, cattle, and the Western spirit he'd first embraced as a young boy in Houston. After he ended his extended explanation, the councilman to the right of Barber cleared his throat.

"Mr. Garrison, my name's Clayton Walker. You may or may not know that my nephew, Justin Walker, is a respected seven-year veteran of the Bison Police Department and, more importantly, a young man born and raised in this town. When our former chief retired, it seemed natural that Justin would succeed him, yet our mayor saw fit to reach all the way down to Houston to fetch us a candidate with a fancy resume and chest full of medals. Now I'm not saying you're not qualified; as Mayor Barber stated, you're probably overqualified for this position. Yet, you've come nearly six hundred miles to appear before this council today. What makes you a better candidate than a man who's spent his whole life here in Kutseena County and the town of Bison?" Walker asked.

"Mr. Walker, Mr. Garrison was recruited and selected by me to fill this position. His credentials are impeccable, and during the selection process, he did not imply that he was a better candidate than any of the others, including your nephew, who, at twenty-eight years old, needs a bit more seasoning before he takes the helm of a police department. Spending time under Mr. Garrison's tutelage will elevate your nephew's professional development," Barber retorted. "Now, does anyone have any further questions, unrelated to their family, for Mr. Garrison, or can I call for a vote?" Barber asked, looking at each council member in turn.

After a long silence, all the members nodded and said they were prepared to vote.

"Very good. As this is an open meeting, each member will announce their vote for the record, and the citizens in attendance, with the mayor voting last. Mrs. Hollingsworth," Barber called to the councilwoman.

"I believe Mr. Garrison is a fine choice. Therefore, I vote for approval," she stated with a smile.

"Mr. Giddings?" Barber called to the councilman seated to his left.

"As I find no weakness in his resume or background, I vote for approval," Giddings announced.

"Mr. Walker," Barber stated.

"I also find no weakness in Mr. Garrison's resume or background investigation, but I cannot in a good conscientious vote for the approval of a candidate that has no ties to Bison, Kutseena County, or West Texas for that matter. Therefore, I disapprove," Walker declared.

"Very well. As the mayor charged with the deciding vote in this instance, I strongly support the approval of Mr. Garrison as the next chief of police for the town of Bison. The vote carries three-to-one for approval. Does anyone have any closing remarks before we go off the record?" Barber asked.

Aside from Councilman Walker's menacing glare, the council's silence responded loud and clear. Therefore, Barber called an end to the special session and closed the record. Sitting closest to Garrison, Connie was the first with congratulatory remarks and a firmer handshake than the previous greeting. The mayor purposely delayed his approach to the town's new chief, allowing Natalie Hollingsworth, Hugh Giddings, and Clayton Walker to greet the chief before he followed with a friendly I-told-you-so look and handshake. Then, Barber glanced toward the back of the room and nodded to Garrison, who followed the mayor's gaze toward the other three members of the Bison Police Department standing along the back wall. Garrison noted two smiles and one frown, which he surmised belonged to the nephew, Justin Walker.

"Let me introduce you to your troops," Barber suggested before leading the new chief down the center aisle of chairs to the back of the room.

"Chief, you've already met your dispatcher and assistant Amanda Stewart during the application process; this is Officers Travis Cooper and Justin Walker. Folks, meet your new chief, John Garrison," Barber said proudly.

Garrison nodded and shook hands with each employee, then paused momentarily to gather his thoughts before saying, "Glad to know each of you. I look forward to working with y'all and making the department the best it can be," Garrison offered.

"It's already the best it can be," Officer Walker quipped.

"Is that a fact? Well, the first thing we'll do to improve things is have you shave that beard. I prefer my officers clean-shaven with an optional mustache," Garrison said, trying not to sound too aggressive after his initial introduction.

"Will you be coming into the office today, chief?" Amanda cheerfully asked.

"Yes, ma'am, as soon as the boss is finished with me," Garrison said, nodding toward Mayor Barber.

"I figured I'd take him around town and introduce him to some of the folks he'll need to get to know sooner than later," Barber announced, then to Garrison added, "First, I need to issue you your badge officially and have you sign a few papers. I'll see you in my office in a few minutes," Barber added before leaving the room.

"I look forward to working with you, Chief. We've heard a ton about you already. I couldn't imagine being a cop down in Houston. That's the real police!" Officer Cooper exclaimed.

"Thanks, Coop. Hopefully, things won't get so crazy around here that we have to use that big-city police stuff," Garrison answered, immediately recognizing the enthusiasm and eagerness of his young officer. "Are we working on anything right now?" Garrison asked.

"Not really. We had a theft at the feed store, and somebody smashed into a parked car in the medical center parking lot. That's about it," Cooper reported.

"What's with the theft at the feed store?" Garrison asked.

"Some jackass walked in early this morning, right

when they opened, and took a twenty-five-pound bag of dog food, then ran out with it over his shoulder. Bob didn't recognize the guy," Walker advised.

"Any video?" Garrison asked.

"Yep, but I can't see the dude's face from the camera angle," Walker answered.

"Hmm . . . It sounds like Bob needs to move his camera. Unless something comes up, how about we all meet at the station at one o'clock?" Garrison ordered more than asked.

Everyone agreed, then the new Bison police chief headed for the mayor's office to get formally sworn in.

CHAPTER 4

MONDAY

After the new chief signed his employment papers, which consisted of the usual payroll, healthcare, and life insurance beneficiary proclamations, Connie Maxwell gave Garrison the oath of office and his badge. Garrison accepted his badge and took a close look. It was a silver five-point star with *Chief* emblazoned across the top, arched ribbon; *Police* displayed on the rocker below the round emblem of an American Bison, ringed with the words *Bison, Texas* in black lettering. There was no number. It felt strange to hold a badge representing a department other than Houston. In his thirty-five years with HPD, he'd earned officer, sergeant, and lieutenant badges, all containing the words *Houston Police*. Now, for the first time since he was a wide-eyed twenty-year-old cadet, he'd carry another agency's insignia. He took a wistful deep breath and thanked Connie, and then Mayor Barber, for the opportunity.

"Okay, Chief, you're officially on the payroll now, so let's meet a few folks around town before you head to your station," Barber said, lifting his Stetson off the hat rack and covering his gray mane. "First stop is the Coffee Mug coffeeshop across the street."

"I saw that when I got in yesterday. Looks like a good place," Garrison admitted.

"Best in town, and the owner is someone you'll want to get to know," Barber advised, pausing to let traffic clear before crossing Center Street, otherwise known as County Road 190.

The two men pushed through the glass door and found all seven quaint round tables occupied, which was uncommon for 10:30 in the morning. Brightly decorated in pastel colors, there was a large painting of hefty yellow sunflowers displayed behind the crystal-clear glass counter, which was stuffed chock full of various pastries and donuts thoughtfully arranged on three glass shelves. An old-fashioned cash register occupied the counter's far end with a tall, middle-aged African American woman finishing up a sale. She glanced at the men and released a smile as wide as Palo Duro Canyon and bright as the West Texas sun. She hurried around the counter and met Barber with a hug, not too affectionate, but the *I'm happy to see you* kind.

"Callie, this is John Garrison, our new police chief," Barber began. "John, meet Callie Johnson, the proprietor of the finest coffee and pastry shop in town."

Callie Althea Johnson looked in her mid-fifties, tall with a narrow face, medium complexion, and straight salt-and-pepper hair pulled back into a large bun. Her brown eyes were rimmed in black eyeliner, and dark red lipstick adorned her lips. She had the poise of an elegant lady who'd taken a wrong turn and ended up in a dusty old Western town.

"A pleasure to meet you, ma'am," Garrison said, offering his hand.

"I'm finally getting to meet the man from Houston that this character here couldn't stop talking about," Callie said, accepting Garrison's hand and nodding toward Barber.

"I hope he didn't bore you too much," Garrison replied, his face blushing a warm red.

"Oh, not at all. Dan said you were Sherlock Holmes, Jack Reacher, and Walt Longmire wrapped up in one!" she blurted, unable to contain her laughter. "Let me get you a table."

"Here you go, Callie!" an old-timer dressed in a white tee shirt and stained denim coveralls shouted from his table near the front window. "They can have this one. I'm running behind schedule already!"

"Thank you, Ben!" Callie waved at him as he hurried out the door. She escorted Barber and Garrison over to the table, pulled a damp cloth from the white apron she wore over her light-blue dress, and quickly wiped the table. "Coffee, gentlemen?"

"Yes, ma'am, two coffees, and I'll have one of those cinnamon rolls warmed up, please," Barber answered.

"And you, Chief?" Callie asked.

"Just coffee for me. I look at a donut and gain five pounds," Garrison said with a grin. "Uh, excuse me, Callie, I know I'm sounding like a cop, but that fella didn't leave any money for you on the table."

"No worries, Chief. Ole Ben paid me an hour ago. He was just sitting and reading the *West Texas Farm Report.*

He picks up and delivers livestock to many of the farmers and ranchers in the area," she explained. "Besides, if he didn't pay me today, I'd get him tomorrow," she added with a wide grin.

"As we've exhaustingly discussed, things here are mighty different than back in Houston. Most everyone knows or at least recognizes everybody else in and around town. Especially Callie. She has a memory like a steel trap. And everyone who comes in here likes to talk, so she listens. That's why I said you needed to get to know her. She'll probably be the best informant you'll have. I know she helped out your predecessor a few times," Barber said, his eyes lighting up as Callie brought two mugs of steaming coffee and a simmering cinnamon roll, half the size of a football.

"Cream and sugar, Chief?" Callie asked, offering a silver tray with packets of sugar, sweetener, and cream.

"Yes, ma'am. I'm a one-sweetener, double-cream fella, and please don't call me Chief. The name's John," Garrison insisted.

"Well, thank you, John, but I like 'Chief' better, if you don't mind," she said, moving away to another table of new customers.

"So, what's her story? She seems somewhat out of place here," Garrison whispered.

"From what I know, she and her husband moved to Odessa from Dallas about thirty years ago. He was one of the first, if not *the* first, African American petroleum engineers to work for the Rockland Oil and Gas Company. Rockland was fairly new back then and was ramping up its place on the Permian Basin. I don't know why, but Callie opened this shop here instead of Odessa. She has a nice place east of town in the county. I believe her husband built it himself," Barber recalled.

"She has a place east of town?" Garrison asked, catching Barber's choice of words.

"Yes. She's a widow now. Her husband died about a year ago."

Garrison dropped his gaze and shook his head for a moment. "What a shame."

"She's a wonderful lady. Emily and I come here every chance we get. All she serves is coffee and pastries. Oh, while I'm thinking about it—don't call her pastries 'donuts.' She'll straighten you out double-quick!" Barber warned his new chief.

"Thanks for the heads-up. I'm sure I'll stick my boot in my mouth plenty for a while around here." Garrison took a sip from his mug. "This is damn good coffee."

"It's Big Bend Coffee Roasters. They're located in Marfa over by El Paso. I believe they have locations all over Texas, but I'd not heard of them until I got here," Barber advised.

The mayor finished his pastry, and the two drained the last of their mugs. The crowd, such as it was, had thinned out to include Barber and Garrison and the three folks who'd come in just after them. Garrison noted the sign dangling from a string on the front door: OPEN EVERY DAY, 6:00 AM to 2:00 PM.

"You have time to let me show you around a bit more?" Barber asked.

"Nope. I need to hustle over to Odessa and order my uniforms, then get back to the station for that one o'clock meeting with my staff," Garrison said, pushing away from the table and tossing a twenty-dollar bill onto the table. "My treat. Thanks for everything. I'll see you and Emily later this evening." He then went to the counter to say goodbye to Callie before leaving.

CHAPTER 5

MONDAY

An Odessa police officer held up his hand, stopping Garrison's truck. Garrison had not expected a noon traffic jam in the middle of Odessa on a Monday. He leaned out the driver's-side window and strained to look past the line of vehicles across the intersection. Up ahead, he could see at least three sets of emergency light bars flashing the dreaded red and blue lights in the middle of what the city designated as the East Business Loop 20. Garrison checked the street sign at the intersection where he was stopped, then called Amanda Stewart—one ring.

"Bison Police, can I help you," Amanda greeted his call.

"Hi, Amanda. It's me, John Garrison—"

"Hello, Chief! How are you?" she asked in her customary Texas drawl.

"Well, I've been better. I'm stuck in a traffic jam in Odessa. It looks like a wreck. I'm on Loop Twenty at South Dixie Boulevard. I may be late for our one o'clock meeting. Please let everyone know I'll be there as soon as possible."

"That loop is always a disaster! I'll pass the word," Amanda assured her boss.

"Anything going on?" Garrison asked.

"There's a disturbance up at the medical center. It seems like a drunk oil worker was brought in, and he's causing a problem for the doctor. Cooper and Walker are over there now," Amanda reported.

"Drunk oil worker at noon?" Garrison asked with a laugh.

"Time a day don't matter around here, Chief. They run them three shifts," Amanda explained.

"All right, then. I'll be there quick as I can," Garrison said, then tapped the red button on his cell phone, disconnecting the call.

The traffic officer blew his whistle and waved Garrison toward the flashing lights. The line of cars snaked up and around the knot of mangled metal. A quick look told Garrison the driver of the Chevrolet Impala had been motoring with their head up their ass and smashed into the rear of the black Mercedes Benz SUV.

They're both totaled, Garrison thought as he swung his FX4 past a wrecker and broke into the clear roadway ahead.

Once out of town, he lay on the accelerator and headed west on Highway 302 to County Road 190, then into downtown Bison, where he pulled into the parking lot at 1:19 PM. He took a deep breath and thought again about what he would say to his new subordinates. He'd mulled through the speech since he left Odessa, but he wanted his talk to be less formal.

All three patrol trucks were parked neatly in a row behind the station, indicating both his officers were present. Dan Barber had told him one of his first orders of business would be to hire a new officer—one had left three weeks ago to join the Odessa PD. Garrison knew exactly who he intended to hire. He'd already made the offer, anticipating his approval by the town council. He knew his selection was spot on, but he wasn't sure of the reaction he'd receive from Walker, Cooper, and Amanda, let alone the council members. He figured he'd leave that announcement for another day, then stepped out of his truck into the blistering heat.

"Sorry I'm late," Garrison announced to Amanda, who occupied the front desk directly in line with the front door.

He turned to the left, stopped, and looked at the layout of his department. His office was to the right, the closed door displaying a small metal sign that read *Chief of Police*. A few feet further past his office were three desks facing the lobby, lined side by side with the officers' backs facing a bank of windows that stretched the room's length. There was a fortified, windowless, steel door to the left of the desks, which he presumed led to the jail holding cell. Cooper sat at the desk to the right, busily typing into an antiquated desktop computer, while Walker sat behind the desk on the far left, looking through notes. The middle desk was empty, its top clean and neat. The station was old but clean, with everything seemingly in place.

Amanda stepped alongside Garrison, shook his hand, and waved toward the office. "Chief Garrison, welcome to your new police station," she announced in her beautiful Texas twang.

Cooper and Walker stopped what they were doing and stood to greet their new boss. Each stepped forward, taking turns shaking Garrison's hand.

"I'm sure it's nothing like Houston, but it's all we got," Cooper said.

"It looks good to me," Garrison assured everyone.

"Let me show you your office," Amanda said, leading the way to his office door and pushing it open.

Garrison stepped inside and smiled to himself. The room was tiny compared to his space at the HPD. There was just enough room for the desk, his chair, and two chairs positioned in front of the desk. A coatrack was in the corner, and a small window was halfway up the back wall. A tall file cabinet sat in the opposite corner of the coatrack. On the desk was the same old-model desktop computer. The police radio and microphone were also familiar; Amanda had the same setup at her desk out front. Covered in dark paneling that looked like it had been there since the Nixon administration, the walls stretched to the drop-ceiling tiles stained the same color as the ceiling in his motel room. Surprisingly, the room did not smell like the stale cigarettes that were undoubtedly responsible for the discolored ceiling tiles.

"How long has this building been smoke-free?" Garrison asked Amanda with a grin.

"About ten years now, I suppose," Amanda answered

with a laugh, knowing what Garrison was referring to. "Chief Stillwell wasn't much on décor."

"We'll see if we can do something about that," Garrison said, then motioned toward the door.

They moved back into the main room, where Garrison asked his three employees to get their chairs and gather in front of the three officers' desks. Walker, Cooper, and Amanda took their seats, Amanda propping a notepad on top of her crossed legs. Garrison greeted everyone again and offered how pleased he was to be the new chief of the Bison Police Department. He admitted he didn't know enough about the town but had studied its history and learned as much as possible from Mayor Barber, as time had allowed. Garrison summarized his thirty-five-year career with the Houston PD and assured the group that he still hadn't seen and done it all. He vowed to do his best to improve the department in every way possible, beginning with making the office a safer environment for everyone. Garrison informed Amanda that he would move her desk away from the front door, and the officers' desks moved parallel to the windows so their backs wouldn't be exposed. He took another long look at the computers and asked Amanda how old they were.

"I think we got them about when the building went smoke-free," Amanda said with a chuckle.

"They were here when I started seven and a half years ago," Walker said, his top lip curled in disgust.

"And they still work?"

"Most of the time," Cooper clarified.

"Mine's only about three years old, Chief. I got a new one since I enter the calls for service, reports, tickets, and such," Amanda explained.

"You do all that?" Garrison asked.

"And more. It's a small town, Chief." She said with a Texas-sized smile.

"That'll take a few days for me to wrap my head around," Garrison offered with a smile of his own. "I understand it's about to get considerably bigger, though."

Amanda nodded. "You got that right. The town purchased two-hundred acres on the south end."

"Mayor Barber tells me the plan is to contract with a builder to erect an apartment building along with a hundred fifty to two hundred new houses," Garrison announced. "That could nearly double our population; I believe."

"Yeah, with a bunch of oil-field workers. That'll bring domestics and fights fer sure," Walker muttered.

"Agreed. I've already told the mayor that if and when that happens, we'll need a couple more officers," Garrison said.

"What'd he say about that?" Cooper asked.

"The usual. We'll have to see if the budget can handle it."

The members of the Bison PD had spoken for another hour when Garrison checked his watch. It was now 3:30.

"What time did all of you start your shifts today?" Garrison asked.

"We all came in at eight this morning for your

appearance with the council. Normally, I'm in at eight, Cooper works afternoons this month, and Justin is on days," Amanda explained. "As you know, we're an officer short, so we don't have a split shift officer at the moment."

"Okay. I'll have a better idea of what we will do tomorrow," Garrison said. "I've received authorization to hire another officer immediately, which will happen quickly. I'll then work on our coverage. I understand we cover the town from eight in the morning until midnight, then calls go to the sheriff's office, and we're on call for anything big. Is that correct?"

Everyone nodded in agreement.

"Have you decided how you will handle that new officer position?" Walker asked, leaning back in his chair, and crossing his arms across his chest.

"I have. I'll let y'all know about that later this week. Right now, Walker can go off-duty. Coop, can you stay until about eight this evening? I'll authorize overtime. I'll be here until at least eight, and Amanda, are you here until four or five this afternoon?" Garrison asked.

"I'm here as long as you need me today," Amanda answered.

"Same here, Chief," Cooper added.

Walker made no such offer. He gathered his phone from his desk, then put the page of notes on Cooper's desk and left the office. Garrison said nothing, just watched his senior officer's actions until he left the building.

"Am I going to have trouble with Officer Walker?" Garrison asked Amanda and Cooper.

"He's just disappointed right now. He'll come around," Amanda suggested.

"I certainly hope so. There's no room for malcontent in a five-person department," Garrison said.

CHAPTER 6

MONDAY

Cooper filled Garrison in on the medical center's disturbance, resulting in a simple report with no arrest. Amanda showed Garrison how to access the information database so he could review the officer reports and submit them after approval. During a break, Garrison checked on the single-holding cell behind the steel single-windowed door he'd noticed when he arrived. It was an eight-foot by eight-foot square with a toilet and small sink in one corner and a sturdy wooden bench equipped with solid metal eyebolts anchored on each end. Attached to each eyebolt was a pair of handcuffs. The walls and floor were painted with a thick coat of gray paint. A drain trap was in the middle of the floor, making it easy to wash out. A single high-watt bulb encased in a metal screen provided lighting from the ceiling.

Garrison closed the cell door and wandered across the room to the opposite wall beside his office. The wall had a full-length shelf with booking devices and forms. A three-stack steel locker was in the corner for evidence and property. A light-blue square was painted on the wall for prisoner photographs. He noticed the fingerprint area had an old-fashioned ink tray and a card rack. He'd not seen that setup for at least a decade.

He returned to his office and began to examine the budget ledger Amanda had provided. There was more money in the account than he'd anticipated. Amanda had explained that everything in the police budget came out of that account except for personnel overtime, which was a separate account and subject to approval by the mayor. At the chief's approval, the three officers and Amanda were eligible for overtime pay. He glanced at the overtime balance. Much lower than he'd like, mainly since it was only June, and there were six more months to go in the year. Further examination of the department fleet confirmed three marked patrol vehicles—all Ford F-150 Police Responders with 400 HP, 3.5-liter EcoBoost engines.

Nice. Not exactly ideal for traffic enforcement, though, he thought.

Amanda stuck her head into the office. "Chief, if you don't need me for anything else, I'll be heading home."

"Thank you for everything today, Amanda. Have a good night," Garrison replied, shocked that it was five o'clock already.

"You'll be able to receive all calls on your phone, and Cooper is out on patrol," Amanda added before disappearing.

Garrison heard the front door open and close, each time the small bell affixed to the top signaling the movement with a ring. He leaned back and listened to the silence. He walked out of his office and looked around at the vacant station. What a difference three weeks made. Three weeks ago, he was in a bustling office in the Homicide Unit, directing a dozen detective sergeants as they worked on five active investigations. The constant ringing of the phones, boisterous chatter of detectives deciding their next move or guessing the punchline of the last joke, and pressure from the captain to report back with an arrest were all a distant memory.

I wonder if it's like this all the time.

He walked over to Amanda's desk and sat down. He'd moved the desk far to the left of the front door near the wall—a far safer position. The desk smelled like a woman. The scent of perfume and air freshener filled the area. In the corner of the desk was a framed photo of Amanda and a man who was probably her husband. Next to the picture was an etched crystal teardrop statuette recognizing fifteen years of service to the police department. He wondered how old she was. She didn't look old enough to have been with the department for over fifteen years. The crack of the radio behind him fractured his thoughts.

"Unit two to base. Anybody there?" Officer Cooper asked.

Garrison spun around and looked for the button on the upright microphone. He found it and answered.

"This is Garrison. Go ahead," he responded, surprised at how uncomfortable he was.

"Hey, Chief, I'm stopping Lincoln-Mary-Adam, five nine seven four, LMA5974, at West Street and the boulevard," Cooper advised.

"Clear, LMA5974, West and the boulevard," Garrison answered, unsure where his officer was.

He hurried to his office, grabbed the map of the town Barber had given him, and spread it across his desk. "The boulevard" was actually Bison Boulevard, the main east-west street that stretched through the entire town. He narrowed down the officer's location, snatched his portable radio, and headed for the door, prepared to act as backup. His truck's tires squealed as he raced out of the parking lot, then he made the turn to head westbound on Bison Boulevard.

Before he knew it, he saw the flashing red and blue lights ahead. Relieved, he eased off the accelerator and cruised up behind his patrol unit, then pulled off the road onto the shoulder near the passenger side of the violator's truck. He instinctively checked his gun, then exited his vehicle. Cooper was standing with the driver near the right rear bumper of the violator's truck, which two additional white males occupied. Garrison stood by, watching the occupants while Cooper finished writing the ticket. Once completed, the driver was released and returned to the vehicle, which sped off.

"Thanks for coming by Chief! I didn't expect that!" Cooper uttered with a wide grin.

"Well, I don't like y'all making a stop alone, I guess," Garrison stated.

"That's okay, Chief. We do it all the time. When there's two of us on duty, we usually check by but handle things alone out here most of the time."

"That's gonna take some serious getting used to."

Garrison patted Cooper on the back before getting into his truck. He was about to pull away when he stopped and leaned out his window. "Hey, Coop. Did the last chief check by with y'all when he could?"

"Not really. Good to see you, Chief! Thanks again!"

Garrison made a U-turn, then headed back to the station. He realized his pulse was racing a bit. He'd not made or served as backup at a traffic stop in a long time, but he'd personally known officers who'd been killed on such stops.

Bad things don't only happen in the big city. I'm not sure I'll be comfortable with this.

CHAPTER 7

MONDAY

Garrison waited until Cooper returned to the station, then went off duty before locking the station doors and heading to Dan Barber's ranch northwest of town. Barber was one of those lucky cops whose wife Emily had shared the dream of owning a small ranch with horses and cattle once the HPD captain retired. Barber had made that dream a reality when he bought two hundred acres in the northwest corner of Kutseena County four years earlier. He'd built one of those log homes advertised in Western magazines, along with a barn and horse stable. His son and daughter-in-law followed three years later to help run the small cattle and quarter horse operation, getting ten acres of their own as an incentive to join Mom and Dad.

Garrison had only been to the place twice. Once while the log home was being built and the other a mere month or so ago when Barber first offered him the job as Bison's police chief. Garrison punched the address into his phone's map application just in case he'd forgotten how to get there. Thirty minutes and one wrong turn later, he turned onto the gravel drive and passed under the yawning front gate's archway that welcomed you to the Westwind Ranch. The drive twisted around two stock ponds and a hay ring before it straightened out and led directly to the house's three-car garage attached to the east side. He parked away from the garage, not wanting to block any vehicles, and paused to take in the sights.

The sun was beginning to dip behind the western horizon, leaving a clear translucent orange and blue hue that would produce a litany of bright stars dotted across an ebony night sky. Garrison soaked in the setting, wanting to achieve the same retirement dream. He knew a lieutenant's pension wouldn't be enough to make this dream a reality. Barber had the assistance of a spouse's retirement and, more importantly, the inheritance from his father, who'd been some high-level official with a major oil and gas company back in Houston. Garrison had neither of those benefits, thus his brief two-week hiatus between his HPD and BPD positions. He did have the so-called drag money he received when he retired. That included a cash payout of his unused sick, vacation, and compensation time, along with the moderate savings he'd managed to hang onto. He figured it'd be enough to find something maybe half the size of his former captain's spread.

The front door opened, and the host couple appeared arm in arm with broad smiles and cocktail glasses held in each free hand. It looked like a scripted scene from some romantic comedy where the irritating friends invite their lonely buddy to their place so they can set him up with a charming widow or something.

"Good evening, Chief! How was your first day on the job?" the mayor asked.

"Well, I would say it was the longest day of my career, but as you recall, I'd be mistaken," Garrison answered with a laugh.

Barber laughed. "Yup. I remember we went forty-one straight hours on that River Oaks homicide about ten years ago!"

"Okay, you two, already with the war stories! Come on in, John, and get something to eat because I know you haven't had anything all day," Emily Barber prompted her guest.

"Yes, ma'am, and no, ma'am. You're right. I haven't eaten today, now that I think of it," Garrison acknowledged.

Garrison followed his hosts into the foyer, adorned with enormous Texas Longhorns above the knotty pine-trimmed arch that led into a massive great room with a thirty-foot-high ceiling split in half by full-sized log beams spanning the entire room. A fieldstone fireplace with its stone-encased chimney reaching to the ceiling and beyond festooned the far wall between expansive triangular windows on each side. The décor was true Wild West with saddle leather furniture and cowhide accents. Four barstools, each with a different size and shape of saddle, sat in front of an extended breakfast bar that separated the kitchen from the great room.

Emily set a steaming plate of barbecue brisket, green beans, and potato salad on the bar, accompanied by a brown linen napkin, silver fork, and knife. Barber pulled a cold bottle of Shiner beer from the refrigerator and popped the top off before handing it to his new chief.

"I have strawberry rhubarb pie if you like after dinner," Emily offered, knowing that was Garrison's favorite pie in the whole world.

Garrison smiled and shook his head. "I can't believe I was stupid enough to stay in town at the motel last night," he grumbled.

Emily smiled warmly. "Actually, I think that was a very classy thing to do, considering you were meeting with the council this morning."

"It was a good move, John," Barber chimed in. "I made sure to let everyone know you were there last night. The council members, even Walker, were impressed."

Garrison chuckled. "Well, I figured I should do that, but I also didn't think it'd be as miserable as it was."

"That motel has been cited for several violations in recent years. I'd hoped ole Joe would spruce the place up a bit. It sounds like another visit will be needed," Barber stated.

"Joe?" Garrison asked.

"Yeah, Joe Millington is the owner of the place. He inherited it from his father about twenty years ago, I guess. I don't know much about the place. Joe's a friendly enough guy, but he's no businessman."

Garrison cleaned his plate, and before he could refuse, which he had no intention of doing, Emily placed a large piece of pie in front of him.

"You're too good to me, Emily. Why can't I find a wife as beautiful and caring as you?" Garrison asked with a wide smile.

Emily's face blushed a faint red as she rinsed the dishes in the sink, then set them in the dishwasher.

"Well, actually, I have a friend—"

"Now, Emily! Not already! The poor guy just moved to town!" Barber managed to say in between bursts of laughter.

"Maybe after I'm settled a bit," Garrison said, scooping the last huge bite of pie into his mouth.

The three friends retired to the den where a big-screen television had a Texas Rangers baseball game playing with the sound muted. Garrison sat in one of the leather wingback chairs facing the television. He checked the score—5 to 3, Rangers, in the eighth inning.

"You still as big a baseball fan as you used to be?" Barber asked.

"Oh yes. Caught every Astros game I could," Garrison confirmed.

"Out here, we pick up the Rangers unless you buy the MLB package; then you get them all, I guess. I've become a Rangers fan here in the last couple of years," Barber admitted.

"I've always paid attention to the Rangers. I usually tried to get to the ballpark when they were in town facing the Astros."

"Where do you plan on living?" Emily asked. "Dan says you don't have a place yet."

"Well, I didn't want to put the cart before the horse, if you know what I mean. Dan said I was a shoo-in for the job, but I wasn't that confident. I'm scheduled to look at a few rental houses in town with a realtor later in the week. Would it be okay to bunk here until I get a place?" Garrison asked Emily directly.

"Of course! Dan already told you that, didn't he?" She gave her husband a look, and he nodded yes.

"I just don't want to intrude," Garrison said.

"Not at all. Glad to have you for as long as you need," Emily assured her guest.

Garrison's cell phone rang, interrupting the jovial visit. He quickly picked it up. "Hello, this is John Garrison,"

The look on his face surely gave him away, indicating to the Barbers the call contained something other than pleasantries. Garrison listened and nodded.

"Where?" . . .

"How many?" . . .

"Okay, I'm on my way. I should be there in thirty minutes. Don't let anyone near the scene and have your deputy step out of the building," Garrison ordered, then hung up.

"What the hell is it, John?" Barber asked.

"Looks like I got a dead body out on the far end of 190," Garrison reported.

"A dead body?" Barber asked.

"Yeah. The sheriff's dispatcher says they got a call from some kids at the abandoned gas station near Curtis

Road. He says there's a guy who looks like he's been shot. Care to join me on this one?"

Barber shot out of his chair. "Yep. There hasn't been a homicide in this town in twenty years!" he exclaimed. "This is a hell of a rude reception, ain't it now!"

CHAPTER 8

MONDAY

Garrison backed his truck farther away from the garage and let Barber pass. Garrison figured he'd let Barber lead the way since it was dark, and he hadn't added grill lights and sirens to his truck yet. To his surprise, Barber had. Barber sped out of his drive and flipped on his lights and siren. Garrison followed just close enough to keep his boss in view but far enough behind to avoid an embarrassing collision.

They wound their way through the county's back roads, then turned southbound on County Road 190. Garrison knew where he was now—it was a straight shot into town, then onward to the south side. Barber's emergency lights and siren alerted traffic to pull off the road now that they were approaching the town. Garrison closed the distance between him and Barber as cars bailed out in each direction. He didn't want someone pulling back onto the highway before he could clear their position. The two trucks blew through town, topping eighty-five as they passed the station, then Callie's coffeeshop.

Less than two minutes later, the sheriff's unit's flashing lights lit up the night sky. Barber slowed and pulled over off the shoulder near the sheriff's car. Garrison followed Barber's lead and parked well off the roadway.

As Garrison approached the scene, his investigative instincts automatically engaged. He noted the deputy standing with four teenagers in front of his unit, away from the old gas station, which was surrounded by a flimsy chain-link fence that had collapsed in several places. Keep-out signs dangled from the tops of the fence that had remained erect. No lights were on inside or near the building, which had intermittently exposed windows and weathered plywood coverings.

"Hey, Bull. This is John Garrison, our new chief," Barber quickly introduced Garrison to the deputy.

"Good to meet you, Chief. Dave Bullard. Everyone calls me Bull," the deputy clarified.

After the customary handshake, Garrison looked into the fenced area of the old station's property.

"What do we have, Bull?" Garrison asked.

"There's a white guy with a bullet wound to the head inside near the back wall. I took a close look to make sure we didn't need an ambulance, but he's beyond that, so I backed out per your instructions, Chief," Bullard reported.

"These are the kids who found him?" Garrison asked, glancing over at the two teenage girls and two boys huddled together in front of Bullard's car.

"Yep. Before your town annexed this property, it was the county's jurisdiction. We'd run out here a few times a week. The local teens like to come out here and party. You know, smoke dope, drink, play music . . . We made a few arrests, but we mostly just sent them on their way. This station's been abandoned for years," Bullard added.

"Let's have a look, boss," Garrison suggested. "Bull, would you mind getting the kids' information? I'll call my guys out here in a moment."

"Already done, Chief. I figured you'd want your guys to take their statements, so I've not done that. Also, I pulled this off one of the boys," Bullard said, handing Garrison a semi-automatic pistol. "Glock nine-millimeter. Says it's his father's gun."

Garrison pushed the magazine release button and checked the number of rounds. He saw a round in the chamber, which he extracted before locking the slide back. He smelled the ejection port and rubbed the inside with his little finger. Smeared gunpowder residue came off on his skin. He looked at Bullard, then Barber, who had closely watched his chief's examination of the weapon.

"It's been fired recently, and the magazine is only half full," Garrison announced. "Bull, would you put the kid with the gun in the back of your patrol unit? I'll get to him after I take a look at the body."

"Sure will." Bullard headed toward the kid.

Garrison and Barber snapped the buttons on their flashlights and lit up the area. Paper and Styrofoam cups, snacks, fast-food bags, and crushed bottles and cans littered the ground around the area. Several plywood sections had fallen from their former positions over broken windows, their rusted nails finally giving way to gravity's pull.

Probably a result of last night's storm, Garrison thought.

He looked for footprints, drag marks, or anything that appeared out of its natural place. The area immediately around the small building was mainly asphalt, broken in some places and cracked in others. That, along with last night's windstorm, would eliminate most ground evidence. He stepped inside and shined his flashlight beam over the body, then stopped a few feet away to scan the immediate area around the body, as did Barber, who'd followed him inside. The two men completed a visual examination of the floor, body, and surface of the room's back wall.

The victim appeared to be a white male, thirty to thirty-five years old, six feet tall, and one hundred fifty or sixty pounds. He wore blue jeans, brown work-style boots, and a soiled sleeveless white tee shirt. He was on his back, his head pointing toward the back wall, arms spread out to each side. A wide circle of blood had seeped from the back of the head, leaving an oblong stain in various stages of coagulation. Garrison approached the body and knelt close.

His high-powered flashlight illuminated the body, the white shirt reflecting a bright glare into his eyes. He angled the light and looked closely at the victim's face. The eyes were wide open, as was the mouth, as if he were gasping for air. There was a single bullet wound near the middle of the forehead with a faint dark-colored ring around it. Based on the amount of blood on the ground behind the head, Garrison figured the bullet had gone clean through, blowing the back of the head off.

Using the flashlight beam, he slowly followed the line from the victim's head up the wall. As expected, Garrison located blood and brain matter splattered on the wall approximately six feet from the floor. No doubt, the victim had been shot while standing. No blood smears or trails were on the floor, confirming the body hadn't been moved after being shot.

Barber had remained quiet, apparently wanting to let his new chief assess the scene without his input. Garrison stood and pulled his cell phone from his pocket. Earlier that day, he'd entered his staff's numbers into his phone, on speed dial. He'd not expected to need them the first night. He tapped Walker's name. A voicemail message announced Walker wasn't available. He left a message asking the officer to call him immediately, then tapped Cooper's name. Officer Cooper answered on the first ring.

"Cooper here. What's up, Chief?"

"I'll need you to return to the station immediately. We have a dead body at the old, abandoned gas station at 190 and Curtis Road. I'll need you to get the camera and evidence kit first, then come on out here pronto," Garrison ordered.

"Yes, sir! Dead body? Who is it? Is it a murder or what?" Cooper asked in a rapid-fire tumble of words. His excitement at having something more than a traffic stop to work on was evident.

"It's a homicide. I don't have an ID yet—a white male was shot in the head. Get out here as quick as you can," Garrison requested, then ended the call.

"I'll wait until Coop gets here before we move the body. In the meantime, I'll see what the kid with the gun has to say. Then I'll take the other kids' statements and get them out of here," Garrison informed Barber.

The mayor nodded. "Sounds good. It looks like this guy's been dead for at least twenty-four hours."

"Agreed. You and I know that, but that kid in the patrol car doesn't."

"No answer from Walker, huh?" Barber asked.

"No," Garrison simply answered, then headed for his truck to retrieve his notepad and clipboard.

Garrison opened the deputy's back door and peered at the kid who'd had his father's gun. Garrison sat down and closed the door. The teen was sweating profusely, and his hands were shaking.

"What are you doing with a gun out here?" Garrison asked flatly.

The boy stared down at his shaking hands. "I brought it to shoot at javelinas, that's all, I swear," he blurted out.

"What's your name?"

"Baker Jenkins, sir."

"I'm John Garrison, the new chief of police. How old are you?" Garrison asked.

"Seventeen."

"You know you can't carry out here at seventeen, right?"

"Yes, sir. But I didn't shoot that guy! He was dead

when we went in! I just brought the gun to show off in front of my girlfriend! I'm telling the truth!" the kid insisted, nearly hyperventilating.

"Look, Baker, I know you didn't shoot that guy in there tonight. But what about last night? Did y'all come out here last night?"

"No sir, not with the storm and all. We were out here for a couple of hours on Saturday night, but there wasn't anyone here," the boy reported, obviously trying to calm himself and speak more clearly.

"What time did y'all leave here Saturday night?" Garrison asked, jotting notes as he spoke.

"About eleven thirty. We all need to be home by midnight on Saturdays."

"You're sure there was nobody here?" Garrison pressed.

"We didn't see or hear anyone. It's not a big building," the kid said.

"I'll be keeping your father's gun. Tell him he can come to the station and get it during the day. I'm not going to arrest you for having it, but if I catch you with it again, you'll spend some time in jail. You're not a juvenile anymore as far as criminal charges go. You understand?" Garrison asked.

"Yes, sir. Thank you, sir," the kid responded.

"Before you go, I want a written statement about what happened here tonight, from when y'all arrived to when Deputy Bullard arrived. Okay?" Garrison handed him a notepad and pen.

"Yes, sir!" And Baker Jenkins began to write.

CHAPTER 9

MONDAY

Much to his mother's dismay, Travis Cooper had wanted to be a police officer since he was a young boy. Every Halloween, he'd dress up as a police officer and hit the neighborhood in search of crime, corruption, and candy. Not necessarily in that order. His determination to make his dream a reality kept him out of trouble as a teenager and inspired him to earn an associate degree in criminal justice from Midland College. A top-ten finish in his cadet class at the Permian Basin Law Enforcement Academy was enough to land him an offer from the Bison PD, which he'd readily accepted two years ago. Now he was working for a veteran of the Houston PD and racing to join the boss at a homicide scene, albeit a brief stop at the station for equipment. He gathered the digital camera and evidence collection kit, then popped the patrol truck's dashboard button that ignited his lights and siren. After a sharp right turn out of the parking lot and a straight code three run down County Road 190, known as Center Street in town, Cooper arrived on the scene.

Garrison figured that was a new response-time record.

"Here you go, Chief!" Cooper stuttered as he set the evidence box down and looked past Garrison toward the old gas station.

Cooper's chest was heaving, and his face flushed with either too much or not enough oxygen. Garrison couldn't tell.

"Deputy Bullard is going to drive the two girls home. The two boys say they're fine to drive home alone. I already have their statements. Mayor Barber has called the medical center, and they're sending the body car out in about an hour or so. Are you with me, Cooper?" Garrison asked his young officer, whose distant gaze made him look like he was lost in a crime novel.

"Yes, sir," Cooper answered.

"I see you have the camera and flashlight. Where's your weapon?" Garrison asked, noticing his officer's belt was bare.

"Oh! Damn! It's in the truck. I'll be right back!" he shouted before running back to his Ford Responder.

Cooper slipped his off-duty holster onto his belt and holstered his Sig Saur P226 9mm pistol. He tucked a pair of handcuffs into his pants and quickly returned to his boss and the mayor. "Sorry, Chief. I won't let that happen again. Guess I'm a little nervous."

"Not a problem. Take a deep breath and settle down. I don't want you to be shocked, so I'll tell you the victim has a gunshot wound to the forehead. It looks like the bullet went through and blew out the back of his head. He's lying on his back, so when we roll him over, it's gonna be ugly. You gonna be okay with that?"

Cooper stood silent momentarily, seeming to process what the chief had told him. Garrison knew he'd likely seen pictures of bloody crime scenes in the academy, but in real life, probably nothing worse than a bleeding laceration on the face of a vehicle crash victim.

"Yes, sir. I'll be fine," Cooper assured his boss.

"Okay, we'll take photos first, then proceed from there," Garrison advised.

Garrison explained they would begin photographing the scene from afar, then work their way closer to the victim's body. They'd do their best in the dark with flashlights, then examine the scene again after daylight arrived. Garrison allowed Cooper to handle the camera while he illuminated the sections of the scene that he wanted photographed. After several minutes, Cooper approached the body. The light hit the victim's face, combining pale white, purple tinge, and dark blue or black toward the back of the head. Cooper swallowed hard and blinked his eyes several times. Garrison watched him carefully; in case he started to vomit and contaminate the scene. The dead man's face looked like one of those zombies in the movies. Cooper gulped a few more times, then clicked several photographs.

"Does it look like he was shot lying on the ground there?" Garrison asked, testing.

Cooper looked at the floor around the body, then slid his light beam up the room's back wall to the splattered stain. "No, sir. I'd say he was standing when he was shot, then fell backward to where he is now."

"Very good. I agree. Now, if the bullet went through his head like we figure, where would you look for it?"

"I figure it'd be lodged in the wall or ricocheted off it somewhere," came the correct response.

"Excellent. Let's look at the area in and around the splatter," Garrison suggested.

The two officers hit the area with their lights and looked closely. Near the center of the globular splatter was a hole.

"That could be it, Chief," Cooper whispered.

"Looks like a fresh hole. Notice the lighter-colored wood inside the grimy surface. We'll wait until daylight and take a closer look. Go ahead and get a couple of pictures right now."

Before Cooper could get started the mayor interrupted the training moment.

"We've got company beginning to arrive," Barber said. "Looks like TV and radio station crews from Odessa are setting up. I'll handle them."

"Do we have crime scene tape in that there?" Garrison asked, pointing to the evidence collection kit.

"Yep," Cooper answered, flipping open the lid and grabbing a large, unused roll of yellow tape.

"Okay, let's run tape all around the perimeter of this place. That'll give us some degree of protection," Garrison stated.

Cooper took the roll and walked it around the fence line that was already providing a makeshift barrier to the scene. He circled and met Garrison, who tied off the yellow plastic ribbon emblazoned with the repeated phrase, POLICE LINE DO NOT CROSS.

"How about gloves?" Garrison asked Cooper, who nodded and plucked two pairs of black latex coverings from the evidence box.

Garrison directed Cooper to kneel on the left side of the body near the beltline, and then reach across and pull the body toward him onto its side. Cooper took hold of the jeans and shirt, then closed his eyes and pulled until the body balanced on its right side. The smell from the cavity in the head erupted with a pungent odor. Garrison was used to it; Cooper was clearly not. He took short breaths, as if that would help him avoid the nauseating odor. The heat wasn't terrible, but the night air hung thick, especially near the gaping wound.

Garrison examined the wound on the back of the victim's head, then motioned for Cooper to return the body to its back.

"Check his pockets for a wallet or identification," Garrison ordered.

Cooper checked the rear pants pockets, then the front. Coming up with nothing, he shook his head. Garrison search the body by squeezing the outside of the jeans from the hips down to the ankles. Cooper followed the chief's search with his light down to a slight bulge around the left ankle. Garrison pulled the pant leg up to reveal an ankle holster with a small-caliber semi-automatic pistol still snapped in.

Garrison pointed to the pistol, and Cooper snapped

photos. Then Garrison carefully pulled the Velcro apart and removed both the holster and gun.

"Always check for a weapon. The last thing you want to do is expose yourself to a pistol or knife blade that could injure you or your partner," Garrison explained, then added, "He's got a pistol in an ankle holster, and powder burns around the bullet wound, meaning . . ."

"Means he probably knew his killer," Cooper finished the statement.

"Correct. We'll wait for the medical examiner, then move him out of here.. Not much else I want to do until daylight," Garrison advised.

Cooper nodded and stepped away. He seemed relieved not to have passed out or soiled the crime scene with his vomit.

Garrison approved.

CHAPTER 10

TUESDAY

Mayor Barber provided an official statement to the media, which wasn't much more than an acknowledgment that the Bison police were investigating a suspicious death. Garrison and Cooper had helped the lone medical-center intern load the body onto the gurney, then into the late-model Ford Econoline van that posed as the medical examiner's body car.

While the mayor worked with the media, the officers then took a cursory look around the inside of the building and followed up with a similar effort around the outside and chain-link fence. To no surprise of Garrison, neither he nor Cooper found anything of interest or evidentiary value. The degree of darkness in the area was new to Garrison, who'd been used to the bright lights of the nighttime big city. He walked out into the middle of Curtis Road, which was nothing more than a narrow ribbon of dirt stretching east and west through the southern border of Bison and did a 360 scan of the area. He then directed Cooper back to his patrol vehicle and joined his young officer in the cab. A couple more media outlets had arrived, keeping Mayor Barber busy. Garrison revisited what he and Cooper had accomplished on the scene and filled his officer in on the teenagers' written statements.

Each statement essentially said the same thing, which Garrison found satisfying, figuring the story was truthful. Except for the kid with the gun, none of them had any reason to lie, although it had been Garrison's experience that even people who didn't need to lie to the police did so for reasons his thirty-five years in the business still couldn't explain.

The story was straight and simple. At approximately ten o'clock, all four teens arrived in Baker Jenkins's car with a six-pack of sour beer and a cheap bottle of wine. No one mentioned marijuana, and Garrison didn't care to ask. Jenkins parked on the east side of the building to keep the vehicle out of sight from cars passing on CR 190, which was far more likely than traffic on Curtis Road. Using flashlights the boys had brought, all four entered the old station via the front door and took turns seeing the body in the order they walked in. After realizing what they'd seen, the freaked-out teens ran out of the building and called the police, then waited inside Jenkins's car. When Deputy Bullard arrived, the girls remained inside the car while the boys met Bullard at the front of his squad car and told him what they had found. All four confirmed Deputy Bullard briefly entered the building, then radioed his dispatcher to contact Bison PD.

Cooper advised he was familiar with the teens' families but didn't really know any of them. Cooper also informed Garrison that he wasn't surprised Jenkins had a gun on him because his father was the redneck type who drove his truck around town with a rifle in his back window and a license to carry his pistol.

Realizing his need for caffeine, Garrison sent Cooper to the truck stop on the edge of town for three large coffees and any snack Cooper thought was best. As the only twenty-four-hour business near Bison, the truck stop was the only option at three in the morning.

Barber had apparently satisfied the media, at least for now, and joined Garrison at his truck for an update.

"What's Officer Cooper up to?" Barber asked.

"I sent him to the truck stop for three large coffees and snacks," Garrison advised. "I'm starting to fade a bit."

Barber chuckled. "I know what you mean. It's not like it was twenty years ago when we could go two days straight on adrenaline alone."

"I hear that. Unless somebody's shooting at me, my adrenaline days are long gone," Garrison agreed. "Unlike Coop, who probably won't sleep for days."

The two men had a good-natured laugh at Cooper's expense.

"I know this isn't the time, but I'm not pleased with Justin Walker not responding to you," Barber admitted. "I'm sure it's a case of sour grapes, but I have no patience for that, either."

"I'm with you on that. When I see him, I'll let him know in no uncertain terms my position on this . . . *and* the fact it better not happen again," Garrison advised his boss.

Barber looked in the truck's side mirror and saw a set of headlights approaching in the distance. "Looks like our coffee and donuts are about to arrive."

"That's the best news I've had since Emily dropped that piece of pie in front of me, which seems like a week ago now." Garrison sighed.

Cooper met the chief and mayor at the back of Garrison's truck. Garrison opened the tailgate and joined Barber for a seat. Cooper kept his headlights on, providing enough light to prep their coffee and pick through a half-dozen day-old donuts from the truck stop.

"Ole Leon made us a fresh pot of coffee, but he apologized for the stale donuts. He says the lady who delivers the fresh donuts doesn't get to the truck stop until about five thirty or so. She brings them from a bakery in Odessa," Cooper reported.

"This is fine. Thank you," Garrison said.

While the men enjoyed their coffee and choked down their early breakfast, Garrison updated Barber on what he had and hadn't found in and around the crime scene. Both agreed they'd do better in a few hours when the sun came up.

"I'm still a little puzzled that there isn't an ID on the body and no other property inside the station. I don't know how long he was there, but it's unusual not to find anything except a pistol in an ankle holster. Maybe we'll find something in the daylight, but it's not like that's a big area to search. We looked it over from corner to corner. All we found were baby armadillos scrounging around. That doesn't make sense," Garrison stated, then gnawed at a donut.

"Maybe he and whoever killed him stopped off to get out of the storm last night. They fought, and the one guy got shot," Cooper chimed in, seemingly exhilarated by the conversation.

"Could be. Hard to tell if there was a struggle with all the trash and crap in there."

"All I know is there hasn't been a murder in Bison in twenty years, and from what I'm told, that one had been nothing more than two drunks tangled up in a domestic when Betty Sue Tucker ran a serrated bread knife through Bobby Tucker's gullet and let him bleed out while she finished off her bottle of Popov before calling the ambulance," Barber said, the words rolling out in a single breath.

"That story's like folklore around here," Cooper said with a laugh. "People still talk about it."

"Sure do," Barber agreed. "When I first came to Bison and started meeting folks, everybody wanted to tell me all about the Tucker murder, as they called it. I must have heard that story a hundred times!" Barber joined in on his officer's laughter.

Once the coffee and donuts were gone, Barber returned to the group of media reporters, who had surprisingly honored the mayor's request not to approach the scene. Garrison sent a text message to Amanda, requesting that she call him when she woke and was ready to talk. He omitted the reason for the request, preferring to notify his secretary directly.

As for Officer Walker, Cooper told Garrison that he lived outside of town in the county, which Garrison decided was too far to send Cooper on a message delivery. A second call to Walker's cell was met with the same voicemail request to leave a message after the beep. Garrison decided to pass on that.

The eastern horizon had begun to lighten with the soft orange hue of another promising day of bright sunshine. A quick glance at his watch confirmed it was approaching six o'clock in the morning. The sunrise would assist in the investigation and help whisk away his burning desire to crawl into his truck and sleep. Twenty minutes later, the sky lit up like a rainbow at the end of a summer shower. Blue, orange, and purple bands of color blended, making the sunrise worthy of a painter's brush. Too bad this morning would be spent investigating the first murder in Bison, Texas, in twenty years.

CHAPTER 11

TUESDAY

Bright daylight provided no genuine assistance to the scene investigation. The abandoned station looked like just that. Empty but for assorted detritus as before, including the fallen sections of plywood that had once covered broken windows and the front door. There was still no sign of how long the victim had been at the station nor any clues to his identity. Garrison did locate the storm shelter's trap door on the floor but nothing of value had been found inside the crudely constructed space. The drawers in the counter that at one time probably held the cash register, displays of candy bars, and cigarettes were empty, but for a used white napkin, the kind you'd get from a truck stop or mega gas station's food court. Garrison tucked the napkin inside a plastic bag for later examination.

He and Cooper extracted the fired bullet from the paneled wall. Garrison speculated it was a 9mm jacketed hollow point, but only careful ballistics examination would confirm that. After discovering he had no swabs or saline to collect serology evidence, Garrison used water and gun-cleaning patches left in the evidence box to collect fluid and blood specimens from the wall and floor. After Cooper took more photographs of the scene in daylight, Garrison was satisfied that was all he would get from the scene. He instructed Cooper to retrieve lumber and nails from Crawford's feed store and return so they could board the place up properly before they left. Mayor Barber sent the media packing after the carpentry work was completed, then joined Garrison and Cooper back at the station.

Garrison walked in first and was met with a horrified look on Amanda's face.

"Chief! I'm so sorry! I just saw your text when I was driving to work this morning. I heard the news on the radio. I figured I'd wait to call you when I got here. Goodness!" Amanda exclaimed, her eyes wide and shoulders slumped.

"That's okay, Amanda. There wasn't much you could have done for us anyway. I had just been trying to catch you and let you know what was going on before you heard it elsewhere. No harm done," Garrison assured her, then walked hastily toward to the evidence processing area, Cooper on his heels.

"John, I'm going to stop by my office, then head home for a few hours of sleep. If you need me, holler," Barber said before disappearing out the front door.

The phones on Amanda's and Garrison's desks were ringing. Amanda quickly dismissed her caller, then answered Garrison's line.

" "Chief Garrison's office," Amanda answered. "Oh . . . Okay . . . Hang on." She held her hand over the phone's receiver and shouted, "Chief! It's Councilman Walker! He wants to know what you're doing about the murder!"

Garrison had been directing Cooper on how he wanted the items they'd collected tagged for future reference. Then he hustled to his office and picked up the receiver. "Chief Garrison," he announced.

The councilman rattled off a slew of questions and exclamations. When he came up for air, Garrison finally spoke.

"We've just returned from the scene where we've been all night. All I can tell is I have an unidentified white male with a headshot wound. Mayor Barber was out there with me. I'd suggest you speak to him about any other details he might want to share. I have none. Now I have a job to do, so I bid you good day," Garrison offered before hanging up the phone, then said to his secretary, "Amanda, if anyone else calls, just take a message."

After securing what evidence they had, Garrison called the medical examiner's office at the county morgue. While on hold, he instructed Cooper to go home and get some sleep, which after initial resistance, Cooper agreed to do. Garrison noted it was nearly twenty after eight.

"Amanda! Find out where Walker is, please!" he called out. He heard Amanda dialing her phone, each key that she pressed a different tone. Then she called out for him to pick up the other line.

He did. "Hello?"

"This is the Kutseena County Medical Examiner's Office. You wanted to talk to us?"

"Good morning. This is Chief John Garrison. Yes, I wanted to know—" he started before being abruptly interrupted by the caller.

"Hey, Chief Garrison! I look forward to meeting you, which I assume will be rather soon, based on the body I have here," the voice trailed off in its enthusiasm. "Oh, uh . . . This is Dr. Vincent Vesley, your medical examiner."

"Hi, Doc, good to talk to you. Do you have any other autopsies in front of mine?" Garrison asked.

The doctor laughed heartily. "Dan Barber told me you were from Houston's Homicide Unit. Don't worry. Here in Kutseena, we push natural deaths aside when we have something like this. Give me a couple of hours, then come on over. I should be finished by then," Vesley advised.

"Thanks, Doc. I guess I forgot I'm not in the big city anymore. I haven't slept in what seems like days. See you soon." Garrison chuckled before hanging up the phone.

Amanda stepped into his office. "Officer Walker is on his way. Says he's running a little late," she reported. "He should be here in about, uh . . . ten minutes," Amanda added before rushing back to her desk to answer the phone, which had not stopped ringing since her arrival to the office.

Amanda's estimate of Walker's arrival was accurate as the senior officer appeared ten minutes later in Garrison's office doorway.

"Come in and close the door," Garrison instructed the officer, whose frown and somber look told the chief his officer knew he was in trouble.

"Sorry—" Walker began.

"Stop right there. First, I'm not the damned bit interested in why you didn't answer two calls last night. Second, if it happens again, I'll suspend you long enough to make it hurt. Third, if this was some protest at not getting my job, I now know why you didn't get it. If you're going to walk around here with a case of the ass, I strongly suggest you find employment elsewhere. But until then, I need to know I can rely on you, as there are only three of us this week. Are you part of this department or not?" Garrison demanded.

"Yes, sir. What'd you need me to do?" Walker answered in a low voice.

"I assume you heard about what happened last night, so I need you to find out everything you can about that abandoned gas station on 190. Who owns it? How long has it been abandoned? Everything you can."

"Yes, sir. On it," Walker said before turning on a heel and leaving the room.

Garrison leaned back in his chair. He was already questioning his decision to take this job. It wasn't the all-night investigation, although he'd hoped those were behind him; he just didn't know if he had what it took to put up with the small-town politics that attached itself like a blood-sucking leech to jobs like this. He closed his door and propped his boots up on his desk. Next thing he knew, Amanda was standing in front of him.

"Chief . . . Chief, wake up. Doctor Vesley's on the phone . . ."

CHAPTER 12

TUESDAY

Garrison jumped like he'd been hit with a stun gun. He jerked his boots off the desk, taking a stack of papers with them. Amanda shrieked and hopped back a few steps, banging into a narrow bookcase along the wall. Garrison shook his head and tried to focus on his secretary.

"Sorry, Amanda, I guess I dosed off for a few minutes," Garrison said, chagrined.

"You more than dozed off, Chief. You've been asleep for three hours," Amanda advised.

"Three hours! How the hell did that happen?" Garrison dragged his hands through his hair. "Damn."

"I told Justin to leave you alone, and I've been screening your calls, but Dr. Vesley called and said he was finished with the autopsy and wanted to know if you were coming by his office."

Garrison stood and winced at the needle-sharp pains that darted through his back, a gift for falling asleep in his chair. He stretched, leaned onto his desk, and took a deep breath.

"Thank you for the shuteye. I'll get myself together and head to the morgue right away," Garrison advised.

"Justin said he's gathered the information you wanted on the gas station, but he's out there now taking a look around," Amanda said, bringing Garrison up to date on his officer's status. "Oh, and Coop hasn't come back yet."

Garrison stumbled into the men's room, took a quick sink bath, and then retrieved the address of the morgue from Amanda before he headed out to see the pathologist. The blazing sun stung his eyes, still fighting to adjust from his impromptu nap. He settled into his truck, which was more like an oven than a truck cab. He started the engine and rolled all the windows down, welcoming the influx of scorching hot air. It may have been a hundred degrees outside, but it felt like twice that inside the entombed cab. He paused momentarily to allow the cool air to begin flowing out of their mini vents, then clicked the transmission into drive and turned north onto Center Street.

The county morgue was just north of Bison's city limits, about a half mile past the Bison Medical Center, which occupied the southeast corner of Center and Coyote Highway at the north edge of town. Garrison felt like a tourist as he took in the names and types of small businesses which dotted each side of Bison's main North and South streets. He took special note of the auto repair shop and the little hamburger stand, which he missed the name of. After seeing the burger stand, he realized the stale donuts he'd had for breakfast hadn't done much for his hunger.

Garrison slowed as he approached the medical center, which was less than a hospital but much more than the massive urgent-care centers he'd become used to in Houston. He made a mental note of the emergency entrance and the parking lots he figured he'd get to know all too well. Just behind the smaller building on the south side of the main center was a round helipad with a large red cross painted in the center. The pad's landscaped perimeter was meticulously manicured with small ground shrubs and flowers. The ever-present orange windsock hung limp at the top of its metal pole, as if it didn't have a care in the world.

Garrison chuckled to himself. *I should be so lucky.*

He recognized the standard county government building up ahead on the right—a single-story, cinder-block-walled structure with plenty of aluminum framing and double glass front doors and simple, low-maintenance evergreen landscaping. adorning each side of the wide sidewalk that led to the entrance. The building was painted tan with brown trim framing the roofline and windows. Several weeds poked their heads up between the shredded wood mulch spread painfully thin. Garrison turned into the first driveway and followed it to the rear of the building, where he knew there'd be a reserved parking space for law enforcement and an entrance near the pathologist's office. He parked his truck in one of two spaces marked with old, rusted metal signs that displayed police. Since the building was equipped with a card access security system, Garrison couldn't enter the back door. A modest knock on the steel door's reinforced window brought a tall, thin man in his mid-fifties, wearing horn-rimmed eyeglasses and a bleached white lab coat, to open the door. Immediately upon letting Garrison inside, the man then turned and walked down the short hallway to an office, all the while speaking into a recording device.

Garrison silently followed the man into the office, which displayed the name, *Vincent Vesley, Doctor of Pathology*, in the center of the door. A wave of the man's hand directed Garrison to a chair in front of a moderate-sized desk containing several gray metal trays filled with assorted documents. A sign on the credenza behind him read *The Dead Speak Loud and Clear Inside These Walls*, an apparent tongue-in-cheek gift from someone the doctor knew. A moment later, Dr. Vesley finished his discussion with his electronic partner and reached across the desk to shake Garrison's hand.

"My apologies, Chief Garrison, but I wanted to get those thoughts recorded before I forgot them, which I find I'm doing more and more these days," Vesley announced with a wry grin.

Garrison shook hands and formally introduced himself.

"I understand, Doc. No problem," Garrison responded.

"This is certainly a rude reception, isn't it?"

"Ha! That's exactly what Dan Barber said last night!" Garrison answered with a laugh. "I'm told there hasn't been a murder in Bison in twenty years, and here I'm greeted with one on my first day."

Vesley peeled off his glasses and waved them around as he spoke. "Well, I've only been here seven . . . no, eight years now, I guess, and I can tell you Bison hasn't had anything close to a murder in that time, but looks like I can't say that anymore."

"What do you have for me, Doc? Other than the obvious gunshot wound to the head," Garrison asked, leaning back in his chair.

"Well, let me start with what I don't have. There are no signs of blunt-force or any other type of trauma anywhere on the body, nor any defensive wounds or needle marks. The back of the skull around the rim of the exit wound shows trauma, probably from the fall after being shot. I have one gunshot wound to the middle of the forehead, which, as you saw, traveled completely through the brain cavity, and exited out the back of the head. I saw you'd bagged his hands. Any reason to believe he shot himself?" Vesley asked with a single raised eyebrow.

"No, sir, none at all. That's just something I do whenever I can in case we want to do an atomic absorption test for gunshot residue," Garrison explained.

"That's what I assumed. I wouldn't say it would be impossible for the deceased to have shot himself in that location, but having a direct entry like he has would be pretty difficult. There are powder ring burns around the bullet hole, indicating a close-range discharge. I'm sure you know that too. I'm ruling this a homicide with the cause of death being the gunshot wound to the head. No surprises there for you," Vesley said with a grin. "I removed the bags from the hands for examination and fingerprinting, but I didn't contaminate them if you plan on conducting your gunshot test."

"I don't think so," Garrison said. "The truth is, I don't even know if we have the test kit or not. I haven't been able to inventory our equipment. Besides, we found a pistol still snapped into an ankle holster he was wearing. I believe it was fired, so it may be the murder weapon."

"The intern that brought him in said he had no identification. Any idea who he is?" Vesley asked.

"Not yet. One of my officers has information on the old gas station where we found him. Maybe that'll lead us somewhere, but I'm not so sure. I get the feeling he was hiding out there or something and was shot by somebody he knew or expected."

"All right, Chief, if nothing else, I'll have to cut our visit short. I've got an elderly woman from out in the county to take a look at. I'll email you when the toxicology is complete, and I've completed my report." Vesley stood, extending his hand.

Garrison took it, and they shook. "Thanks, Doc. I look forward to a future visit when we're not talking business."

Garrison climbed back into his oven-disguised-as-a-truck-cab and just sat there for a moment. *That wasn't much help. The only thing I didn't know was the lack of needle marks*, he thought while waiting for the cool air to begin flowing.

The sound of his phone blew up his thoughts. A quick look showed the caller was Justin Walker.

"This is Garrison," he announced.

"Chief, it's Walker. You'd better come down to Curtis Road right away. The county boys found an abandoned SUV about a mile east of the old station. Looks way out of place. They figured they'd better let us know before they started messing with it."

"Okay. A mile east of the gas station. Got it. I'll be there right quick!" Garrison advised.

CHAPTER 13

TUESDAY

Garrison's disillusionment over not having his truck already equipped with emergency lights and siren burned inside him like the blistering sun beating down on Bison. Despite knowing the SUV wasn't going anywhere, he wanted to get to it as quickly as possible without blowing red lights or speeding past the town hall where, knowing his luck, Councilman Walker would see him and raise hell. He navigated around the few cars that found their way in his path and hit the brakes when the light in the center of town turned red on him.

Of course, it's red, he thought, tapping his right thumb nervously on top of the steering wheel.

The light flashed green, and his Ford's tires squealed when he hastily punched the accelerator. A short burst of speed later, he was hooking a left turn onto Curtis Road. Stones and gravel peppered the wheel wells, sounding like ripping Velcro in all four. A dense cloud of dust ballooned behind the crimson Ford FX4 as it sped down the narrow dirt path. Garrison scanned the area on both sides of the road, looking for any possible hope of a witness. No chance unless someone drove by when the SUV was abandoned. There wasn't a farmhouse or ranch building anywhere near the road. He could make out a couple of houses and an outbuilding or two well off in the distance, but there'd be no witnesses there. He looked down the road and saw Walker's responder and two county cars on the south side of the road with a black SUV.

Garrison smiled to himself. *Three units at an abandoned vehicle in the middle of nowhere.*

He parked his truck about fifty feet behind Walker's vehicle, then approached the scene, scanning the ground for anything unusual. Seeing what his chief had done, Walker quickly jumped into his responder and backed it away from the SUV, where he had positioned his vehicle far too close to its rear bumper. Walker exited his truck as Garrison walked past.

"Sorry, Chief. Wasn't thinking."

"Remember, the scene is always bigger than we think," Garrison answered with a forced grin.

Walker introduced the two deputies, one of which was a sergeant, before all four officers took a closer look at the SUV.

"This thing is . . . way out of place out here, Chief, and with your shooting just down the road, we figured it's probably involved," the sergeant advised.

"What do you have on it, Walker?" Garrison asked.

"A Hummer H2, unknown year. The registration comes back to an '84 Chevrolet Blazer with a salvage title. "The VIN shows invalid," Walker reported.

Garrison looked closely through the windshield at the VIN plate affixed to the lower left corner of the dashboard. The plate was a professional counterfeit, but the rivets were not factory. Garrison slid on latex gloves and pulled back on the chrome handle. The door was unlocked and opened smoothly. A robust odor of ammonia burst from inside the vehicle. Garrison checked the inside of the door frame and confirmed the vehicle identification decal had been removed. Garrison checked to ensure his officer had gloves on, then motioned for him to move around to the front passenger door.

"Take a look inside the glove box and under the front seat. I'm sure we won't find anything since someone went to the trouble of wiping it down with ammonia, but just in case," Garrison instructed.

Garrison opened the center console and found it empty. Under the seats and the vehicle's rear area were also clear. Walker shook his head, confirming the glove box was empty. The carpet was pristine, and the black leather looked like new. The vehicle looked like it had just come out of the showroom, despite the last Hummer H2 being made in 2009. Garrison stepped back from the vehicle and removed his gloves. He looked under and all around the immediate area of the Hummer. Nothing.

"Did you see any tire tracks when y'all drove up?" Garrison asked the deputy.

"No, sir. With the drought and that windstorm, any tracks would've been wiped out pretty quick."

Garrison looked around. "They had to have another vehicle. No way anyone's walking away from here."

"Not unless they live in one of these farmhouses, which we can tell you they don't," the sergeant added.

"They went a mile east before dumping the Hummer,

which tells me they probably headed to Odessa or Midland. No sense driving a mile east, dumping the Hummer, then turning and heading back west," Garrison ruminated.

The sergeant took off his hat and scratched his head. "They could catch a flight out of Midland to anywhere they needed to go."

"Could you fellas call for a wrecker? We'll have it towed to our station," Garrison asked the deputies, who nodded and immediately keyed their radio, telling a waiting wrecker driver to come in. "Walker, make sure the wrecker driver wears gloves and doesn't touch too many surfaces. I'll see you back at the station."

Garrison thanked the deputies, getting a business card from each, then spun his truck around and headed for the station. He had a bad feeling about his first investigation as Bison's police chief. He felt hollow. His stomach churned, and his chest felt empty. He knew at some point his angst would crush him, causing his blood pressure to explode into one of those week-long headaches he seemed to live with constantly. He despised failure and the feeling he got when he believed it was imminent. He recalled some of the cases he'd failed to solve, and the anger and anguish he'd allowed to permeate his life. That was the main reason he was divorced, although he knew there were others.

This murder was obviously a professional hit with the suspect, or suspects, ensuring there'd be no viable evidence at the scene or the vehicle. He knew from the unsolved cases in Houston that these types of crimes rarely got solved. An unsolved murder would be just what Councilman Walker would grab hold of and run with. The first murder in forever in this town, and the fancy new chief from the big city couldn't figure it out. Garrison may have been from the big city, but he knew how these small towns operated. A quick vote of no confidence, and he'd be up before the council, getting voted out of his job faster than he was voted in. At least he hadn't bought or rented a house yet, and he did have his pension, though it sure wasn't enough to live on.

CHAPTER 14

TUESDAY

Looking like she was about to bust, Amanda met Garrison at the front door. Her frown had pulled the corners of her blue eyes down, exposing lines no makeup could hide.

"Chief, Mayor Barber called. He wants an update. He says Councilman Walker has been in and out of his office every ten minutes demanding an update. Sheriff Mitchell called. He asked that you give him a call when you can. Cooper is on his way in, and Maria Fernandez called asking you to call her ASAP," Amanda gushed in one long breath.

Garrison forced a smile and patted his secretary's shoulder. "It'll be all right, Amanda. Don't let any of this cause you grief. We'll figure this out, and we'll all be heroes," he said with superficial confidence.

Amanda took a breath and smiled, the worry lines disappearing like magic. "Thanks, Chief. I'm just concerned you won't get the chance here you deserve, is all," she admitted.

"That's up to me. Not my staff. Now, could I get you to do me an enormous favor?"

"Certainly," she eagerly answered.

"I know it's not your job, and I promise I won't take advantage, but could you order me something for lunch? I haven't eaten in quite a while," Garrison hesitantly asked.

"Of course! What would you like?"

"How about that burger place on North Center? Is it any good?" he asked.

"Clyde's? Absolutely! The best in town. Although the Pump Jack Bar owner will tell you differently." She giggled.

"The Pumpjack Bar?" he asked, happy to get business off Amanda's mind.

"Yep. It's out on Bison Boulevard at the east end of town. We'll get you out there one of these days." She then spun on her heels and headed to her desk to call in the lunch order.

"Please get yourself something too. My treat," Garrison added.

"Thanks, Chief, but I've already eaten. It's after two, you know."

Garrison checked his watch. It was pushing two thirty. He'd not even thought about the time since last night. He glanced over the brief notes Amanda had given him. They were the standard "while you were out" sticky notes. Garrison looked at Amanda's neatly printed writing. It was beyond legible. The letters had a slight slant to the right, a touch of the feminine. He looked back at Amanda, who was on the phone placing his order.

She's going to be a treasure, he thought.

Garrison fell into his office chair and looked at the phone. He wanted to call Fernandez first but knew he'd better let the mayor know what was happening.

"Mayor Dan Barber's office, how may I help you?" Connie Maxwell greeted Garrison's call.

"Hello, Connie, it's John Garrison. Is the Mayor available?"

"Sure thing, Chief, hang on."

Seconds later, the mayor picked up. "Hello, John. What the hell's going on? You have anything yet?"

Garrison told him what had transpired at the medical examiner's office and about the recovered Hummer on Curtis Road.

"Sounds like a pro, doesn't it?" the mayor asked.

"Yep. That's what it looks like," Garrison agreed.

"Damn it! Walker's being a jackass about this already. All right, keep me posted when you have something. And don't worry about Walker. I'll deal with him."

After that call had ended, Garrison dialed Maria Fernandez's number.

"Hey John, how's it going out in paradise?" Fernandez asked.

Her voice was soft, pleasant, and downright sexy, even though she made no attempt at sounding that way. Her voice was familiar and comforting.

"It hasn't exactly started out as paradise, I'm afraid," Garrison said with a twinge of laughter.

"Oh? Somebody smash into a steer or something?" Fernandez laughed into the phone.

"Actually, I've got a murder on my hands," he informed his former Houston homicide partner and recruit, who was scheduled to join him in six days.

"You're kidding!" she blurted.

Garrison's tone turned serious. "I wish I were, but we had a guy get himself executed Sunday night during a tornado."

"Executed? During a tornado?"

"Shot one time in the forehead at close range. Whoever did it, collected all the evidence, then dumped their SUV down the road. They took the time to wipe it down with ammonia. And I know what you're going to ask ... No, I've got nothing else," Garrison said. "Any chance you could get out here before next Monday?"

"Um, okay, I guess so. I'm packed, and my stuff is in storage already. I can leave tomorrow. How long of a drive is it again?" Fernandez asked.

"It's a solid eight hours unless you have to stop every hour to use the bathroom!" Garrison chuckled, having been on long road trips with her before and knowing her demands.

"All right, all right! Whatever! I'll leave early in the morning and try to get there sometime tomorrow afternoon. Where should I stay?"

"Whatever you do, don't stay at the motel here in Bison. Look for a hotel in Odessa. It's only about thirty minutes from here. We'll figure the rest out after you get here," Garrison said, feeling the weight already lifting from his shoulders.

"Okay, I'll call you when I'm close," Fernandez advised before ending the call.

Garrison leaned back in his chair and stared at the various papers on his desk. He didn't know what most of the documents were about, but he felt his confidence building back up inside. Maria Fernandez wasn't only one of the most beautiful women he'd ever met, but she was one of the best homicide detectives he'd ever worked with. By her own account, she was tall for a Mexican woman at five-eight and had shoulder-length, coal-black hair that was always elegantly styled. A narrow section of long tresses constantly tumbled over her left eye. She was a regular at the nail salon and was only seen with expertly applied makeup. Her fellow detectives initially teased her about being high maintenance for a cop. To that, she responded firmly that just because she was a cop didn't mean she had to stop being a woman. That put an end to that.

Like him, she had joined HPD at the young age of twenty, but unlike him, she had the good sense to retire after twenty-five years instead of the thirty-five he'd hung around for. When he discovered he'd need to hire an officer immediately, he didn't hesitate to ask her to join him at Bison PD. At first, she scoffed at his offer, then gradually changed her mind, telling him with no husband or children to answer to, she might as well see what West Texas policing was like, especially with him being the chief and their former captain the mayor.

Garrison heard the rumbling of a wrecker's diesel

engine roll into the parking lot behind the station. He grabbed the evidence box and headed past Amanda, who said his lunch would arrive in a few minutes. Garrison and Officer Walker watched the Hummer get eased off the flatbed and placed perfectly in the parking space indicated by Walker. Garrison signed the tow slip, then heard Amanda's voice on Walker's radio.

"Unit two, come in . . ."

"This is unit two. Go ahead, Amanda," Walker answered into the small mic he had clipped to the epaulet on his left shoulder.

"Just got a report of a traffic crash on South Center in front of Hollingsworth's feed store," she advised.

Walker looked at Garrison, who nodded. "Go take care of that. Let me know if you need any help."

Garrison set his hat on the Hummer's roof, then reached into the vehicle and carefully pulled the hood release lever. He popped open the hood. He checked the front of the engine block, looking for the seventeen-digit VIN. As expected, it was obliterated. He crawled under the engine compartment and took a look.

Damn skid plates!

He retrieved his toolbox from his truck and then crawled back under. He removed the plate and searched the lower sides of the engine block. Sure enough, there were seventeen digits that did not match the VIN plate on the dash. He took down the combination of numbers and letters, then hurried back into the office, where a white paper bag sat on the corner of Amanda's desk. The aroma drifted up and wrapped around his head like a warm, cozy hug.

"Damn! That smells good!" he announced while handing Amanda the crumpled piece of notepad paper containing the scribbled digits. "Could you run this right away, please," he asked, digging his dirty hand into the bag, and retrieving the greasy delight.

Two bites in, the burger sent titillating flavors roaring over his starved tastebuds. He couldn't be sure if it was the fact he was starving or if ole Clyde really did make the best burger in Texas, but Garrison was convinced this was the best damn hamburger he'd ever eaten. He looked down into the bag and saw a nest of entangled French fries ready to be devoured. He leaned his head back and closed his eyes, savoring every second.

"You gonna be all right, Chief?" Amanda giggled as her fingertips clicked across her keyboard.

"I don't know. This is better than a Whataburger, and I didn't think that was possible," Garrison admitted, wallowing in his oral glee.

The printer behind Amanda began to rumble and vibrate, its mechanisms snapping into action. She spun her chair around and waited for the machine to spit the data pages onto the gray plastic rack. Five pages later, she snatched them up and handed them to Garrison, who was now working on the helpless fries with greasy fingers.

"What's it say?" he managed to mumble over a mouthful of fried potato strips.

"2009 Hummer H2. Reported stolen by El Paso PD

three years ago. The notes say it was a steal from the Mexico side." Amanda stopped there.

Garrison swallowed hard and gave her a thumbs-up. "Perfect! Call El Paso PD and ask for everything they have about the case. I gotta wash my hands and get back to the Hummer."

"Shouldn't you have done that before you ate?" Amanda asked, emphasizing the "before" through a wide smile.

"I know, I know! You're right, but I was starving!" he shouted before heading to the men's room, thinking, *Finally, a lead . . .*

CHAPTER 15

TUESDAY

Garrison felt energized. His belly was full, he had a lead, and his former partner would arrive tomorrow. He looked up into the blazing sun and smiled. Even the sun's flaming embers seemed to have eased a bit. He tossed magnetic fingerprint powder over the usual spots on the Hummer: door handles, hood release, rear gate handle, and such. As expected, he found nothing on the exterior and expected the same from the inside. Despite his doubts, he worked on the dashboard, rearview mirror, console, and steering wheel. Nothing other than a powdery mess resulted. He scrutinized the windows. A thin layer of West Texas dust covered every inch of the outside glass. The inside looked like it had just come from the detailer's shop. Garrison peeled off his latex gloves and saw Cooper pulling into the parking lot.

"Get some rest, kid?" Garrison asked his junior officer.

"Not much, Chief. Too damn excited, I guess. Find out anything? This Hummer involved?" Cooper asked.

"We think so. We found it on the side of Curtis Road, about a mile east of the gas station. It'd been wiped clean, though—no prints, as I expected. I found the real VIN on the bottom of the engine block. It's a 2009, reported stolen by El Paso PD three years ago. I have Amanda working on getting some details from El Paso."

"Whaddya need me to do?"

"Walker's out on a wreck right now," Garrison said. "When he gets back, I need to see what he found out about the history of that old gas station. When he comes in, I'll need you to head out on patrol and answer any calls."

"Patrol! Aw, come on, Chief. This is what it's all about, not patrol." Cooper's shoulders had immediately dropped upon hearing the instruction.

"Answering the public's calls for service is what it's all about, Coop. Don't worry, you'll have plenty to do on this before it's over," Garrison assured his eager officer.

Garrison wrapped yellow crime scene tape around the Hummer, then followed Cooper inside, where Amanda was finishing her call with El Paso PD.

"The El Paso records clerk said she'd send whatever they had as soon as possible," Amanda reported.

The radio behind her ignited with the sound of a siren.

"Unit two! Come in, Amanda!" Officer Walker shouted above the wail of his patrol unit's siren.

"Go ahead, unit two. I have the chief here," Amanda calmly answered.

"The county is chasing a stolen truck that did a crash burglary at Bentley's tire store. They're westbound on Bison Boulevard coming into town. They're asking for assistance."

Amanda looked at Garrison, who immediately nodded in approval. He looked at Cooper, who was already running for the door.

"Tell Walker he's clear to engage, but let the county be primary if he can," Garrison told Amanda.

She repeated Garrison's orders to Walker and let him know the Chief was heading his way. Walker acknowledged; his siren now clicked to the familiar Yelp mode used in pursuits.

Garrison grabbed the keys to the third patrol truck and hurried out the door. He fired up the engine, pulled out on Center Street, and blocked all northbound traffic with his vehicle. If he remembered the town map, which he hoped he'd committed to memory correctly; the pursuit would come right through downtown in front of the town hall. He then sprinted across the street and stopped the southbound traffic with hand signals. He heard the sirens in the distance, their piercing sound increasing each second.

Emotions of excitement, concern, and worry collided inside him. He'd been in more pursuits than he could remember, some ending in fiery crashes and death, but he wasn't the chief of police for any of those. He glanced across the street and saw Mayor Barber standing in front of town hall with council members Walker and Giddings.

This should be fun, Garrison thought.

The blaring sirens bounced off the buildings as they entered the east side of town. Garrison watched the suspect vehicle, a red Ram pickup truck, its bed filled with tires, rip past him like a bullet from the barrel of a gun. Garrison caught a glance of the three suspects crammed inside the single cab—all white males in their early twenties.

Garrison committed their faces to memory as unit one, the Kutseena County Sheriff's Dodge Charger blasted past him with unit two, Walker piloting his Bison PD unit close behind. A few car lengths back, Cooper flew past in a flash. Garrison winced, realizing his men were traveling over 100 mph through town. Garrison ran to his patrol unit and sped off after his officers. His patrol truck had surprisingly good acceleration, which allowed him to keep the pursuit in view. His radio barked nonstop.

"Approaching Crawford's tack store!" Walker called out.

"Right behind unit two!" Cooper, now the third unit in the pursuit, shouted into his mic.

"Garrison to unit two, what's your speed?"

"One oh five!" Walker responded. "They're zigzagging now, trying to wreck out the county unit!"

"Give 'em some room, boys!" Garrison ordered. He could see the clouds of dust erupting from both sides of the highway, confirming Justin's call that the suspect vehicle intentionally crossed the oncoming lane to hit the gravel shoulders.

"Just past West Street!" Walker called out, confirming they'd left the Bison town limits.

"Damn it!" Garrison roared. He knew he should probably call off his units since they'd left Bison's jurisdiction, but he hesitated, hopeful the pursuit would end quickly.

"Suspects wrecked out! Suspects on . . ." Walker's radio transmission was cut short.

Garrison's heart sank as he jammed the gas pedal to the floor, trying to get more speed to catch up to the chaos.

"Suspects bailed out. Running on foot northbound through the pasture," Cooper said, then after a pause, added, "Unit two wrecked out! Walker's wrecked out!"

Garrison screeched to a halt behind Walker's unit, which had a caved-in windshield courtesy of a creased roof and smoking engine. He rushed to his officer, who was kicking the inside of the driver's door, trying to escape. Garrison yanked on the door handle as hard as he could, rocking the bent metal door until it gave way and flew open. Walker scrambled out of the wreckage and leaned on Garrison, blood flowing from a deep cut on his forehead.

"You gonna make it?" Garrison shouted above the blaring sirens from the vehicles of Cooper and the deputy, who were still chasing two of the suspects on foot through the pasture.

"Damn, tires flew everywhere when they rolled. One of them smashed into my windshield . . . Son of a bitch! My head hurts!" Walker exclaimed through a wide bloody grin.

Garrison unclipped the radio mic from his officer's shoulder epaulet and called Amanda.

"Amanda! This is Garrison. We'll need an ambulance out here. One officer injured, and possibly the suspects too," Garrison calmly advised his dispatcher before he led Walker to the side of the road.

"Two suspects in custody!" Cooper shouted in between huffing and puffing into the radio.

"Two suspects in custody," Amanda repeated her officer's radio transmission.

Garrison quickly turned off the sirens and then approached the suspect's truck, which had rolled several times and was propped up on the driver's side, smoke was wafting up from the engine compartment and all four tires. Garrison drew his Smith & Wesson Model 25-5, .45 Long Colt revolver, and glanced inside through the cracked windshield. The suspect driving the truck remained inside. His face was crushed from smashing into the windshield, as evidenced by the bloody spider-webbed impact in the middle of the glass. Garrison was no doctor, but he'd seen enough dead bodies to know the suspect was dead. The sound of a distant siren broke the momentary tranquility.

Ambulance, good deal, Garrison thought, watching Cooper and the deputy march the two suspects through the grass, dirt, and heaps of cow manure toward the highway.

"Put one in each patrol unit," Garrison ordered Cooper, who directed his suspect to his unit while the deputy sergeant did the same with his.

"Walker, okay?" Cooper asked.

"Nasty cut on his forehead, but he'll live to brag about it," Garrison quipped. "Third suspect is dead inside the truck."

"Dead?"

"Dead," Garrison repeated.

"Sheriff Mitchell is on his way," the sergeant advised as he approached. "Looked like the driver was dead."

"Yup. Dead," Garrison repeated for the third time, then walked toward the ambulance that had just arrived.

CHAPTER 16

TUESDAY

Garrison supervised the loading of the wrecked BPD responder onto the same flatbed tow truck that brought the suspect's Hummer to the station earlier in the day. The ambulance transported Walker to the Bison Medical Center and the two additional county deputies who'd arrived with Sheriff Billy Mitchell transported the two surviving suspects to the county jail. Mitchell had to work the fatal crash investigation with the state troopers since a death occurred during a police pursuit. Garrison was thankful he didn't have to deal with the investigation since he'd just authorized his officers to assist the county deputy in his pursuit. His statement to the trooper in charge was short and sweet, as was Officer Cooper's. Officer Walker's would have to wait until later.

After introducing himself, Sheriff Mitchell asked Garrison not to leave until he could speak with him. Garrison stayed in his patrol unit until he saw Mitchell approaching, then stepped out of his truck to meet the sheriff.

"Thanks for standing by. I know you want to get to the hospital to check on Walker, but I got a call from the

Ector County Sheriff's Office this morning. They found a dead body in the county west of Odessa. A white male in his thirties. He was shot one time in the forehead at close range. They found him this morning when some Rockland Oil and Gas Company men checked out a new drilling and fracking site. They said he'd been dead a couple of days. It sounded like your case. That's why I called you this morning," Mitchell reported.

"I'm sorry I didn't get a chance to call you back. It's been a helluva couple of days for me," Garrison apologized.

"No problem. I reckon it's no coincidence our victims were found a day apart and killed the same way," Mitchell mused.

"Nope. Probably connected, especially if Ector's victim was killed Sunday night like mine."

"Well, I told those Ector County boys you'd probably be giving them a call sooner than later," Mitchell advised. "And thanks for joining in on this chase with Smitty. Your predecessor would've kept his mouth shut and his officers out of it."

"Oh?" Garrison asked, raising an eyebrow.

"Oh, back in the day, he'd have been out on the Boulevard shootin' at the bastards, but the last couple of years, he got gun-shy. I guess he didn't want to risk his pension." Mitchell shrugged.

"I don't figure on getting a pension, and if this keeps up, I won't be around long enough to collect my first paycheck," Garrison half-heartedly joked.

"Well, your beginning here in Bison has been

somewhat of a rocket launch, that's for certain, but don't get too discouraged. You're buddy the mayor is a good man. He'll keep ole Walker off your ass."

"You familiar with Councilman Walker?" Garrison asked.

"Oh hell, everybody's familiar with that grumpy son of a bitch." Mitchell laughed. "I'll see ya around. We'll get a beer, and I'll tell ya everything about Bison's history and the people in it," He then shook Garrison's hand before leaving the scene.

After checking with the trooper to see if he needed anything else from him, Garrison sat in his truck momentarily, taking in everything that had transpired in his less than two full days as Bison's police chief. This was supposed to be an easy retirement job, but had he known what he was in for, he wouldn't have let Barber talk him into the job. He'd spent most of his career as a detective sergeant responsible for his own actions. The brief time spent as a lieutenant before he retired was a cakewalk compared to this. After thirty-five years of walking that fine line between confidence and conceit, he suddenly found his confidence being sternly challenged.

All right, enough self-pity, he thought.

Garrison pulled into the parking lot outside the emergency entrance and paused to chuckle at the irony. He'd driven by on his way to the morgue earlier when he'd noted the medical center layout, thinking he'd be a regular visitor someday. He certainly didn't see today being that day. Garrison found Officer Walker propped up in a hospital bed with a thick, white bandage on his forehead. Cooper, Mayor Barber, and Councilmen Walker crowded the small area encircled by a hospital curtain. The constant beep from a monitor sounded from above the patient's head, where a nurse dressed in pink scrubs and white athletic shoes was turning knobs and watching a green jagged line dance across the screen of a small monitor.

"How are you doing?" Garrison asked Walker, ignoring the rest of the peanut gallery.

"I'm good, Chief. Got a little headache, is all," he announced with a smile. "I hear we got 'em all."

"We did," Garrison simply answered.

"I heard one of the suspects died. That right, Chief?" Councilman Walker snarled.

"That's correct." Garrison knew to keep his answers brief with that man.

"And was it worth risking my nephew's life over?" the councilman pressed.

"I decided to join the chase!" Walker said to his uncle. "The chief just let me finish it!"

"And let your officers go a hundred miles an hour right through town!" the councilman blurted.

"Now, councilman, since when did you start defending criminals?" Dan Barber sternly asked.

"Since he was outvoted yesterday morning," Garrison answered, not caring how his response would be received. "Talk to you a moment, Mayor?" Garrison asked before stepping out of the curtain-walled room without waiting for an answer.

Barber followed his police chief into the waiting area.

"How are we looking on the murder case?" Barber asked in a whisper.

"We got the Hummer identified. It was stolen three years ago in El Paso or across the border. I'm waiting for the reports. But the Ector County Sheriff's Office found another dead body west of Odessa. Same MO Single gunshot at close range to the forehead. It looks like it also happened Sunday night, along with our other one. It's gotta be related," Garrison reported.

"Damn," Barber mumbled. "If it is, and I'm sure you're right, this is even bigger than we thought." He rubbed his fingers over his goatee-covered chin.

"Billy Mitchell told me they didn't find the body until this morning. I'll go over there tomorrow and find out what I can. Oh, and one more thing, Fernandez will be here sometime tomorrow afternoon. I'll need to get her sworn in ASAP so she can get started on this with me."

Barber laughed and looked back toward the emergency room. "Ole Councilman Walker's gonna have a fit when that happens."

CHAPTER 17

TUESDAY

After five o'clock, Garrison parked his responder behind the station and pushed the electronic lock button until the familiar beep assured it was secure. He paused and looked at the wrecked F-150 assigned to Walker. He wasn't sure, but he guessed it would be a total loss. That'd leave the department with two patrol vehicles and three officers when Fernandez arrived the next day. He'd already figured he needed to use his personal truck until he garnered the funds for an additional vehicle. He and the mayor hadn't previously discussed that—or much else about the daily goings-on, for that matter. He'd eventually take the time to further examine the budget account he'd inherited, but at the moment, he had no idea when that would be. Despite the late hour, he also noticed Amanda's car was still in the lot. He found the front door unlocked and Amanda still at her desk.

"Hi, Chief. I called Cooper. He told me about Justin, and I saw his patrol truck. Kind of a mess, huh?" she asked, the premature age lines creeping back around her eyes.

"Walker's all right; that's all that matters. I'm sure he'll be out for a few days, though. I haven't had the chance to mention it to y'all, but we'll have a new officer here tomorrow. That'll help."

"A new officer! Fantastic! Anyone I know?" Amanda asked, replacing her frown with a smile and, thus, slaying the stubborn lines hugging her blue eyes.

"No, no one you know. Her name's Maria Fernandez. She worked with me in Houston. She also just retired, and I convinced her to join me out here," Garrison said, rolling his eyes.

"Wonderful! It'll be nice having another woman around here!"

"I just hope she isn't treated poorly, being an outsider and all," he said, looking at Amanda for assurance.

She waved her hand, dismissing his worries. "It'll be fine, Chief. Some folks might have a problem with it, but no one that really counts."

"Councilman Walker counts," Garrison scoffed.

"Councilman Walker only likes the decisions he makes, nobody else's. He'll have to get over it," Amanda said. "Now that you're back, I'll go home, if that's all right."

"You bet. Thanks for staying late. I'm hoping to get a good night's sleep tonight."

"Good. Make sure you do," Amanda ordered with a smile, then headed out the door.

Garrison looked around the empty station and soaked in the tranquil silence. He looked into the waste basket and saw the balled-up white bag his lunch had come in. His shoulders slumped, and he cursed himself for his oversight—he'd not paid Amanda for his damn lunch. He pulled a twenty-dollar bill from his wallet and put it in her desk drawer.

After plugging the portable radio into the charging dock, he went into his office and collapsed into his chair for the second time that day. A neat manila folder sat on his desk with the words *Lonestar Fuel* printed on the cover. Garrison opened the folder and found numerous documents Walker had gathered in his background investigation of the old gas station on Curtis Road. According to the research, the station had once been a Texaco, which closed twenty years ago. Paul Howard then purchased it in 1989 and opened it as the Lonestar Fuel Depot that same year. According to an old newspaper article, the station closed after Howard died in 2002 and has been vacant ever since. The deed remained in the Howard name until 2010, when it was foreclosed on and eventually deeded to the county for unpaid back taxes. It remained abandoned.

That's a nice dead end, Garrison thought, closing the folder and leaning back in his chair.

He shut his eyes and walked through the crime scene again in the dark and daylight. He searched his memory for anything he might have overlooked. Regarding the physical evidence, he was confident he'd not missed anything. He couldn't remember a homicide scene with so little evidence. Usually, homicides were messy actions committed by careless individuals whose only thought, after doing the dirty deed, was getting away before the police arrived. He'd had a couple of well-thought-out and planned cases, but those were pretty rare, despite what the movies and television shows depicted. Professional hits were also rare, but it was damn near impossible to solve them when they happened. This appeared to be in the latter category.

Why in the hell would there be two execution-style murders out here in the middle of Nowhere Texas? What's out here that's worth killing two men for?

Cattle ranches, farms, hunting leases, and oil . . .

Oil was damn sure valuable enough to kill for, but most of that was over in Ector and Midland counties. He thought Bison seemed a bit too far away for any oil company espionage.

The clang of the front door jolted Garrison from his crime-solving thoughts. Officer Cooper appeared in his office doorway.

"Hey, Chief. The doctor's letting Walker go home. He has a concussion, but everything else seems okay, except for the twenty stitches he took in the forehead," Cooper reported. "Looks like his ride is done."

"Yeah, I figure the truck is totaled. Glad he's okay. Can you stay and work the afternoon shift until eleven?" Garrison asked.

Cooper leaned against the doorframe. "Sure, I figured I'd be here until then, anyway. Walker's been working days. Any idea when we can get a new officer?"

"Tomorrow, in fact."

"Tomorrow! Damn, that's quick! Who is it?" Cooper asked with the same excitement Amanda had displayed earlier.

"Her name's Maria Fernandez. I worked with her

in Houston. I'd planned to have her start next Monday, but I've asked her to join us sooner. She should be here sometime late tomorrow."

"Oh. Is she new or .. ?" Cooper began.

"Or old like me?" Garrison finished with a chuckle.

A shade of red colored Cooper's cheeks. "I wasn't going to put it that way, Chief!"

"Neither. Fernandez just retired from HPD. She's forty-five or so," Garrison said, tilting his head back and looking up at the ceiling, trying to think of her correct age. After a moment's wrinkled brow, he was sure. "Yep, forty-five."

"Wow. Things are really changing around here," Cooper muttered.

"You going to be okay with another outsider from Houston?" Garrison asked bluntly.

"Are you kidding? I think it's awesome!"

"Glad to hear that. I want all of us to get along well and form a good team," Garrison admitted, looking back at the file on his desk.

"I'm all in on that! In the two days you've been here, I've had my first homicide and high-speed chase. You already got my vote for Chief of the Year. I'm going to get something to eat. Want to join me?" Cooper asked, his body half-turned as he began to step away.

"No thanks. I'm heading home. Don't get into anything. I'd like us all to get some sleep tonight. Call me if you need me, though," Garrison said with a wry grin.

"Got it, Chief! Got the blinders on!" Cooper shouted as he strolled out the front door.

CHAPTER 18

WEDNESDAY

arrison pulled into the parking lot of the Coffee Mug Café and noted there were already four trucks there ahead of him, despite it being just past 6:00 AM. He watched Callie gracefully move from table to table, juggling a coffee pot in each hand. He smiled, thankful for the full night's sleep Bison had afforded him.

"Good morning, Chief," Callie offered in a jazzy-smooth voice. Regular or decaf?" she asked, lifting each pot, respectively.

"Regular, please. I usually need the energy boost this early," Garrison chuckled.

On the way to his table, Callie swept past a server station exchanging the pot in her right hand with a large white mug heavy enough to use as a weapon.

"I heard there was another murder over by Odessa," Callie said quietly as she filled Garrison's mug.

He leaned back in his chair and smiled at the business owner. "Mayor Barber told me if I needed an update on the state of Bison, I should come to you," he mused.

"Ha! Is that what His Honor said?" Callie laughed as the bell on the front door announced the arrival of another customer. "Excuse me," and she hustled away to take care of other business.

Garrison gazed out the wall of windows facing Center Street and watched the shadows grow as the bright sun introduced itself, promising another scorching day in West Texas. He nursed his coffee, not wanting Callie to waste her stock on refills for him. Garrison was a rare one-cup cop, having only started drinking bean juice about five years earlier. Even then, he liked double cream and sugar.

After finishing off his mug o' joe, he headed across the street to the station. With Walker out on injury, Garrison would be the only dayshift officer Bison had to offer today. After locking the front door behind him, he entered his office, booted up his computer, and looked over a few department files with information he'd need to know. He found the login for the electronic budget file. After navigating through a couple of simple security screens, he found the most recent balance sheet. To his surprise, it was updated on the first of the month, thanks to Amanda. His second and more critical surprise was the current balance in the account. It was much larger than he'd anticipated.

No wonder this place needs a face-lift. Apparently, the former chief didn't like to spend money.

Garrison was working on a new budget report when he heard the lock turn on the front door. The click of heels against the tiled floor announced Amanda's arrival. He confirmed it was 7:00 AM, an hour earlier for his secretary. He went out front to greet her.

"Good morning. A little early for you, isn't it?" Garrison asked, noticing Amanda's red eyes and lack of her usual expertly applied makeup.

"I just decided to come in early in case you needed me," she replied, turning her face away from Garrison.

"I see. I appreciate that. Is everything all right, though?" Garrison shifted his weight from hip to hip and glanced at the floor, uneasy with the probing question. But he felt it had to be asked. Something was clearly wrong.

"Everything's fine, Chief. I'll be all right," she insisted, signing on to her computer.

Garrison decided he didn't know her well enough to impose, so he quietly returned to his office and closed the door, giving Amanda some privacy. Before he could get back into his budget report, he heard Amanda speaking on the phone, her voice uncharacteristically raised and agitated.

"I don't care what you have to say, and I'm not interested in your apologies! Don't call me here at work!"

Garrison had been around enough police personnel to recognize a marital quarrel, recalling she was married.

But he stayed seated and continued with the report, realizing there was enough funding to replace the wrecked truck and purchase another. His telephone rang, piercing the early morning tranquility.

"John Garrison, Bison Police."

"Good morning, Chief. This is Bill Zimmermann. I'm a lieutenant with the Ector County Sheriff's Office. You have a few minutes for me?"

"Sure do, Lieutenant. I heard you have a body over

there that may be connected to mine here," Garrison began.

"Well, sir, according to what Sheriff Mitchell told us, it looks that way. I was wondering if you'd like to meet with me and the coroner to compare notes," Zimmermann said.

"What time?" Garrison asked.

"The autopsy is scheduled for 9:00 this morning, so I told the doc I'd be there around eleven."

"Sounds good. I'll see you at the morgue at eleven," Garrison answered before hanging up and quickly stepping out to Amanda's vacant desk.

A moment later, Amanda exited the ladies' room, where she'd taken time to fix her hair and put on a fresh application of pink lipstick. "I'm sorry, Chief, I needed a few minutes," she admitted, flashing a faint smile.

"Of course. Can you put together a copy of the homicide file? I'm going to Odessa to meet with a sheriff's department lieutenant about a similar investigation."

"Give me a few minutes," she said, smiling broadly.

"Great. Please include these with it." He handed her the gas-station history file.

Twenty minutes later, Garrison heard Dan Barber's voice in the lobby. He finished taking an inventory of the evidence supplies and met the mayor, who was bantering with Amanda about his dachshund's prior night's antics.

"Good morning, Dan. What can I do for you?" Garrison asked, having left the Barber's house before he woke.

"Just curious. Any update on that case over in Ector?" Barber asked.

"Heading over there this morning. I talked to Lieutenant Zimmermann earlier. The autopsy's scheduled for nine AM. I'm meeting him about eleven or so."

"Sounds good. I'll be getting the approval documents to you today so you can replace your wrecked truck," Barber added.

"Fine. Send me approval for the purchase of two while you're at it."

Barber paused and looked at Garrison closely, then nodded. "I'll approve a set amount of funding. How you use it will be your decision," he advised before smiling at Amanda and heading for the door.

Garrison returned to his office and scrutinized the photographs from his murder scene. He was satisfied with the documentation of the scene but kept thinking he'd missed something. He had that feeling of a headache without the pain. Blank thoughts banged around in his head like a silent pinball machine. The suspect had cleansed the scene like no other he'd investigated, except for the gun on the victim's ankle. All the evidence was removed, yet whoever killed the victim had missed the gun.

How'd they miss the gun? Or did they?

CHAPTER 19

WEDNESDAY

Garrison sped down Highway 181, cussing the fact he didn't have a direct freeway connecting Bison to Odessa. It was a well-maintained highway that split an endless brown sea of water-starved, flat scrubland pockmarked with pump jacks and oil derricks instead of the trees and colorful foliage he was used to back in southeast Texas. Both sides of the black asphalt strip contained dirt access roads and paths that looked like a drunken spider had spun a haphazard web. Lanes in both directions were littered with oil tankers with various company names faded on the sides of what were once bright silver rhombus cylinders mounted on double-wheeled axels. After expending an excess amount of effort dodging the haulers, he finally gave in, realizing with every truck he passed, there were two more in his way. He settled in behind what appeared to be a moving billboard of hazmat placards below the words, "You should be driving this truck" and "Now hiring" in fresh bright-red paint.

He chuckled, thinking it was probably less stressful driving a liquid bomb than being the Bison police chief these days. After what seemed like an eternity, he reached

Highway 302 and headed for downtown Odessa to the Ector County Medical Examiner's Office. He had no idea where he was going; he'd had to type the address into his cell phone's map app. After decades of being comfortable with his city and its surroundings, he now knew what a fish out of water felt like.

Turning into the half-empty parking lot, Garrison noted the size and simplicity of the facility. Unlike the eight-story behemoth structure without an empty parking space he'd had to deal with in Houston, the single-story, tan-brick building with abundant parking spaces was a welcome sight. Garrison had arrived an hour early, figuring he'd watch the remainder of the autopsy, then get acquainted with the pathologist.

After entering the lobby, he detected the same odor that all morgues seemed to generate. Never able to describe it, he'd always told inquiring minds it was a unique smell they'd have to experience for themselves, though he didn't recommend it. A young man clad in dark-blue medical scrubs directed him down a hallway to steel double doors on the left. Garrison pushed through the heavy barriers, which led to a short hall and another set of double doors, these of the glass variety. Garrison waited until he caught the attention of the doctor's assistant, a young woman who he figured to be an investigator. After holding up his badge, the push of a button unlocked the door.

The doctor paused and turned to Garrison. "Can we help you?" she asked, holding what Garrison recognized as the stomach of the cadaver.

"Yes, ma'am. I'm the Bison police chief, John Garrison. Sorry to disrupt your examination."

"Oh, hello, Chief! Zimmermann told me you'd be here today. I'm about finished. You're welcome to stay and witness the rest of the exam," the doctor offered.

Garrison nodded but said nothing before stepping to the top of the tub, out of the way, to watch the rest of the process. The polished floor gleamed in the spacious room; the lights were bright; and the stainless-steel body carts, referred to as "tubs," glistened. Despite witnessing these exams more times than he cared to remember, he never felt comfortable. They were indeed easier to deal with than when he was a rookie, but seeing the inside of a dead human was never a pleasant experience.

He noted the time of his arrival and jotted down a few notes regarding the body's appearance, including the apparent bullet hole in the center of the forehead. The white male victim appeared to be between sixty-five and seventy-five years old, and by the looks of the body, he hadn't been in good health. The skin was separated from the bone around the eyes and chin and wrinkled along the forehead, confirming the head's interior had already been examined. Since the wound was to the head, the only additional information Garrison was particularly interested in was the toxicology report for the presence of drugs or alcohol, as well as the contents of the stomach. Knowing what the person had last eaten often led to viable leads in an investigation. Garrison watched the pathologist dissect the organs like a high school student exploring the guts of a frog in biology class. After thirty minutes, Garrison joined the deputy medical examiner and investigator in an adjacent office.

"Well, Chief, as you know, the cause of death was a gunshot wound to the head. The bullet passed through the head and exited the back of the skull. I didn't find any bullet fragments. There was nothing else out of the ordinary. No sign of blunt-force trauma or assault from any other object. Getting the toxicology report and confirmation of the stomach contents will take a while. I can tell you there was the presence of unidentified meat and corn in the stomach. I'd say the time of death was between 10:00 PM Sunday and 2:00 AM Monday," the pathologist reported.

"Any identification of the victim?" Garrison asked in between scribbling notes on his pocket memo pad.

"No. He arrived as an unknown. No one here in the building recognized him, but I'm going to guess he's a local. I'll provide fingerprints for Lieutenant Zimmermann. I can confidently say he wasn't in good health, especially his lungs. He used both smoke and chewing tobacco and was missing several teeth."

"Thank you for the information. It was good to meet you both. I don't have business cards yet, but here's my contact information," Garrison said, handing the investigator a piece of notepad paper with his name and telephone number.

Garrison entered the lobby and saw it was only 10:30. He decided to wait for Zimmermann outside and call Amanda to check on his distraught secretary.

"Bison Police Department, how can I help you?" Amanda's voice was soft but firm.

"It's John, Amanda. I'm still over here at the morgue waiting for the Ector lieutenant. It'll be a while before I get back."

"Okay, Chief, but we've had a couple of calls, and I didn't want to call in Coop without talking to you first."

"What's come in?" Garrison asked, his anxiety level rising with the question.

"Bob Crawford called. He said someone spray-painted a penis on the side of his store last night, and Doris Lawton called from the Pump Jack and said two bikers walked out on their bill last night at closing. I told them I'd send someone as soon as possible," Amanda reported.

Garrison bit his lip and looked up at the clear blue sky before closing his eyes tight and rubbing his temples.

I don't give a damn about a painted penis and a twenty-dollar burger bill! I've got a damned murder case to solve!

"Are you there, Chief?"

Amanda's question brought Garrison back to reality.

"Yes, ma'am. Go ahead and call Coop and see if he can come in early. If he can't, they'll just have to wait until I get back," Garrison said sharply, unable to completely mask his irritation with the insignificant complaints.

"I'm sorry, Chief. Folks here aren't used to having to wait."

"I know, I know. I'm sorry to take my frustration out on you. I know you have more important things to deal with than me being a jackass," Garrison apologized.

Amanda laughed then, and that relieved his worry that he'd upset her. "I'll be back as quickly as possible," he added.

"No worries, Chief. I'll call Cooper," she managed to mumble, mingled in with muffled laughter before she hung up.

CHAPTER 20

WEDNESDAY

arrison sat on a wooden bench before entering the morgue and reviewed his notes. He was surprised the victim hadn't been identified by someone from the sheriff's office or the morgue. He figured everyone knew each other out here in the sticks, although Odessa was anything but the sticks. Still, as old as the victim was, he'd figured identifying him would have been easy, and the time of death matched that of his victim down at the gas station. The four-hour gap would have been plenty of time for the same killer to leave Bison and make it to the area where this victim had been found, assuming this victim was killed where he was found and not transported from another location.

Most important, Garrison wanted to know if this victim had been found with a gun. He hoped he'd get plenty of answers from Zimmermann. Garrison looked up from his notes to see a silver Chevrolet Tahoe with Ector County Sheriff emblems on the sides pulling into the parking lot. Two deputies stepped out of the vehicle. Both wore plain clothes, with gold badges clipped on their belts next to semi-automatic pistols holstered on their sides.

Garrison stood and greeted his fellow lawmen. "John

Garrison," he announced as he extended his right hand to the deputy who'd been the driver.

"Detective Jason Lee," the driver announced, accepting Garrison's handshake.

"Bill Zimmermann," the lieutenant said, collecting another handshake. "Good to meet you, sir. Lee is the lead detective on this case. He has more information for you than I do. Let's step inside. We can use an office behind the reception desk."

The three officers stepped inside the small office before Zimmermann closed the door.

"I don't mean to be rude, but before we get into this, I'd like to know if your victim had a gun on him when he was found," Garrison asked.

Zimmermann and Lee exchanged a glance, and both smiled. "We wanted to know the same thing," Lee admitted. "Yep. Had a Smith & Wesson M & P Shield in an ankle holster. Yours?"

Garrison nodded. "Yep. Same gun in an ankle holster. The scene was clean as they come, except for the slug buried in the wall and the pistol in the ankle holster."

"We're quite sure our victim was dumped where he was found. It looks like he was shot elsewhere. Not enough blood on the ground, but we can't figure out why he still had a gun on him," Zimmermann mused.

"Because he was shot with that gun you found on him," Garrison stated without hesitation. "I'm convinced my victim was also shot with the gun we found on him. I didn't think of it at the time or even the next day, but that gun bothered the hell out of me. Why clean up the scene so well but leave a bullet and gun behind?" Then it hit me. The killer left the murder weapon behind on purpose."

"Damn, I wouldn't have thought of that," Lee admitted, scratching his bearded chin. "Why leave the damn murder weapon at the scene, especially holstered to the victim?"

"I haven't gotten that far yet, but in a way, it makes sense. No chance of finding the murder weapon on the suspect, and my guess is both guns were wiped clean before they were holstered. Did you preserve your gun for prints?" Garrison asked, not worried about insulting his fellow law enforcement officers.

"Sure. We'll need to send it to the state police lab, though," Lee advised.

"Same here," Garrison verified.

Lee handed Garrison a folder containing his report and photographs from the scene. "This is all I have right now. Maybe Cooper or Justin will recognize this guy," Lee suggested, indicating he knew Garrison's officers well enough to call them by their first names.

Garrison opened the folder and spread several photographs on the small round table. He looked over each photo carefully. Lee and Zimmermann also reexamined the images. After scanning the photos, Garrison nodded.

"I agree the body was moved, at least from these photos. What's out there where the body was found?" he asked, noting open, flat land around the body in the distance.

"This is near Notrees off 302 in the western part of

Ector County. The Rockland Oil and Gas Company owns the land. They operate a drilling and fracking operation out there," Lee advised.

"Rockland has been around for over thirty years," Zimmermann added.

"The Kutseena County border is right near there," Lee said. "I asked around Notrees, but nobody reported seeing or hearing anything. We also believe we know who the victim is."

"Oh?" Garrison asked, leaning forward in his chair.

"Yep. I'm fairly sure it's Hank Dawson. He's an old hermit who lives on a big spread just west of where we found him. I never dealt with him, but I know the Kutseena deputies have. His place is in their county. I think he owned quite a bit of land that bordered Ector County."

Garrison nodded, crossed his arms, and leaned back in his flimsy plastic chair. He looked at Lee and Zimmermann with narrowed eyes and a frown. "If you're right, why would someone want to execute an old hermit living in the middle of nowhere?" he asked rhetorically.

Zimmermann matched Garrison's gaze. "Care for a wild theory?"

"Absolutely! I'm just the new guy in town. What do you think?"

"If we're right and this is Dawson, he's about the only private landowner left around the county line. The oil companies have bought or leased most of the land for their operations. Now, I don't know how much land this Dawson had, but if he was stubborn and unwilling to sell or lease . . ." Zimmermann intentionally paused.

"Then maybe his next of kin would," Garrison finished the thought. "I'll get these photos of him in front of everyone I can who may have known him. If I get an identification, I'll call you immediately," he advised Lee, who nodded. "Right now, I have to get back to town. I'm the only cop on duty, and I've got a couple of impatient complainants with a spray-painted building and a hamburger theft." He sighed and rolled his eyes.

Zimmermann and Lee laughed loudly, and Garrison joined them.

"Welcome to small-town policing, Chief!" Zimmermann managed to say in-between laughter he was barely able to control.

"Yep, a small town with big-city crime all of a sudden," Garrison responded.

Zimmermann nodded and curbed his laughter. "And you know, plenty of folks are gonna say you brought it with you from Houston," he added.

"I know; I just hope they're wrong. Thanks for everything. I'll be in touch," Garrison said before leaving Lee and Zimmermann behind to talk to the pathologist.

CHAPTER 21

WEDNESDAY

Garrison sped back to Bison, dodging fuel tankers, various pickup trucks, and cargo vans displaying the names of an array of oil and contractor companies. He was anxious to show the victim's photo around town to get a positive identification. He wasn't thrilled with the idea of showing townsfolk a crime scene photo of a man with a bullet hole in his head, but he figured he'd cover the forehead with his finger and go with it. He was confident Lee and Zimmermann's guess that the victim was this Hank Dawson was correct, but he felt a sense of urgency to confirm their suspicion. If it were Dawson, Garrison would finally have a solid lead. Halfway to Bison, Garrison changed his course and headed for the sheriff's department and Billy Mitchell. They could identify the man, and it wouldn't matter what the photos contained.

Garrison stepped through the front door of the Kutseena County Sheriff's Department, an impressive building. It appeared to be a newer facility and was wrapped in brown brick. Polished tile displayed the county logo in a large circle in the middle of the lobby floor. A deputy sat behind a tall, horseshoe-shaped desk, a decal the department's arm patch affixed front and center. Compared to the ultra-bright lights he found in the morgue, the antique-finish, cone-shaped light fixtures hanging from the ceiling made the lighting easy on his tired eyes. The spacious lobby was quiet except for the thud of Garrison's bootheels against the shiny floor.

"I'm John Garrison, the new chief of Bison PD. Is Sheriff Mitchell available? I don't have an appointment, but it's important," Garrison informed the deputy before he could offer a greeting.

"Yes sir, let me check," the deputy answered pleasantly as he picked up a phone and punched in a four-digit extension.

"Sheriff Mitchell will be right up," the deputy announced after a brief exchange with someone on the phone.

"Thanks, I appreciate it."

The deputy leaned over the desk and extended his hand. "I'm Seth Morrison. Good to meet you, Chief."

Garrison shook the deputy's hand. "Same here," he added with a nod.

The door to the right of the desk swung open, and Billy Mitchell filled the doorway. "Come on in, Chief. I didn't expect to see you again this quickly. You must have news," he said with a grin.

"I don't know if it's news yet; I'm hoping you can identify Ector County's victim," Garrison explained, following Mitchell down a short hallway to a large office in the corner of the building.

Garrison sat in one of two hand-tooled, brown leather, winged-back chairs in front of Mitchell's wide oak desk.

"What'd you have?" Mitchell asked, leaning across his desk, and looking at the folder Garrison had placed there.

Garrison spun the folder around and opened it, showing the best photo of the victim's face.

Mitchell's face darkened with a deep frown and narrowed eyes. He let out a sigh before looking at Garrison. "It's Hank Dawson," he murmured, as if not to disturb the dead.

Garrison nodded. "That's who Jason Lee and Bill Zimmermann thought it might be."

Mitchell looked through the remaining photographs before leaning back in his chair and looking out one of the two large windows that formed a broad corner view of the parking lot. Garrison kept silent while Mitchell appeared to gather his thoughts. Mitchell's shoulders slumped forward, and his head leaned to one side. He rubbed his clean, shaved chin and gazed at the window.

"Hank Dawson was a hermit. He lived alone in his family's house on five hundred acres on the county's east side. He was a Vietnam vet that didn't adjust well after he came home. I'm aware of no wife, no kids, no family left. His mother died about ten years ago, and his father a few years before that. He wasn't terribly friendly to anyone who trespassed on his land, but he never really gave us much trouble. Kept to himself. We'd drive out there occasionally to check on him. He was always friendly with us. Where'd they find him?"

"Out in the county near a town called Notrees. I'm told the property belongs to the Rockland Oil Company," Garrison answered.

Mitchell turned back to face Garrison. "That's just across the county line from his spread. Rockland owns almost everything along the county line there."

"Do you know if Rockland or anyone else wanted to buy Dawson's land?"

"Oh, hell, Rockland and every other wannabe oil company that came along. Dawson's father had offers on that land for years, decades probably. The old man wouldn't sell at any price, for whatever reason."

"Dawson run any cattle or other livestock out there?" Garrison asked.

Mitchell nodded. "Sure. Years ago, the old man ran some cattle and goats, but I don't think Hank was too interested. The last time I was out there, maybe about a year ago, I didn't see any signs of livestock."

"Y'all ever arrest him?"

"Yep." Mitchell picked up a pen and clicked it against the desk. "A couple of times, in fact. For being drunk and disorderly in town and for drunk driving. I'd have to check the records to make sure. I know we hadn't dealt with him for quite some time. Like I said, he was friendly toward us when we'd stop by."

"It looks like he was dumped at the scene. There wasn't much blood where they found him. He could've been killed at his place, then brought to where they found him," Garrison suggested.

"Well, if that's the case, it's my homicide scene. Let's

hustle out there right now. I'll get a couple of deputies to join us." He pushed out from his desk and stood.

"Sounds good. I need to call my secretary and see if my one healthy officer made it in yet. I'm new to this balancing service calls with my investigations," Garrison chuckled as he rose to standing.

"Oh, don't I know it! We can't keep our constituents waiting! Or are they customers now? This new policing is confusing to me," Mitchell said, shrugging his shoulders.

Garrison checked in with Amanda, who confirmed Cooper had arrived and was handling the incoming calls. In addition, Amanda advised that Walker had called in and said he wanted to return to work tomorrow but didn't have the doctor's authorization. Garrison instructed Amanda to call him back and tell him a doctor's approval was a must, nonnegotiable. Then he advised her as to where he was going and why before ending the call.

Sliding behind the wheel of his truck, Garrison then joined the Kutseena County Sheriff caravan enroot to the Dawson ranch for what was sure to be the actual murder scene.

CHAPTER 22

WEDNESDAY

After Mitchell had ordered one of his patrol deputies to head to Hank Dawson's place right away, he pulled Deputy Morrison off the front desk and had him ride with Garrison, who was now doing his best impression of a NASCAR driver to keep up with the county sheriff. Mitchell's dual sirens wailed like screeching African monkeys as they sped down county roads Garrison hadn't heard of yet. Having no clue of his whereabouts, he was glad to have Morrison along, calling out the road names and general location of where they were in the county. Garrison's personal F-150 was no match for Mitchell's SUV, which pulled away at a double-quick rate.

"What the hell's he got there?" Garrison yelled over to Morrison, who laughed.

"New Ford Interceptor! That bad boy will do one-fifty!"

"Damn! We didn't have anything like that back at the Houston PD!" Garrison chuckled. "Damn good thing you know where we're going because I'm lost!"

"He's coming up to Screaming Eagle Road. We'll turn

right, and it'll take us right to Dawson's place," Morrison reported.

"Did you know Dawson?"

"Yep. Pretty cool guy. I guess he was a real badass in Vietnam. He wouldn't talk about it much unless he was drunk, which was most of the time we saw him. Didn't come around much, though."

"You know if he had any friends in Bison or Odessa?" Garrison asked.

"Naw, I don't think so."

Up ahead, Mitchell slowed and turned onto Screaming Eagle Road, allowing Garrison to catch up a bit. The two vehicles were the only ones on the road, despite the time of day and sunny conditions. After a few minutes, Garrison saw a sheriff's car parked at the entrance of a dirt drive he assumed led to Dawson's property. Mitchell entered the driveway and stopped at the rusted, pipe-style gate and entrance arch. Garrison pulled his truck behind Mitchell's and waited while Mitchell briefly conversed with his deputy.

Garrison looked past the two lawmen and saw the probable topic of their exchange. The big gate was closed and locked with a heavy link chain and a padlock the size of a baseball. Just inside the gate was a cattle guard grate that, at one time, assured livestock wouldn't wander out if the gate were left open. Made of round pipes spread just enough apart to cause a hoof to become unstable, the guard stretched entirely across the width of the gate opening and about nine feet deep into the property.

After a few moments, Mitchell waved at Garrison,

pointing toward the five-strand high barbed wire fence that connected the iron pipe of the gate to a line of wood posts that seemed to go on forever. Garrison backed his truck away from Mitchell's Interceptor and waited while the sheriff retrieved a pair of wire cutters from the back of his vehicle and cut through each of the five wire strands.

Beyond the entrance about a hundred yards away was a single-story ranch house. There were a few trees on the property, which appeared to be surrounded by what once were grazing pastures, now overgrown with ground scrub and thick weeds about a foot tall. The lack of water and intense heat from the sun's fiery assault stunted the vegetation's growth. Obviously, there hadn't been any livestock on this land for quite some time.

The deputy pulled the cut wires back as Mitchell finished his wire pruning, giving the officers a clear path into the property. The circumstances being what they were, Garrison brushed aside their lack of a search warrant, comfortable a possible murder scene and the possibility of additional victims met the exigent-circumstances exception to the search-warrant rule. Besides, he was only assisting the sheriff's department in their investigation, and Mitchell had already decided to force entry onto the property.

Garrison noticed a medium-sized plastic storage bin, its lid firmly secured with a black bungee cord stretched from handle to handle, sitting in the weeds to the left of the gate. Once a dark blue, the sun-bleached plastic was now a dull gray but for the bluish area near its bottom. Garrison jumped out of his truck and approached the bin.

Remembering Deputy Morrison had said Hank Dawson was a Vietnam veteran and hermit, Garrison approached carefully, examining every inch of the container and surrounding area. Nothing appeared out of order. He carefully unhooked the bungee cord from the hole in the right handle and slowly lifted the top. Stopping about two inches up from the rim, he looked over his shoulder at Mitchell, who had been joined by his two deputies on the opposite side of the Interceptor.

"Good knowing ya, Chief!" Mitchell called through a wide grin over the hood of his vehicle, a protective barrier.

Garrison said nothing. He lifted the lid another two inches and leaned down to look inside. The bin contained a loaf of bread and a box of donuts in the center. *Harmless.* Garrison removed the lid entirely and stood over his findings. Figuring it was safe now, Mitchell and his deputies joined Garrison and peered into the bin.

"What the hell?" Mitchell said aloud, tucking both thumbs behind his belt buckle and leaning back.

Garrison thought momentarily and looked across the pasture to the ranch house.

"This is either coming in for Dawson or going out from him. My guess is somebody dropped food off for him, so he didn't have to go into town," Garrison speculated.

"Well, let's go see what we're in for," Mitchell said before turning around and heading for his Interceptor.

Mitchell led the way through the opening cut into the fence and slowly drove down the dirt path leading up to the west side of the house. Garrison noticed the path contained only old, sunbaked tire ruts ahead of Mitchell's vehicle, possibly because no vehicle had recently traveled the path or because of the storm the other night. Garrison figured it was probably the former of the two options. *If that was true, how did the murder suspect get to the house?* That got him to running through some theories, but those would have to wait.

The trio of vehicles stopped about fifty feet from the house and parked. Garrison joined Mitchell, who directed his deputies to carefully check the house's perimeter, then the barn and shed behind it.

"Now, don't turn any doorknobs or open any windows yet. I wouldn't put it past Hank to have a couple of booby traps," Mitchell ordered his deputies.

Each deputy disappeared around opposite corners of the house. Mitchell and Garrison proceeded to the front of the house, framed in a covered wood-planked porch. The front door stood between a large window on the left and a smaller one on the right. The door—a thick, heavy-looking, windowless, wood slab painted a dark brown—was closed, its edges tight around the frame. The porch was cluttered with various garden tools, an old whiskey barrel, and two antique wooden rocking chairs that looked to have been there since the Kennedy Administration. Several cigarette butts were scattered around the chair to the left of the door, telegraphing that Hank Dawson sat there often.

Garrison took a 360-degree turn, scanning the areas near and far from the house. The barren ground in front of the porch was void of grass or other vegetation and contained dozens of tire ruts traveling in every direction.

The tracks, some deep, some shallow, looked to have been made by various tires—could have been truck, car, or SUV. There was a round pen to the west of the house and two cattle pens on the east side. The pen's wooden posts were rotted and split, with the rails in a similar condition.

Garrison and Mitchell walked to the east side of the house, where they found a small garden with wilted, tomato plants and cucumber vines. Unlike the surrounding dirt, the garden soil had been tilled and mixed with what appeared to be topsoil or peat moss. Whatever the mixture, it was fertile and friendly to the hearty plants it lodged. Other than the rain from the recent storm, the garden's flaccid plants indicated it hadn't been watered in a few days, which was a deadly oversight under the summer Texas sun.

The intermittent shouts of "Clear!" and "Nothing here!" from the deputies disrupted the quiet sound of the warm breeze whistling past the creaky wooden boards, once neatly affixed to the frame of the house but now showing their age. Both deputies joined Garrison and Mitchell near the garden.

"Got a broken bedroom window on the east side, and Hank's pickup is parked between the barn and tack building. By the looks of the thick dust on the truck, I reckon it hasn't moved in a long time," Morrison reported. "We didn't check the doors."

Mitchell looked along the east side of the house and saw a door. "I'm more inclined to attempt entry through the side door instead of the front," he remarked to Garrison, who nodded in agreement.

Mitchell took a position next to the side door, Garrison right behind him, and waved to his deputies to do the same on the opposite flank. The deputies drew their weapons, one standing, the other kneeling, covering high and low potential danger.

CHAPTER 23

WEDNESDAY

Mitchell carefully grasped the doorknob and gently turned it to the right. The knob rotated cleanly, but a deadbolt lock on the inside resisted Mitchell's firm push. Mitchell said nothing, just shook his head, and then motioned with his right boot that he would kick the door in. Garrison and the deputies nodded and prepared to rush through the opening quickly.

Mitchell stepped back, tucked his right boot under his thigh, and threw all his weight forward behind his right leg. His boot smacked the door just under the knob. The bolt gave way, and the door flung inward, whipping to the right. Mitchell quickly entered the hallway, his deputies right behind. Garrison paused before following, noting the entrance led to a long, narrow hallway with open doors on both sides. The hardwood floor was free of rugs and heavily worn from years of boot soles trampling over its surface.

Mitchell quickly turned left into an open doorway; Deputy Morrison dashed through the first door on the right, and the second deputy took the next open door on the right. Garrison followed and, careful not to run past open doors that hadn't been cleared, crouched low, his

Smith & Wesson .45 Long Colt revolver pointed straight down the hallway in case an assault came from that direction. The intense heat inside the house brought beads of sweat streaming down Garrison's face, burning his eyes. He felt himself sweating through his shirt.

At least the place doesn't smell like a rotting body. He didn't know what they'd find in the house, but he was comforted by the fact there wasn't a human body roasting inside the place. Once a cop experienced that odor, they never forgot it.

Mitchell joined Garrison back in the hallway. "Kitchen's clear," Mitchell announced.

Both deputies appeared in their doorways with thumbs up, signaling their rooms were safe. Mitchell waved to his deputies to follow him, then began a slow, deliberate heel-to-toe walk down the hall. A wide archway on the left led to the large front room and two more open doors farther down on the right. Mitchell paused at the edge of the arch and peeked around the wall, first looking left, then right. He then rolled around the rim of the arch to the left. Deputy Morrison crouched low, immediately crossed, and entered the room to the right, gun ready if needed.

Garrison was impressed with the tactics Mitchell and his deputies used. He'd seen and read about many rural law enforcement officers killed or injured due to a lack of training and equipment compared to the opportunities afforded officers of big urban departments. His respect for Sheriff Mitchell increased with every order and movement he and his deputies made. Garrison kept his attention on the two open doors farther down the hall.

After they cleared the front room, Mitchell and his deputies rejoined Garrison in the hallway.

"Don't smell anything," Mitchell whispered.

Not yet.

Garrison said nothing, just nodded in agreement before the foursome continued down the hall toward the last open doors. At the back of the group, Garrison grasped the back of Deputy Morrison's gun belt and kept watch to the rear in case they missed someone or something. When the search party paused, Mitchell turned into the first open door on the right. One of the deputies followed behind him. After a few moments, Mitchell exited the room and proceeded to the next open door. The scent of dried blood was evident. Recognizing the distinctive odor, Mitchell carefully peeked around the door frame and froze. Keeping his gun close to his body and firmly in his right hand, he held up his left, ordering the trio to stop. Mitchell looked around the room, then warily entered with the deputy. Deputy Morrison remained at the doorway while Garrison kept watch back down the hallway.

"Take a look at this, Chief," Mitchell called out, apparently confident the house was vacant and safe.

Garrison walked into the doorway and stopped to examine the scene. A single twin bed covered in what had once been white sheets but were now soiled with grime and bloodstains was pushed into the far corner. A small, black, metal-based lamp and a large, dark-green, glass ashtray overflowing with cigarette butts and cough drop wrappers sat beside the bed atop an old night table. A heavy-looking wood chest of drawers rested under another overfilled ashtray and an empty whiskey bottle sat against the opposite wall. There were dirty clothes strewn about the floor, with one exception. A blood-stained path from the bed to the doorway was clear of debris. The room had two windows—one opposite the door and the other above the night table. Mitchell pointed next to the chest of drawers. Garrison stepped inside the room and followed the sheriff's direction. Propped in between the chest and the wall was a Remington 870 Express twelve-gauge pump shotgun.

"I reckon he never heard 'em coming," Mitchell said.

"Nope, sure looks that way," Garrison agreed.

Careful not to touch anything, Mitchell closely examined the pillow on the bed. He confirmed a small hole in the pillow. He then knelt and looked under the bed, and so did Garrison. A bullet hole in the wooden floor appeared directly under the pillow.

"Looks like he was shot here in the bed. It also looks like the killer left the bullet embedded in the floor for us," Mitchell announced.

"Not surprised. I'll bet the bullet matches the gun found on Dawson," Garrison said.

"For what it's worth, this back window is unlocked," Deputy Morrison said.

"So is this one," Mitchell confirmed after examining the window above the night table.

"Since we know they didn't come in through the side door, they must have come through that broken window next to the side or front door. They damn sure went out the front door because the blood trail leads straight to it, and it's not locked," Mitchell reported having checked for that during the search. "Seth, bring in our crime scene kit from my unit. Chief, you want to look closer at anything before we get started here?" Mitchell asked Garrison.

"No, sir. If it's all right with you, I'll take a few pictures, then head back to my office."

"That'll be fine. We'll take care of business here, and I'll call you when I get back to the station," Mitchell advised as they walked toward the front door.

The two men stood on the front porch and looked around for anything out of place.

"There it is," Garrison said, tapping Mitchell on the arm.

Mitchell followed Garrison's gaze and saw what he had found. Two rows of beat-down weeds led off in the distance to the east of the house. Obvious tire tracks.

"They came from there," Garrison declared.

"Uh-huh. Let's have a look," Mitchell mumbled, then instructed Deputy Morrison to photograph all around the outside of the house. "The chief and I will be right back."

Garrison gazed out the windshield of Mitchell's Interceptor at the two-track trail that twisted through the east pasture of the Dawson ranch. Garrison couldn't be sure, but the tracks appeared to have been caused by a single vehicle—probably an elevated four-wheeled drive due to the center weeds standing tall in-between the two lines of vegetation pressed down under the weight of the tires. Mitchell guided his Interceptor adjacent to the path, careful not to destroy any possible evidence left behind.

Halfway through the field, there hadn't been any sign of apparent evidentiary value. The fence along the east side of the ranch came into clear view. As both lawmen expected, a gaping hole in the aged, barbed-wire barrier provided ample space for a vehicle to pass through.

Mitchell stopped the Interceptor about fifty feet from the fence line and turned off the motor. Both men examined the area before exiting Mitchell's vehicle. Garrison looked beyond the fence and saw the property bordered a drainage ditch that gently rose to the gravel shoulder of a two-lane highway.

"That's Highway 15. It's the Ector County line," Mitchell advised.

"Where does it go?" Garrison asked, stepping through the opening in the fence and looking into the ditch.

"It connects I-20 on the south side to Highway 302 on the north side near Notrees, where they found Dawson."

"And both 302 and I-20 go into Odessa," Garrison said confidently.

"Correct."

Knowing it was useless, Garrison stepped into the ditch and followed it up the far side, onto the gravel shoulder of the highway. The highway was a dark ribbon in both directions. Heat waves bounced off its burning surface, distorting the air above it. Garrison returned to the opening in the fence and checked the wire tips.

Clean cuts had been made with a wire-cutting tool. He followed the wires from the ground up to where they had been pulled back from the wooden posts. Kneeling, he closely examined the wire attached to the post. The wire was a four-barb double twist. He carefully ran his finger across one of the barb points facing inward toward the opening—a black line transferred onto his skin. Just then, Mitchell walked up behind Garrison.

"Paint?" Mitchell asked.

"Yep," Garrison answered triumphantly. He reached into his soaked shirt pocket and removed his notepad. Thumbing through, he found a dry piece of paper near the middle and tore it out. After folding the paper into a triangle, he took his pocketknife and scraped the tips of several barbs. Flecks of black paint fell into the paper folds.

"It's a long shot, but we might have enough to identify what type of vehicle this came off of," Garrison stated.

"There's not much there, but damn, I didn't think to look for that," Mitchell admitted.

Garrison groaned as he stood up. "Well, I figured they'd drive through without lights on, and I know how damn dark it gets out here in the sticks."

"That Hummer you found over by your scene have any scratch marks on it?"

"Nope," Garrison confirmed.

"Okay, we know they used at least two vehicles, then. And this one went north on 15 here to 302, then east toward Notrees, where they dumped ole Dawson.

I'll check with the car rental companies in Odessa and Midland and see if anyone returned a vehicle with scratch marks."

"Thanks. It's getting late. I'd better get back to town," Garrison said with a sigh. "I'm expecting my new officer to call anytime now, and I'm sure everyone wants an update."

CHAPTER 24

WEDNESDAY

The sharp sound of his cell phone rang through the dashboard, splintering Garrison's thoughts as he sped back to Bison. His video panel displayed the name "Maria Fernandez" and offered to accept or decline the incoming Bluetooth call. Garrison tapped the accept box and greeted his friend and new officer.

"Hey, Fernandez, everything okay?" Garrison asked.

"Yep, just got to my room at the Hampton Inn on 191 in Odessa. Figured I'd check in and see what was up," she announced.

Her voice caressed Garrison's ears like a sweet songbird on a summer morning. He felt the hair stand up on his arms and was embarrassed at his goosebump reaction.

"I'm on my way back to the station. I just left the scene of the second murder victim in our case. The sheriff's office is handling it since it was in the county, but I'm certain it's related to our victim in town," Garrison reported.

"Okay, I'll leave here in a few minutes and meet you at the station."

"Great. You have the address?"

"I'm a detective, remember? I'll figure it out and see you soon." She laughed before disconnecting the call.

Garrison took a deep breath, then looked down at himself. His shirt was soaked with sweat, his pants nearly the same, with dirt stains up and down each leg.

Great, I look and smell like crap, and I don't have a change of clothes at the office, he thought, fully aware he was fretting about his appearance far too much. After all, Maria Fernandez was a fellow officer and subordinate, not the blind date Emily Barber wanted to arrange for him. Still, he was certain Fernandez knew about his attraction to her, even though they'd never acted upon or even spoken of it.

Garrison pushed his thoughts of her out of his mind as he turned onto Center Street and headed for the Bison PD. He cruised through the Bison Boulevard intersection and hung a right turn into the parking lot, the overheated rubber on his tires screeched out like a crow's caw. He hurried into the office just as Amanda was shutting down her computer in preparation to leave for the day. Garrison scanned the old wall clock and noted it was nearly five thirty.

"Hi, Chief, I heard you squeal into the parking lot, so I thought I'd head home, if that's okay," Amanda said . . . without the bright smile Garrison had quickly become accustomed to.

"Certainly. Thank you for waiting until I got back. Are there any messages?" he asked.

"I put 'em on your desk," Amanda announced, taking a discernible long look at Garrison's clothes. "What in the world have you been up to?" A wry grin invaded her stoic expression.

"I know. I'm a poor sight for a chief, and our new officer is on her way to meet me. Is there any place where I could buy a new shirt and pair of pants in town?"

Amanda's faint grin burst into a gaping smile, and she tilted her head slightly. "Oh, that's right. Officer Fernandez is supposed to arrive today. I forgot all about her!" She suddenly stopped and plopped her hands on her hips. "Oh, wait . . . I get it now . . ."

"No. it's not like that at all!" Garrison said, hoping his tone was firm enough to ward off any hints of attraction for his new officer.

Amanda giggled. "Okay, Chief. Please leave it to me. You get cleaned up the best you can, and I'll run over to Crawford's store. He carries a nice selection of work shirts and pants. What sizes do you wear?"

"No, I'll do it. No need for you to waste your time on dressing me, of all things," Garrison insisted.

"It's not a waste of time, and I don't care to rush home right now anyway," Amanda stated flatly.

Garrison paused, then quickly slipped a credit card out of his wallet and offered it to his secretary, who threw up both hands and shook her head.

"No need. Crawford'll run a tab. A large shirt and thirty-six waist?" Amanda asked.

"Better make it a thirty-eight, but thanks for the compliment," Garrison said, returning the credit card to his wallet. "It's only been a few days, and I'm already deeply indebted to you."

Amanda quickly headed for the front door, her heels snapping with purpose against the polished tile floor. She stopped at the door and turned back to Garrison.

"Does she know?" Amanda asked.

"Know what?" Garrison raised an eyebrow.

"You can't fool us girls, Chief. We always know!" Amanda laughed, shaking her head before disappearing through the doorway.

Great. Now I've made an ass of myself in front of my secretary. Keep it up, John, and you'll be out of a job before they print your first paycheck.

He pulled a handful of paper towels from the rack and soaked them in cool water before taking a second sink bath in as many days. After twenty minutes, he finished and checked the messages Amanda had left on his desk. Milt called from the bait shop down by the lake, as had the DPS office in Austin. The front door opened, and the familiar sound of Amanda's clicking heels announced her speedy return. This time, she greeted him with that familiar smile.

"Okay, Chief, I wasn't sure of the best color for you, so I brought two Wrangler shirts, one in navy blue and the other dark red, along with a pair of regular-fit Wranglers. All men look good in a pair of Wranglers. And don't worry about the cost. Bob Crawford said you can stop by and pay later this week," Amanda proclaimed. "I also took the liberty of stopping by the drug store and picking up toothpaste, a toothbrush, and a deodorant stick. You want to make a good impression."

Garrison accepted the garments and toiletries and

set everything on his desk. "Just know, whenever the employee evaluations come along, I'll recommend a hefty raise for you!"

"Again, not necessary, but I'll gladly take it. See you tomorrow," she said before strolling out of the station.

Garrison utilized his new toothbrush and deodorant, then changed into his new attire, selecting the navy shirt—his favorite color was blue. He sat down and picked up his radio. He realized he'd not heard Cooper on the radio.

"Unit three, this is Garrison. You out there?" he asked into the mic.

"Unit three, I sure am, Chief. I'm down here at the bait shop talking to Milt. Anything wrong?" Cooper asked.

"Negative, just checking in. I'm here at the station if you need me," Garrison advised. He keyed the mic again. "I have a message from Milt. Anything going on out there?"

"No, sir. He says for you to come down and introduce yourself as soon as possible. He knows all the best fishing spots if you're interested."

"Tell him I'll try to stop by tomorrow or Friday, and yes, I'd love to know the best spots."

"Will do, Chief. I'll be in later after dinner," Cooper said, then signed off.

Garrison flipped open the homicide file and looked through the pages again. He'd read what little they had about the scene and the victim for the umpteenth time, hoping he'd notice something he'd previously missed. Another review of the photographs produced no new thoughts or conclusions. There were dead ends at the gas station, Hummer, and probably the Dawson scene. Whoever had committed these murders was a meticulous professional.

He heard the front door opening, then closing. No clicking heels this time. Garrison picked up his Long Colt revolver from the desk and peeked out his office door.

CHAPTER 25

WEDNESDAY

Maria Fernandez looked like she had prepared for a magazine cover photo shoot instead of having traveled all day. Her long, black hair was straight and flowed over her sculpted shoulders, except for the narrow tress dangling over her left eye. Her white sleeveless shirt, tucked snugly inside form-fitted khaki slacks, clung against her slender body. Her makeup was expertly applied, and her manicured fingernails were polished with a dark red that matched the lipstick coating her perfect pouty lips.

Garrison quickly returned his revolver to his desk and greeted Fernandez with a tight hug that included an extra squeeze he knew was inappropriate, but he didn't care. He was pleased to see her, as an officer and a trusted friend.

"Well, are you happy to get another officer in here, or is it something else, Chief?" She giggled, guessing they were alone in the office.

"Yes," Garrison said, not committing to either question, or perhaps to both. He looked into her brown eyes and added, "It's been a bit overwhelming around here, and you know I don't usually get overwhelmed."

Fernandez looked around the station. "This is a

bit nicer than I anticipated. And look at you. You've embraced the rancher look already!" she exclaimed with a wide grin as she gave him the once-over.

Garrison felt himself blushing. He held out his arms and looked down at his shirt and pants. "I had to buy these at the local tack store. I destroyed my other clothes at the scene this afternoon."

"Tell me all about it," she demanded.

Garrison turned and waved a hand toward the empty desk at the back of the room. "That there is your desk, Detective. Go have a seat, and I'll grab the file from my office and join you. My office is a little cramped."

While Officer Fernandez headed that way, Garrison stepped into his office, thankful Amanda had provided the toothbrush and deodorant. He snatched the file from his desk and pulled a chair next to Maria's desk, which she'd already begun to rearrange. He placed the file on the desk, then glanced around the room.

"What is it?" Maria asked, following Garrison's gaze.

"I just realized we don't have a refrigerator or anything to drink around here."

"That's fine. I don't need anything right now. You won't keep me here all night, will you?" she asked with a chuckle.

"No, actually, I was going to suggest we drive out to Mayor Barber's ranch as soon as you've looked through the file."

"Sounds good. And by the size of this file, it won't take long," she said, opening the folder and looking through the photos before bothering with the reports.

Garrison returned to his office, searching for the nearest appliance store. As expected, it was over in Odessa. He quickly looked over the refrigerators, then called the store. Twenty minutes later, he'd completed the purchase and arranged for delivery on Friday morning. Pleased with himself, he returned to Fernandez, who was closely examining the photos.

As if anticipating Garrison's questions, she confirmed she'd already read the reports, including the history of the gas station and the Hummer theft. Without taking her eyes off the photo array, she asked, "Any word from DPS about the victim's ID or the ballistics on the gun?"

"I have a message from DPS. I'll call in the morning. I'm hoping they'll have that information," Garrison advised.

She gave a small nod and pushed some hair away from her face. "They purposely left the bullet in the wall," she announced. "And the gun."

"Yep," Garrison agreed. "I don't know why these idiots don't always do that. It ensures we can't find the murder weapon in anyone's possession."

"Pretty fancy gun to just leave behind. Somebody's got big money," she added.

"We think one of the oil companies may be involved," Garrison said.

She pushed the photos away and sat back in her chair. "We?"

"The Ector County lieutenant and lead detective," Garrison explained. "The victim out in Ector owned five hundred acres of prime land that he refused to sell."

"But why kill a homeless dude in an abandoned gas station?"

"Despite his appearance, I don't think he was homeless, but I've got no answer yet," Garrison admitted.

Garrison looked out the window and saw Cooper pull into the parking lot behind the station. "Good deal. Another one of our officers is here. Travis Cooper. I'll introduce you."

Fernandez craned her neck to see out the window. "Nice trucks," she muttered.

"Don't bother getting used to them. I'm switching them out for the Ford Explorer Interceptors as soon as possible." Garrison laughed, knowing she was not interested in driving a police pickup truck.

"This job's getting better already!" she teased.

Cooper walked into the station and upon seeing Fernandez at her desk, smiled and quickened his pace. She flashed a broad smile and extended her slender right hand.

"Coop, this is Maria Fernandez. Maria, this is Travis Cooper," Garrison said.

"Nice to meet you, ma'am," Cooper said with a wide smile.

"Nice to meet you, and please, don't call me 'ma'am.' I'm Maria, Fernandez, or just Dez if you'd like," Maria said.

"I've heard a bit about you from the chief. Another Houston homicide detective here in little ole Bison. Man, things are changing!" Cooper exclaimed, clearly unable to suppress his excitement.

"Let's get this homicide out of the way and hope we don't need these skills for a long time," Fernandez said.

"I'll second that!" Garrison added.

Cooper frowned. "I don't know . . . Family arguments and speeding tickets aren't exactly exciting."

Fernandez laughed. "We'll see if you still feel that way in twenty years!"

Garrison slapped Cooper on the shoulder. "Everything under control out there in Bison?"

"Yes, sir. Milt said somebody used one of his rental boats last night, but they brought it back and didn't tie it up."

"Any damage?"

"No, sir. Milt had no complaint. Just once in a while, someone doesn't tie the boat right, and it drifts out into the middle of the lake. When that happens, he calls us, and we help him get it back to the dock. Like I said, not exactly exciting stuff," he said with a grin.

"Boring is good," Garrison said. "Okay. I'm going to head home. You on until eleven?"

Cooper rocked back on his heels. "Yes, sir, unless you need me to stay longer?"

"Nope. Call me if something comes up."

Cooper held up a finger. "Oh, one more thing, Chief, I talked to Walker. His doctor said he can come back, so he'll be in tomorrow morning."

"Oh, good. I'll talk to him then. I'll be busy getting Fernandez sworn in most of the morning, so it'll be good to have him back." Garrison retrieved the homicide file and his revolver, then escorted his new officer out of the station.

"I'll be glad to drive you to Barber's place and then back here if you'd like. He's not that far," Garrison offered.

"Not necessary. I'll follow you. I don't know how long I'll stay," she answered, walking to her car without waiting for further comment from Garrison.

Garrison pulled out of the station parking lot; Fernandez's Dodge Challenger was close behind. He could feel the stress evaporating from his body as he steered his truck along the highway. Come tomorrow, Walker would be back at work and Fernandez would officially be joining the force. Garrison's team would finally be at full strength. Now if he could get good news from DPS tomorrow, he'd feel much better about things.

CHAPTER 26

THURSDAY

The floor of the East Texas horizon burned a bright orange beneath an otherwise aphotic sky as Garrison cruised down the two-lane blacktop highway that led from the Barber Ranch back to Bison. The headlights of Fernandez's flaming-red Dodge Challenger looked like two white eyes inside Garrison's rearview mirror. The prior night's visit with Bison's mayor and his wife had oozed deep into the night, sparking Emily Barber's insistence that Fernandez dispense with the idea of driving back to Odessa at the late hour. Even with Garrison as a temporary visitor, the Barbers' ranch home was equipped with three guestrooms, exquisitely decorated in the southwest motif. Plenty of space for another person. The early morning reconvening of the group had brought further insistence from the ranch owners that Fernandez disregard the hotel and stay at their place until she found appropriate housing. To everyone's satisfaction, Maria had agreed after a brief but thoughtful hesitation, assuring her hosts her stay would be temporary.

The piercing ring of Garrison's cell phone burst from

his dash like a gunshot, causing the police chief to jump in his seat.

Damn it! I've got to figure out how to change that damn thing! He glanced at the screen—it was Fernandez. He accepted the call. "Hello," he answered, instinctively looking into his rearview mirror as if he could see her talking.

"Any idea who was supplying our dead rancher with food?" Fernandez's voice chirped through the F-150 speakers.

Having supplied her with all the information he could remember about the two homicide scenes the night before, Garrison thought momentarily. He'd not given that much thought after the initial discovery yesterday afternoon. His unfamiliarity with the town, county, and everything else put him at a severe disadvantage.

"You still there?" she asked.

"Yes, sorry. I don't know. I'll call Sheriff Mitchell this morning and see if he has any ideas," Garrison answered.

He pictured the items he'd found inside the bin outside Dawson's gate—a loaf of Hearth Texas bread and a box of donuts. The Hearth Texas brand was familiar, but the donuts were local—plain white box with no brand name and a clear cellophane window on the top. Garrison remembered Dan Barber's comment about Callie Johnson being a great informant. He decided he'd stop at the Coffee Mug and ask her before he went to the station.

Dawn arrived with the promise of another clear, sun-drenched, searing day. Garrison pulled into the Coffee Mug Café lot and parked next to a line of pickup trucks decked out with big toolboxes, brush guards, and pipe racks. Fernandez followed Garrison into the lot, which smacked of a farm and ranch convention. Her Challenger looked like a red rose in the middle of a cluster of thorns.

"Think my car will be safe out here?" Fernandez asked, glancing around the corral of banged-up work-mobiles.

"Nope," Garrison chuckled as he walked past his bewildered officer.

Garrison opened the glass door and stepped aside, allowing Fernandez to enter. The small café was busy, with every chair of every table occupied by a hardened sunbaked man clad in an assortment of weather-worn denim and tee-shirts that had once been briskly white and seen better days. The chatter stopped as Fernandez paused and looked around the room. The aroma of freshly brewed coffee and delectable pastries engulfed the space. From behind the sparkling glass counter, Callie Johnson turned toward the front and greeted her two new customers with a wave, then tugging on her white apron to smooth out any wrinkles infiltrating its sharply pressed facade. Callie quickly scanned the room and frowned when she realized no seating was available. Garrison waved and shook his head, clutching Fernandez's arm before stepping over to the counter to engage Callie.

"I'm sorry, Chief; I'm sure I'll have a table for you momentarily," Callie announced.

"No need Callie. We can't stay. Maria, this is Callie Johnson, the owner of the café. This is my new officer, Maria Fernandez," Garrison completed the introductions.

The two women gently shook hands and nodded.

Garrison looked down into the glass case and immediately recognized the pastry boxes on the top shelf. He interrupted their conversation.

"Are these boxes unique to your café?" Garrison blurted out, pointing into the cabinet at the boxed pastries.

"Excuse you, Chief!" Fernandez said, feigning shock at his rudeness.

"I apologize, ladies, but these donut boxes . . . "

"I don't sell donuts, Chief!" Callie scolded Garrison, offering a grin, letting the chief know she wasn't really offended.

"Oh, hell. Could we get a couple of coffees to go, ma'am?" Garrison asked politely, rubbing his forehead.

"Yes, sir, you sure can. Regular or decaf? And no, those boxes are not unique to us. I buy them in bulk from a supplier in Midland," Callie said.

"Two large regulars please, both with cream and sugar," Fernandez said, popping up two fingers on her right hand.

"Girl! Look at those nails! Where'd you get those done?" Callie shouted, clutching Fernandez's hand, and gazing at her manicured fingertips.

Garrison looked down at the floor, smiled, and shook his head. He waited for the fingernail conversation to end, then pulled a five-dollar bill from his pocket and set it on the counter. Callie placed the two cups of coffee next to the bill.

"Why did you want to know about the pastry boxes?" Callie asked.

"I saw the same type of box in a plastic container out at Hank Dawson's place. I'm trying to find out who was giving him food," Garrison explained.

Callie's smile faded. "Why? Is there something wrong?" she asked in a low voice.

Garrison looked around and leaned close to Callie. "We found Hank Dawson dead in Ector County."

"Oh no!" Callie exclaimed, covering her mouth with her hand and stepping backward, bumping into the huge coffeemaker. Her bright countenance dulled, and the luster drained from her brown eyes. She looked around quickly as if she'd lost her whereabouts. Fernandez hurried around the counter and clutched Callie on the elbow, then guided the café owner to a nearby chair. Garrison quickly joined the women behind the counter. Several customers vacated their seats and rushed to the counter to see what was happening.

"Are you all right, dear?' Fernandez asked.

Callie looked up with tear-filled eyes. "What happened to Hank Dawson?"

"I don't know if this is the time to ..." Garrison began.

Callie sniffled but insisted, "No. It's okay. I'm fine, but I'd like to know."

Garrison turned his back to the crowd near the counter and whispered into her ear. "He was shot. We're sure he was killed at his ranch, then moved to an oilfield in Ector County. Did you know him very well?"

Callie dabbed tears from her eyes with a napkin Fernandez had placed in her hand. She nodded slightly, then looked past Garrison toward the folks at the counter.

"I'm fine, everyone. Please return to your breakfast," Callie assured her customers. Her forward gaze into space made her look like she was in a trance. "I didn't know him well, but he used to come here regularly before my husband died. After that, he stopped coming around. I was concerned about him, so I drove to his place one afternoon. I brought a box of pastries and a loaf of bread. His gate was locked, so I left it hanging on the fence. When I returned the next week, the container was next to the gate, so I put the food inside. I've been doing that for about a year," Callie explained.

"When was the last time you saw him or knew he'd taken the food from the container?" Garrison asked.

Callie took a deep breath and regained her composure, slipping a faint smile in between words. "I saw him about a month ago. He was out near the gate when I drove up. He thanked me and offered me money, which I refused. I told him to come to the café and see me. He said he would but never did. I know he took the food last week. I put the pastries and bread in the container on Sunday," Callie recalled.

"Solves that mystery," Fernandez mused.

Garrison's phone buzzed inside his pants pocket, and he took a look. Amanda's name appeared across the screen. "Good morning, Amanda."

"Good morning, Chief. I came in early today and called down to Austin. They have a positive ID on our murder victim," she reported.

CHAPTER 27

THURSDAY

G arrison opened the station door and stepped aside to allow Fernandez to enter. Amanda's face brightened when the two officers walked into the lobby. Without a word, Amanda quickly stepped around her desk. She handed Garrison a message slip, the old-fashioned kind office managers purchased back before voicemail was available on computerized desk phones.

"Good morning, Maria," Amanda said, and their new officer returned the greeting. Then to Garrison, Amanda added, "Here you go, Chief. The trooper said to call anytime this morning."

Garrison hastily dialed the Department of Public Safety number. After two rings, a deep voice answered, "Crime lab."

"Good morning, this is John Garrison, the chief of Bison PD in Kutseena County. I understand you have information regarding identifying our murder victim."

Garrison grabbed a pen from an old, coffee-stained Bison Police mug that sat on his desk and now served as a pen and pencil holder. He slid a notepad in front of him and jotted copious notes as the DPS crime-lab official spewed information containing the victim's identity and personal data, a brief criminal history report, and a Texas driver's license number. Much to Garrison's relief, the firearm and tool marks evidence was also available, confirming his suspicion that the bullet dug out of the gas station wall was fired from the Smith & Wesson pistol in the ankle holster on the victim's leg. Garrison provided his email address, thanked the lab official, and placed the phone receiver in its cradle. When he looked up, Fernandez was leaning against his office doorway, waiting for his report.

"DPS is going to send me the entire file via email, but I have what we need to get moving on this," Garrison said.

"Well, who is he?" Fernandez asked.

Garrison checked his watch. "I'll tell you all about it after you get sworn in. Let's get over there before we're late." He stood abruptly and squeezed past Fernandez in the doorway. Only then did he pause and look back over his shoulder. "Something wrong?" he asked her.

"No, not really. I just figured this was my last chance to change my mind," Fernandez said, flashing a broad grin.

"Nope, that time passed. I need you too much now. Let's go before his honor starts pestering Amanda with phone calls, wondering where the hell we are," Garrison muttered on his way toward the door.

Fernandez waved at Amanda and then followed Garrison outside. The short walk to the Bison administration building proved informative for the chief.

"Your secretary's going to be available soon," Fernandez said.

"What?" Garrison asked, opening the glass door to the city offices.

"Seems like Amanda caught her old man screwing a dealer from the casino. She told me she filed for divorce."

Garrison stopped inside the door and looked at Fernandez with raised eyebrows. "Well, that explains her behavior the last couple of days."

"I guess he moved out yesterday," she said. "I didn't know we had a casino around here."

"It's about sixty miles west of here, just inside the New Mexico state line. Less than an hour's drive, I'm told if you're interested." Garrison chuckled, and she joined in.

"I just might be!"

Connie Maxwell saw them enter the building and waved them toward her. Shifting a stack of papers in her hands, she knocked on the mayor's closed office door to let him know he had visitors.

Garrison made the introductions, then the door swung open. Mayor Barber stepped back and waved the trio into his office. "I was about to call Amanda and see where you two were."

"I know. I told Fernandez we'd better get over here before you started searching for us." Garrison laughed. "We have a good excuse. I was on the phone with the DPS Lab." Once everyone was inside, he closed the door behind him.

"Great. I'll look forward to hearing that report. But first, we have some business to tend to, provided you've come to your senses and decided not to work for this—"

"She's decided no such thing," Garrison cut in, a teasing twinkle in his eye. "Connie, please proceed so we can get out of here and do some real police work."

She giggled and said, "That sounds like a good plan."

Connie had Fernandez raise her right hand and repeat the Bison Police Department's Oath of Office, which, once recited, resulted in Barber presenting Bison's newest officer with her five-point star badge. The two ladies then left the mayor's office to get some paperwork signed, leaving Garrison behind to brief the mayor on the murder investigation.

"What do you have for me?" Barber asked.

"I confirmed the gun we found on the victim was the one used to kill him. I also verified his identity and personal information. I should have the full report when I return to the office, but it looks like he was a convicted burglar and thief. He also had a couple of drug charges and a weapons arrest. His last known address was in El Paso. His driver's license had been expired for about a year," Garrison reported.

"What's your next move?" Barber asked, leaning back in his big leather chair.

"Well, she doesn't know it yet, but I'm sending Fernandez down to El Paso to find out what she can about our victim. I'm going to meet with the Ector County detective and get an update on their investigation before I stop by Sheriff Mitchell's office and see where they're at on the Dawson case."

Barber nodded and checked the calendar on his desk.

"There's a council meeting Monday night at seven thirty. I'll need you to appear and update the council," Barber advised.

"It's an ongoing investigation. I don't want to give any updates— "

"I know, I know. But out here, you see, we have to do things a little differently to make people happy. Just write up some innocuous statement that sounds good but doesn't really say anything."

"Damn it, Dan! You know I'm no good at kissing council members' asses! You knew that before you hired me. I don't know about this. I don't have the resources," Garrison sighed, his words fading while he rubbed his forehead.

"You're right. I knew that part of the job wouldn't be your strength, but I also knew you were the best man for the job, and I damn sure didn't see a murder case coming your way on day one, either. Just do what you do. Now that Fernandez is here, you have a damn good investigator to lean on. I am confident you'll solve this case and become a hero around here. As far as resources are concerned, let me know what you need, and I'll do my best to get it for you," Barber assured his bewildered chief.

"I sure hope you're right about solving this thing. I haven't seen a hit like this in years," Garrison admitted. "And the last one like this, we never solved, if you remember."

"I remember," Barber answered. "This will be different."

"It better be, or your town council will arrange it, so you won't have to worry about me anymore," Garrison stated before leaving the mayor's office.

CHAPTER 28

THURSDAY

Garrison and Fernandez burst through the police station's front door and found the rest of his staff waiting at the front. A large vase of flowers, complete with a helium-filled blue balloon adorned with *Congratulations* in white letters, hovering lazily over the flowers, sat front and center on Amanda's desk, while she, Walker, and Cooper stood there with big smiles on their faces. The Bison Police welcome committee greeted their newest member with a round of applause.

"Oh my!" Maria exclaimed, placing a hand over her heart. "This wasn't necessary!"

Justin reached out and shook her hand. "Justin Walker, ma'am, nice to meet you," he offered.

"Thank you!" she said. "Those flowers are beautiful!"

"We'd like to take credit, but Amanda made it happen," Cooper admitted.

"Well, we had to do something, and with everything going on around here, this was the best I could do," Amanda said behind a giggle.

"It's a wonderful gesture; I love them!" Fernandez assured Amanda and the men. "I'll move them to my desk, if y'all don't mind."

Walker picked up the large glass vase and carried the bouquet to her desk.

Meanwhile, Garrison patted Amanda on the shoulder. "Thank you for doing that," he whispered before heading toward the back to join the others.

"How's the head?" Garrison asked Walker, whose thick, gauze bandage was pressed snuggly against his forehead with a wide slice of white tape.

"Oh, fine, Chief. The damn cut hurts worse than my head."

"Glad to have you back so soon. Pretty quick turn-around for a concussion, isn't it?" Garrison asked, concerned his senior officer had convinced his doctor to let him back to work too soon.

Walker chuckled. "Doc said he wasn't completely sure I had a concussion. Said I might have just been knocked silly, is all."

"You damn sure were that," Garrison stated before turning to Cooper. "Don't you ever sleep, Coop? It's a little early for you this morning."

"Didn't want to miss the festivities, Chief!" He grinned, then pointed at Walker. "Besides, I didn't know if he was on light duty."

"Nope, full duty," was Walker's firm retort. "I don't want to sit around here all day."

"Well, you two will have to double up if you're going to stick around, Coop. We're down a truck, and Fernandez will need a truck to go to El Paso," Garrison announced.

"Oh?" she asked, leaning back in her chair.

"Yep. In fact, since we're all here, might as well have a

meeting," Garrison said, pulling up a chair. "Amanda, can you join us, please?"

Amanda tossed a notepad onto her chair, then pushed it over to the group.

"Okay, we received the ID of our murder victim this morning. His name was Richard Hardin, age twenty-six. The last known address was in El Paso. His TDL was expired, and if I remember correctly, the cell number DPS found for him had been reissued about six months ago. Instead of just calling El Paso PD, I figured it would be better if one of us went down and dug around a bit."

"I agree with that," Fernandez said. "El Paso ain't going to do much for us with just a phone call."

"I'd like you two—" he pointed at Walker and Cooper "—to handle the calls here in town while I go over to the sheriff's department and see what Sheriff Mitchel has come up with. Then I'm heading over to Odessa and meet with Detective Lee and see what, if anything, they've done. I'm guessing that once Mitchell told Lieutenant Zimmermann the murder scene was in Kutseena County, they probably shut down their investigation. Amanda, please note that I'll need to address the city council on Monday night and give them an update. Hopefully, we'll have more to report than we do right now, which isn't much. Not that I plan on telling the council much anyway. As far as I'm concerned, they don't need to know anything more than we're working on an open investigation and giving it our full attention. I'll put a victim profile sheet together and have one for each of you later this afternoon. Any questions?"

"If it's all right with you, I'd rather drive my car to El Paso. Less conspicuous," Fernandez said.

Garrison thought for a moment before answering. He didn't like the idea of his officers using their personal vehicles for business, but this was Bison and not Houston. After all, he was using his personal truck. "Okay. That's fine. I can reimburse you for the gas, but I don't know about mileage."

"No problem. I don't care about mileage at this point," Maria advised. "How long of a drive is it anyway?"

"A good four and a half hours unless you want to pop state trooper radar guns along the way," Walker answered with a wide grin.

"She'd probably do that anyway." Garrison laughed. "Just don't go getting any tickets!"

Fernandez dropped her hands onto her hips in mock dismay. "So, what are you saying, Chief?"

"I'd hate to let you go before we can order your uniforms," Garrison said, still chuckling. In fact, all the staff at Bison PD was laughing at this point.

The station's phone rang, ending the jocularity. Amanda quickly hurried to her desk. "It's the county dispatcher!" she called out. She took notes, then confirmed the call and disconnected. "We have a domestic disturbance over at the Vina residence," she reported with a touch of disgust to her tone and expression.

Noting Amanda's response, Garrison looked at Walker and Cooper for help. "Are they regulars or something?"

"Yep, they get drunk and fight bad enough that

the neighbors call every couple of months," Walker confirmed.

"A little early in the morning to be drunk and fighting," Garrison said, glancing at his watch and seeing it was only 9:45 AM.

"Probably still drunk from last night," Cooper scoffed. "We'll go see how bad it is this time." He grabbed his radio off his desk and headed toward the door with Walker right behind.

"Okay, be careful out there. Let me know if y'all need backup, and if you need to make an arrest, don't hesitate," Garrison chimed in, unsure of how his predecessor handled these marital fights. "Amanda, can you write down the address for me, so I know where they're heading?"

"Here you go, Chief. They're going to Armadillo Avenue, just off Center and Jack Rabbit Road across from the hospital," she advised, handing Garrison the address on a message slip.

"That's up in the varmint section of town, Chief!" Cooper called over his shoulder before the front door shut.

"I see we have a single holding cell," Fernandez stated. "I'm guessing we don't hold prisoners here for very long."

"No. I had the chance to talk to the sheriff, Billy Mitchell. He agreed to let us bring our prisoners directly to the county jail and book them there. I'm not sure how these guys handled that before, but after I looked around this place, I knew I didn't want prisoners here if I could help it," Garrison explained.

He stepped into his office, pulled his radio out of its charger, and turned it on before returning to Fernandez's desk.

"I'll need to assign you one of these. We have a couple of extras," he informed her.

"You want me to write up that victim profile sheet?" she asked.

"That'd be great. I'll check and see if the lab sent the email with the report. I'll forward it to you. Amanda, can you show her how to sign into her computer and set up her email?" Garrison asked before disappearing into his office.

"Unit two arriving," Waker called in.

"Unit three is with him," Cooper added.

Amanda confirmed with, "Units two and three received."

Garrison set his radio down on the desk and located the email from the DPS lab. He began reading through the attached reports, then focused on the criminal history report for victim Richard Alan Hardin, a white male, date of birth April 22, 1995. A data scan confirmed one burglary-of-a-habitation conviction, two theft convictions, and two convictions for possession of a controlled substance, penalty group one, less than one gram (cocaine). All before age twenty-five, with what looked like eighteen months incarcerated in prison. Garrison clicked on the next page when his radio's emergency tone pierced the quiet office.

"Unit two! Unit two! Shots fired, Chief! Shots fired!" Walker's voice shrieked out of the radio. The call catapulted Garrison and Fernandez into a sprint toward the station door.

"You have keys?" she shouted as they ran out of the building.

CHAPTER 29

THURSDAY

Garrison threw his radio onto the front seat, then jumped into his truck, Maria pouncing onto the passenger seat as Garrison slammed the F-150's accelerator to the floor. The truck's oversized tires squealed like a wounded pig as he spun the red Ford's rear end halfway into the left turn lane in front of Callie's café.

"Son of a bitch! I don't know where the hell they are!" Garrison yelled.

"Armadillo Avenue and Jack Rabbit Road across from the hospital . . . Whatever that means!" Fernandez shouted back, hanging onto the truck's pillar handle, attempting to stay in her seat.

Garrison blew his horn as he sped through the red light at Bison Boulevard, prompting another driver to screech to an abrupt halt halfway into the intersection. Garrison pounded his horn while swerving around two cars.

Cooper's voice exploded from the radio. "Suspect's on foot, running northbound from the house! It's Max Vina!"

"You two all right?" Amanda asked in a surprisingly calm voice.

"We're okay," Cooper advised. "Vina fired a couple of

rounds into the ceiling, then ran out the back when Luna let us in the front door. Walker's chasing him. I'm here with Luna. Better send an ambulance!"

"Base to unit two. What's your status?" Amanda asked.

"I'm in the neighborhood just north of Armadillo. I've lost him," Walker reported, his sharp words punching through rapid, heavy breaths.

Garrison slowed his speed and turned left onto Jack Rabbit Road.

"Give us a description of the suspect," Fernandez called into the radio, disregarding the formalities.

"Five-eight, two hundred pounds, black goatee, wearing a white tee-shirt and brown cargo pants," Walker answered.

"Ask Coop if he found a gun at the scene. He's unit three," Garrison said.

"Unit two, did you recover a gun at the scene?" she asked.

"Negative. Vina may still have it. Luna says it's a nickel, model 1911, forty-five auto," Cooper advised.

"Justin, you copy that?'

"Yep, received. Still looking on foot."

"Unit three , ambulance en route, should be there quick," Amanda reported.

Garrison slowly drove past the Vina house. Cooper's patrol truck was parked halfway up the dirt driveway. He and Fernandez scanned the surrounding driveways and what they could see in the backyards.

"Drop me off here," Fernandez ordered.

Garrison stopped. She jumped out, tucking the radio

inside the back of her khakis at the small of her back before pulling her Glock 9mm pistol from its injection-molded tactical holster. She then disappeared behind a house before he continued down the street. The ambulance's siren wailed behind him, and he turned onto a cross street named Opossum Road.

I see why they call this neighborhood varmint town, he thought.

He brought his truck to a quiet stop along the ditch line, then slid out on foot, joining the search, uncomfortably cognizant that he didn't have a radio. He heard the incessant yapping of a dog three houses away and decided to give that yard the first look. He peeked around the corner of a white single-story "shotgun shack" house, then slowly crept down the cracked asphalt driveway, quickly scanning the back corner of the house, garage corners, and neighbor's yard, then back to the rear corner of the house. As he cleared the back edge of the house, he saw a pop-up-style camper parked on a barren dirt area that may have once hosted grass. Two black boot soles were slightly protruding out from under the rear of the trailer.

He stopped and knelt at the corner of the house; his revolver clutched in a two-handed grip. He brought his gun to eye level and followed the view over the front sight, which he put right on the boot heels. He saw brown pants and a white tee shirt under the camper.

"Bison PD! I see you under the camper, Vina! Come out with your hands where I can see them! Now!" Garrison shouted.

Garrison leaned slightly forward after no response, keeping his suspect in sight. He pressed his finger firmly against the trigger.

"This is Chief Garrison, Vina! Don't make us come and get you! Come out from under there now!"

Vina yelled out some unintelligible response in Spanish, then began to creep backward on his stomach along the ground like a crippled frog, pulling his body with the toes of his boots. The house's back door opened, and Garrison turned his head sightly. A skinny woman in a floral dress stepped out.

"What the hell's going on out here?" she screeched before screaming at the sight of Vina pushing himself out from under the camper.

"Police! Get back in the house!" Garrison shouted.

The woman jumped at Garrison's order, whirled, and ran back inside.

"Keep moving, Vina! Keep your hands where I can see them! If I see a gun, I'll kill ya! Understand?" Garrison roared.

"No pistol! No pistol!" Vina shouted, standing up with both hands raised high into the air, facing Garrison.

"Turn around so I can see the front of your waist! Now!" Garrison demanded.

Fernandez and Walker appeared at the opposite corner of the house, their guns locked on Vina. Neither spoke a word. Vina turned slowly and saw the other officers with weapons aimed at him.

"No pistol!" Vina shouted again.

"Walk back toward me!" Garrison ordered, sweat

streaming down his face like he'd been caught in a rain shower. "Keep walking backward toward me, hands up!"

Vina kept his hands high and carefully stepped backward toward Garrison's voice.

"Stop right there!" Garrison ordered before driving his left hand into Vina's back, plunging the suspect face down into the dirt. Garrison quickly spun around and pushed his left knee into Vina's back as he holstered his gun and ripped handcuffs from his cuff case.

His officers ran to assist, Walker grabbing Vina's right arm and pulling it behind his back, where Garrison snapped the metal bracelets on each wrist. Garrison nodded to Walker. Then, each officer reached under Vina's arms and lifted him to his feet. Walker quickly searched the man from head to foot.

"Nothing," Walker confirmed.

"What'd you do with the gun?" Garrison demanded.

"I threw it down after I ran out of the house. I don't know where," Vina answered.

Fernandez checked under the camper. "Nothing here!"

She began searching the ground around the camper, moving farther away with each circle.

"Let Amanda know we have the suspect in custody, and we're all okay," Garrison instructed Walker, who quickly relayed the message via radio. Then Garrison focused on Vina again. "Show us which way you ran from your house."

"Okay. This way," Vina answered, then nodded toward the other side of the house.

Garrison walked Vina along the path he indicated

he'd run. The officers followed, scanning the ground and bushes along the way. They moved back and forth through the fenceless yards of several houses before arriving at the Vina's backyard.

"Here it is," Fernandez announced, pointing toward the nickel-plated Taurus .45 pistol under an overgrown holly bush.

Walker started to bend down to retrieve the pistol when Garrison spoke up.

"Leave it, Justin. I'll want a couple of photographs first, then we'll collect it with gloves on."

"Yes, sir." Walker backed away from the weapon, looking sheepish. "I knew that," he muttered, as if chiding himself.

"Fernandez, stand by the gun. We'll get what we need inside, then return here immediately. Do you have a camera in your unit?" Garrison asked Walker, who nodded in the affirmative. "Put him in your unit. I'll send Cooper out to watch him. You come back and photograph the gun, then collect it. Make sure you wear gloves just in case we need to send it off to DPS."

Garrison entered the Vina house through the back door and found Cooper in the kitchen with the paramedics, wrapping a wide bandage around Luna's head near her left eye socket. Garrison looked up at the ceiling and located two holes about a foot apart above the sink counter. He waved for Cooper to join him in the backyard.

"What'd she say?" Garrison asked him.

"She said they were arguing about him not going to work today. He went to the bedroom, got his gun, and was going to leave when she grabbed his arm and told him to stop. He hit her with the pistol in the front room, then went into the kitchen. Cut her pretty bad. She followed him and told him she was going to call the police. The neighbors beat her to it, and we arrived right about then. When she opened the front door, he fired the shots, then hooked it out the back door," Cooper reported, his words coming fast. "Walker took off after him, and I stayed here because she was bleeding badly."

"You have everything you need for the report?" Garrison asked.

"Yes, sir. She said she didn't want to prosecute. I told her it didn't matter; he was going to jail anyway. And I got a couple of pictures of her injury with my phone before they wrapped her up."

"Good job. Fernandez found the gun in the yard. I told Walker to take photos of the gun before we seized it. I also want photos of these bullet holes. Don't bother searching for the bullets. You stay with Vina while Walker takes care of that, then you two transport him directly to the county jail. I'll talk to Mrs. Vina, then Fernandez and I will meet you back at the station. Any questions?" Garrison asked.

Cooper's face cracked in two with a wide grin. "No, sir! Man, I'm glad you showed up! Ain't never had this kind of action before!" He then hurried toward the front of the house to meet Walker.

"One more thing," Garrison said, and Cooper stopped in his tracks.. "Who was driving?"

"I was," Cooper confirmed, his grin fading.

"Don't ever pull into the driveway on a call like this or

any other. I don't care how often you go to a location and never have a problem. You never know what the hell's going to happen on any given day. I need you two to be as safe as you can out here. Make sense?" Garrison asked.

"Yes, sir. Sorry. We should've known better."

Garrison spoke to Luna Vina, explaining that the law required them to arrest her husband and take him to jail whether or not she wanted to prosecute. Walker snapped photos, then he and Cooper left with Max Vina. Garrison and Fernandez walked back to Opossum Road, where he'd parked his truck.

"I thought you said this was a retirement job," she heckled.

"I thought it was. I was wrong," Garrison scoffed, shrugging his shoulders.

CHAPTER 30

FRIDAY

ernandez flipped the sun visor up, then guided her Dodge Challenger SRT Hellcat onto the westbound ramp from Highway 115 onto Interstate 20 toward El Paso. She pressed the gas pedal sending the 717 horsepower 6.2L HEMI V8 engine into a frenzy, launching her onto the open freeway. She rocketed past the Rattlesnake Bomber Base Museum, thinking she might want to check that out someday, and settled into the leather seat for what she hoped would be less than the four-and-a-half-hour ride the mileage calculator predicted. Garrison had provided a full victim profile report, compliments of the DPS Fusion Center's crime analysis investigators. Although she was certain the address, place of employment, and listed telephone number would all be either bogus or outdated data, they'd at least give her a starting point in tracing their victim's activities before he ended up dead in Bison.

Fernandez cruised along, dodging a never-ending hoard of semi-tractor trucks that hauled everything from rusted metal to livestock. An occasional car or SUV dotted the two-lane thoroughfare, but most of the time, she had a vibrant view of nothing but a clear ribbon of road. Two hours into her expedition, Fernandez entered the dry, dusty valley of Scroggins Draw, where she aimed her fire-red chariot toward the Interstate 10 exchange ramp and continued westbound on the desolate highway. She glanced at her cell phone screen and confirmed she couldn't rely on cell service anytime soon. The serenity of the trip allowed her to roll through the facts of the case thus far. Unfortunately, the known facts didn't afford much insight into the suspect's identity or motive. Everyone believed the two murders were linked, but there wasn't any real connection between the ex-veteran rancher and the two-bit thief.

An hour passed with nothing more than the humming of Goodyear tires clutching the pavement's surface. The late morning heat was beginning to radiate off the freeway's double-lane skin. A lonely metal highway sign, displaying Sparks, Texas, Population 4529, and peppered with bullet holes ringed in jagged silver jutted up from the parched roadway's gravel-littered shoulder. Fernandez saw a Love's Travel Stop ahead and heard it calling her name, so she backed off the throttle and eased into the confines of the trucker's lounge and fuel dump. The endless West Texas wind that turned the abrasive terrain into a continuous sand-blasting mechanism had pummeled the building's once lustrous paint into a drab achromatic palette.

After a brief respite, Fernandez put the truck stop in her rearview mirror and headed into El Paso. Her first stop was at an apartment complex on the west side of town. Listed as the last known address of victim Ricky Hardin, Fernandez found the location was a decades old single-story building that had once been a motel. The dilapidated crumbling structure was surrounded by a broken asphalt parking lot dotted with potholes and brown weed-filled cracks. Fernandez parked in front of a filthy gray door with "office" painted on it in worn black letters. Fernandez looked around and noted an apparent homeless clump of humanity sleeping on the walkway in front of room six and a giant gray rat rummaging through a heap of trash next to a faded green, rusty dumpster. A tall, scrawny white male with dark eyes and a pock-marked face, clad in a ragged black tank top and tattered jeans that had lost their denim blue hue years earlier, answered her knock at the door. Barefoot and chewing on what looked like a burnt chicken bone, the dude looked like one of those zombies staggering around on television programs.

"What?" came the singular mutter from what Fernandez believed was the meth-head manager.

Fernandez flashed her badge before the zombie's face, then held up a photo of Ricky Hardin.

"You know this guy?" she asked.

"Nope," the zombie answered as he attempted to slam the door shut.

Fernandez stepped onto the threshold and stopped the door, the heel of her cowboy boot clanging against the tarnished kick plate.

"Take another look," she hissed, shoving the photo closer to the zombie's face.

"Looks like Ricky," the zombie blurted, spewing greasy chicken bits all over the photo.

"Last time you saw him?" Fernandez curtly asked, keeping her questions as brief as possible, figuring the guy couldn't process more than a few words at a time.

"Gotta be six months or more. The owner kicked him out for not paying," he admitted.

"You know anything about him? Friends? Relatives?" Fernandez pressed.

"Nope. He was a meth head and vodka sponge. All I know," the zombie muttered.

Fernandez stepped back and let him slam the door, the rotted frame struggling to remain intact. She looked at the room doors contemplating whether asking around would be worth it. She quickly decided it wouldn't and checked the file for the next address—a janitorial company along the river on El Paso Drive where Hardin may have worked.

She sped along the edge of the Rio Grande River, a ribbon of water that weakly separated the United States from Mexico. Border patrol vehicles were randomly stopped along the path, agents clad in drab green uniforms milling about, searching buildings, shacks, and ditches. Now past noon, the heat was nearly unbearable. The temperature display on Fernandez's dashboard read 104. Despite the air-conditioner set on max, the sun's merciless beams penetrated the windshield turning the Challenger's interior into a pottery kiln. Ahead, two occupied border patrol trucks blocked the right lane, their emergency lights flashing from red to blue to amber.

Another uniformed agent directed her to drive around the commotion. While passing the scene, she observed an old, battered panel van, its rear doors open, and what looked like a dozen Mexican males sitting on the road's gravel shoulder. She shook her head; grateful she wasn't charged with the interminable task bestowed upon the border agents.

A short distance down the road, Fernandez located the address and turned off El Paso Drive onto a section of rocks and dirt that passed as the entrance to a corrugated tin building that once housed the ELP Cleaning Services Company. Clutching the last functioning hinge, a rusted metal front door swung lazily in the breeze. A window frame beside the door was cluttered with jagged pieces of filthy glass. Marie snapped a photo of the abandoned edifice, then made a quick escape from the downtrodden area, disinterested in what she might discover inside. She'd already confirmed the three telephone numbers connected to Hardin's name were no longer in service. She found a top-rated Mexican restaurant nearby and decided to call Garrison.

"This is Garrison," the Bison chief answered.

"You owe me one, Garrison!" Fernandez laughed into her cell phone.

"That bad, huh?" Garrison chuckled.

"Worse! I could've been kidnapped, taken over the border, and never seen again!" she exclaimed.

"I highly doubt that!" Garrison chided. "You find out anything?" Garrison asked.

"No. The apartment was a run-down motel with a

meth-head zombie manager, and the cleaning company was an abandoned building on the border. I don't see me learning anything worth a damn here," Fernandez admitted.

"Okay. Are you going to stay the night or head right back?" Garrison asked.

"I'll be on my way right after I eat. The least you can do is buy me a late lunch out here!" Fernandez chuckled.

"I can't argue with that! Head right to Barber's place. There's nothing new here. It looks like we'll have to wait a while for answers from the search warrants Sheriff Mitchell sent out," Garrison reported.

"See you this evening," Fernandez said before tapping the red dot on her phone to disconnect the call.

CHAPTER 31

MONDAY

Two weeks had passed since Fernandez's unproductive visit to El Paso. There hadn't been any additional information on victim Ricky Hardin. His background was as cloudy as Garrison's investigation of his death. As Garrison expected, Ector County closed their investigation on Hank Dawson once they confirmed he'd been killed at his ranch in Kutseena. Billy Mitchell informed Garrison that his investigation was delayed, pending the responses to the search warrants he'd sent in hope of identifying Dawson's cellular telephone carrier, financial records, and anything they could get from the veteran's administration. On their third search of Dawson's property, Mitchell's deputies located a single receipt from the Kutseena County credit union, indicating Dawson ran his money through there. There were no documents, bills, or contracts for a cellular telephone, nor was an actual phone found. In addition, Mitchell reported no family members had been identified.

Garrison and his officers had settled into a casual routine. The past two weeks had been quiet, but for a couple of domestic quarrels, another theft of service from the burger joint, and a drunk driver passing through town on his way to Odessa from the New Mexico casino on the other side of the state line. The downtime allowed Garrison to meet with most of the business owners in town, the Kutseena County District Attorney, and his assistant prosecutor, as well as the five members of the Bison volunteer fire department. Mayor Barber had kept the council members pacified, allowing Garrison to concentrate on putting his police department together. Two new Ford Explorer Interceptors were ordered, much to the delight of Cooper and Walker. Fernandez and Garrison procured their uniforms, and Amanda survived the two weeks of being estranged after filing for divorce from her philandering husband.

Garrison sat at his desk reading through what passed as the Bison police department policy book. He jotted down notes along the paragraph border of each policy, both alarmed and amused at their lack of critical content. He heard the front door open and heard Amanda greeting Fernandez. He checked his watch and saw it was nearly three o'clock in the afternoon—shift change. Walker would be going off duty, and Fernandez would be coming on. Garrison paused when a frowning Fernandez appeared in his doorway.

"I hate this damn monkey suit!" Fernandez announced. "I thought about this. I haven't been in uniform in fourteen years," she mused, to accentuate her displeasure.

Garrison looked at her and nodded.

"I know. I'm not thrilled about it either," he admitted.

"Well, you're the chief. Change the uniform policy or

something," Fernandez suggested, quickly switching from a solemn frown to a mischievous grin.

Garrison leaned back in his chair and grasped his hands behind his head.

"What would you suggest, Officer Fernandez?" he asked semi-seriously.

"I'm glad you asked that chief. I thought we could keep the uniform shirt but switch to jeans and a standard belt. It's not like we carry all that crap the HPD officers had to drag around," she noted. "And besides, I've noticed you've not worn your uniform since you addressed the town council a couple of weeks back," she uttered.

It was true; Garrison had no desire to run around Bison in full uniform. He'd gotten by in plain clothes for over three weeks without any remarks from Barber or the council members. He figured Barber wouldn't care, but Councilman Walker would eventually view it as another unprofessional decision by his unwanted police chief.

"I'll take your suggestion under advisement," Garrison offered before Amanda's voice cracked through his radio.

"Unit one, we have a report of a fight in progress at the Pumpjack bar. Several motorcycle riders are fighting out front."

Fernandez spun around and headed for the door, with Garrison close behind, while snapping his radio onto his belt.

"Any weapons seen?" Garrison asked Amanda as he hurried past her desk.

"No report of weapons, chief! Be careful!" Amanda shouted after him and Fernandez.

Garrison and Fernandez jumped into an F-150 Responder and sped out of the lot, its lights flashing and siren squawking. Garrison hit the brakes at Bison Boulevard and watched Walker's Responder race by. Garrison spun the steering wheel and pounded on the throttle, sending the truck into a hard right turn.

"Damn it!" Fernandez shouted; her voice muted in the blare of the siren.

Garrison saw Fernandez slide off her seat, her left arm slammed into the center console, and her knee smashed into the radio before she pushed herself back into her seat, grabbing for the seat belt.

Garrison then accelerated to catch up to Walker. "Sorry, have to do it!" he yelled.

She shouted back, "No worries! I could use some paid time off!"

"Not in the budget!" he retorted with a grin.

The two Responders reached the Pumpjack Bar and Grill in moments. Garrison looked past Walker's vehicle and saw half a dozen men, clad in leather vests with large circle emblems on their backs, battling in front of the bar. The combatants were taking turns pounding each other into the ground.. The sound of the encroaching sirens sent two of the bikers to their motorcycles, and they quickly sped off, leaving the other four insolent knuckleheads continuing to kick, claw, and punch each other into obscurity. Noticing the police, one of those four eventually fled on foot eastbound on Bison Boulevard, leaving his motorcycle behind.

Walker slid his patrol car sideways into the parking

lot, with him bailing out of his Responder before its forward inertia ceased. His boots hit the gravel-littered parking surface a fraction before he plunged into the middle of two oblivious combatants. Garrison and Fernandez followed close behind, Garrison sliding on a knee and clutching a biker's vest as he flew past, pulling the pugilist away from his opponent. The biker, a big man with long salt-and-pepper hair flowing from beneath a dangling bandanna, turned and mindlessly swung a right cross punch toward the chief, who blocked the assault with a stiff left arm.

"Police! Stop!" Garrison managed to blurt out before grabbing the big man by the throat and pushing him backward.

Fernandez raced to assist Walker, who'd rolled another suspect over onto his back. He managed to get a handcuff on the suspect's right wrist before the suspect threw his left elbow back and knocked Walker off his knee onto the asphalt.

A tall, bald-headed fighter rushed toward Fernandez. She pivoted her hips and kicked the outside of his left leg, smacking the meat over his common peroneal nerve, and he fell to the pavement with a crippled left leg and a face distorted in apparent agony. Fernandez quickly pulled her prisoner's hands behind his back then snapped her handcuffs closed on his wrists. She then spun and lunged back toward the short, sinewy, white male biker, who was swinging a right fist decorated with silver handcuffs toward Walker. Fernandez grabbed the biker's arm and let her body drop to the pavement, bringing the suspect down with a crashing thud. Walker clicked the handcuff shut on the prisoner's left wrist, then looked at Garrison, who was locked in a physical battle reminiscent of a WWE wrestling match.

"Watch them!" Walker yelled before he sped to his chief's aid, lowering his shoulder as he took aim. He hit the suspect like a linebacker on Sunday. Forcing the long-haired biker's chest into the parking lot's gravel surface, he clicked the handcuffs on each wrist. The familiar rapid clicking sound of the cuff bar's metal teeth ended the fracas.

All three officers were panting, doing their best to catch their breaths. Garrison looked around and saw Fernandez standing over two bikers, displaying bloodied noses, eyes, and mouths, not to mention the bleeding scrapes on their arms, courtesy of the knife-like gravel the Pumpjack Bar's parking lot provided. Garrison pointed toward the patrol trucks and escorted his prisoner to his while Justin aided Fernandez in securing the other two in Justin's Responder.

"I'll check inside and see what the hell started all this," Garrison informed his officers before disappearing into the cave-like front door of the saloon.

Garrison paused and allowed his eyes to adjust to the dark ambiance inside the Pumpjack bar. A few patrons sat at tables staggered around the triangular room, and a bartender stood behind a long, dark wood bar topped with a copper-covered slab, on which the slender red-headed Pumpjack owner propped her bare elbows and waited for

Garrison with a wide grin. He'd just met the owners of the bar a week earlier.

"Good afternoon," Garrison managed.

"Hello, Chief. Everything go the way it should've out there?" she asked, grinning from ear to ear.

"Well, the bad guys are in custody, and my officers appear uninjured."

"How about you? Those shredded jeans don't look too good," she replied, gazing down at his right leg.

"Sorry for the unprofessional appearance," he responded with a wide grin of his own.

After getting the bartender's report, Garrison emerged into the daylight and closed his eyes, waiting for them to adjust before joining his officers.

"Either of you hurt?" he asked.

Both officers shook their heads.

"Great. Same old crap. Members from two different gangs. They started drinking and decided to see who was tougher. We'll take them over to the county, charge them with disorderly conduct, and leave it at that," Garrison advised. "We can leave the bikes here. Fernandez, ride to the jail with Walker." Then he slid into his vehicle and spoke into the radio to Amanda, "Unit one, we'll be en route to the county with three."

"Got it, Chief. While you're at the jail, check in with Sheriff Mitchell. He called and said he's got vital information about the murder case."

CHAPTER 32

MONDAY

Garrison strolled down the wide hallway to Billy Mitchell's office, where he found the door closed. Two loud raps on the thick wooden slab brought the Kutseena County sheriff to the door, which swung open on three silent silver hinges. Mitchell was dressed in his neatly pressed uniform, complete with three military creases on the back of his shirt.

"Good afternoon, Chief. I heard you had a little trouble out at the Pumpjack," Mitchell chuckled, glancing down at Garrison's shredded jeans.

"A little," Garrison answered as he followed the sheriff into his office. He plopped down in one of the plush leather chairs opposite Mitchell's polished desk. "Got any good news for me?"

"Some good, some not so good, I reckon," Mitchell responded as he flipped open a manila folder on his desk. "The grand jury issued my subpoenas for Dawson's credit union account and VA file, but since I had no information for a cell phone account, that was denied as expected. Also, Dawson had no next of kin and no will. That means his estate will go to the state of Texas as escheated property." He turned the folder around so Garrison could read the top document.

Garrison leaned forward and perused the letter before settling back into the relaxed confines of his chair. His right knee began to throb. The skin on his damaged knee burned, and sharp pains darted around under his right kneecap. He winced and flexed his right leg, bending at the knee several times.

"I hate to admit it, but I'm getting too old for that fighting crap," he mumbled.

Mitchell laughed. "You've been involved in more shit in less than a month than your predecessor was in the last five years of his career."

"That's not a goal I cared to achieve," Garrison admitted. "How long before the state takes Dawson's place?"

"A couple of months. Why?"

"I'd like to go out there one more time and look around, if you don't mind."

"Not at all. The property is my responsibility until the state notifies me that they've assumed ownership. Once that happens, it'll probably be put up for sale, which should be entertaining since every oil company on the planet will make a bid," Mitchell speculated. "You want a deputy to go with you?"

"No, not necessary. I want to poke around one more time to satisfy myself. I'll head out right now since I'm halfway there already."

Mitchell reached into his desk drawer and removed an envelope marked "Dawson Key." He handed the envelope to Garrison.

"Just drop it off at the front desk when you get back," Mitchell stated. "I'll let you know what we find out from the credit union and VA."

Garrison limped out of the building into the blazing west Texas sun. The heat radiated off every exposed surface, sending blurry ripples of fiery air upward everywhere he looked. He realized he hadn't considered the heat since Amanda had dispatched the fight call. There was such a thing as an officer's "fight or flight" instinct when stress takes over, and the mind focuses on the immediate threat and nothing else. That had obviously taken place during the bar brawl, but now all he could think about was how hot it was. He smiled and shook his head before climbing into his Ford Responder and turning the air conditioner to max.

After checking in with Amanda, he cruised down the highway toward Soaring Eagle Road, where he took the turn. He parked in front of the west gate of the Dawson ranch and sat for a moment. The faded food bin looked lonesome next to the steel-poled gate, surrounded by sunburnt weeds. The gate was wrapped with yellow evidence tape, and a No Trespassing sign, "by order of the Kutseena County Sheriff's Office," hung lazily from the top rail on two loops of twisted barbed wire. Garrison looked across the pastures watching the tops of the tall weeds sway gently in the hot breeze. The distant sound of vehicles passing on the highway bordering the ranch's east side polluted the otherwise serene silence.

Garrison decided not to cut the evidence tape and, instead, climbed the gate and jumped onto the opposite side, his aching knee protesting when his size-ten, bull-hide roper boots hit the dirt. He paused again at the house's front porch and studied each inch of the platform, hoping he'd see something they had missed on the original visit. Nothing. He unlocked the front door, a heavy wood slab with a formidable dead-bolt lock and solid frame. He crept around each room, trying to put himself in Dawson's shoes, giving his best impression of a former military veteran who didn't seem to trust many civilians and chose to live a hermit's life. He and Mitchell both had been a little surprised that Dawson hadn't rigged any booby traps inside the house. Then again, perhaps they'd been overthinking things. Garrison saved Dawson's bedroom for last, carefully perusing the murder scene, which now lacked the bedding and shotgun Mitchell had seized as evidence. The room remained intact and in the same condition they'd initially found it.

Then he remembered the lack of a handgun. At least, it hadn't been on the list of seized items the sheriff's office had shared with him.

Funny that a vet and rancher wouldn't keep at least one handgun around.

Not here in Texas, where owning a handgun was practically a rite of passage. Garrison stood silent and closed his eyes, reviewing what he knew thus far.

He must have had a secret hiding place.

He slipped his cell phone out of his pocket and called Mitchell.

"Yes, sir?" Mitchell asked.

"Did you look for a hiding place anywhere after I left? Dawson had to have a stash of something around here."

"Son of a bitch! I didn't think of that. I'm on my way!" Mitchell shouted into the phone before disconnecting the call.

Garrison knelt on the floor, then crawled under the bed and began to check the wooden boards. No hidden compartment revealed itself, so he sat up and slowly scanned the room.

It has to be here in this room. He wouldn't want it to be too far away from where he spent most of his time. Come on, John, think.

He limped over to the small closet in the corner and peered inside. Nothing on the walls. He pushed aside a pile of dirty laundry and checked the floor. Still nothing. He turned and looked around the room again. He slid the chest of drawers aside and inspected the back wall and the floor. Nothing. He spun and looked at the bed table. It was a small rectangular wooden box with a single drawer at the top that had contained nothing of value when they first searched the place. Garrison stepped over to the dusty table and pushed it away from the bed. Like a lighted beacon in the night, there it was, a twelve-by-twelve cut outline on the floorboards with a hollowed-out notch at the edge closest to the bed. No doubt, it was Dawson's version of a safe.

CHAPTER 33

MONDAY

Garrison sat on the wooden steps of the Dawson front porch, watching Billy Mitchell's Ford Explorer slowly maneuver through the tall weeds that permeated the once dirt and gravel driveway. He'd decided to wait for the sheriff before opening what he'd hoped would be a paragon coffer of answers beneath Dawson's bedroom floor. Mitchell stopped in front of the house, bringing a swirling cloud of red dust with him.

Garrison forced a cough and waved his hand in front of his face, unable to hold back a laugh. "Appreciate ya, Sheriff!"

"Hey, that's West Texas magic dust, my friend!" Mitchell retorted as he slipped out of his vehicle, camera in hand. "Find anything?"

"Yep. A trap door in the floor under the bedside table," Garrison boasted. "I haven't opened it yet. I did take a few photos with my phone." He opened the front door, allowing Mitchell to enter first.

The two lawmen proceeded to the bedroom and stopped to look over Garrison's discovery. Mitchell snapped several photos, then set the camera down on the table.

"Well, since you found it, you do the honors," Mitchell said, waving his hand over the secret entry.

Garrison slipped two fingertips into the crudely gouged section of wood and carefully pulled up. The section of flooring easily lifted away. Mitchell pushed the rubber button on the back of his mini flashlight and illuminated the dark interior. The compartment was larger than its twelve-square-inch portal. Scrap pieces of barn wood topped with a faded red-and-black-plaid flannel shirt lined the makeshift safe. Garrison reached inside and moved folds of red cloth, the kind that quick oil-change technicians use to clean their hands and uncovered a Colt Python .357 magnum revolver with a six-inch barrel. Next to the Python, wrapped in an identical cloth, was a Colt Government model 1911 .45 automatic pistol. A quick check of each gun confirmed they were fully loaded.

Garrison set the weapons aside and removed four full fifty-round boxes of Federal brand ammunition, two boxes for each firearm. Under the ammo was a creased paper folder containing Dawson's birth certificate, birth and death certificates for each of Dawson's parents, and Dawson's DD-214 discharge papers from the US Army. Under the sleeve of the plaid shirt was an Alcatel pre-paid cellular flip-style telephone, sealed inside a clear plastic package, and a six-by-nine-inch, brown, leather-covered notebook secured with several rubber bands.

Garrison removed the plaid shirt, and a Zippo-brand cigarette lighter fell to the floor. Mitchell retrieved it and took a close look. The lighter contained Dawson's name just below an engraving: *Vietnam 1969*. Mitchell handed the lighter to Garrison.

"The guy survives Vietnam only to be shot dead while he's sleeping in his bed," Garrison muttered as he set the lighter next to the other items retrieved from the storage crypt.

Mitchell photographed the items separately and as a group, then went to his vehicle to grab some evidence bags. They carefully secured each item inside the brown paper bags, then took a cooling-off break in Mitchell's air-conditioned Interceptor.

Wearing nitrile gloves, Mitchell removed the rubber bands on the leather notebook and opened it so they could both view the contents. The yellow-tinged pages contained notes written in ink and pencil and loosely organized by date.

Garrison noticed the handwriting on the first several pages was markedly different than the recent entries. Still, all contained the same information—the date, company name, and amount of money offered to buy the Dawson ranch. Mitchell slowly turned the pages until he reached the final entry on page fifty-three. After reading Hank Dawson's last entry, Garrison looked at Mitchell, whose wrinkled forehead caught beads of sweat inside its deep crevasses.

"What the hell do you make of that?' Mitchell asked.

"I figured Clayton Walker had deep pockets and ties in the county, but I didn't realize he had that kind of money," Garrison answered, looking over the entry again:

"Thursday, May 28, 2021. CW Investments (Clayton

Walker) offered $10,000 an acre. Five point five million dollars. Wants mineral rights. Still less than Rockland's offer."

"Clayton is old oil money," Mitchell explained. "His father owned plenty of land around here way back in the day. Hit some oil, then sold off most of the land to the companies wanting to drill a hole every five feet. Clayton and his brother inherited all that when their mother passed. After he and his brother had a falling out, Clayton began to dabble in land and property investments for quite a while now."

"A falling out?" Garrison asked.

"From what I heard, he and his brother, your officer's father, got into it over how to spend daddy's money. His brother sued Clayton, and it ended up in court. I don't know what happened, but his brother, who lives up in Lubbock, stopped coming around. I don't know how much Clayton ended up with, but I figure it was more than I'll ever see." Mitchell chuckled. "I'm just an ole country cop, but the offer date looks more important than the amount. The twenty-eighth of May 28 was what . . . ten days before you end up with a dead body and Dawson was killed?"

Garrison scratched his head. "Well, it sure doesn't look too good for Mr. Walker, does it?"

"Nope. I'll need to talk to him sooner than later. You might want to join me," Mitchell suggested.

"That's going to be a problem. I'll talk to the mayor about it first."

"All right. Let's get out of here before we uncover any more prickly evidence," Mitchell ordered.

CHAPTER 34

MONDAY

The Ford Responder glided down the road at a steady pace. Garrison had engaged the cruise control to give his aching right knee a much-needed rest. What began as tolerable pain had amplified into pounding agony. To make matters worse, he could feel the knee had swelled, causing the enlarged joint to push the damaged skin firmly against his tattered jeans. He could barely move his lower leg, and when he did, the pain was excruciating. He decided a visit to the medical center was in order.

After completing the forms, Garrison was swept into examination room number one, where a nurse young enough to be his daughter was waiting. Her long, dark hair was pulled back in a ponytail which swung back and forth behind her neck, peeking out over each shoulder as she moved. She ordered him to remove his pants, put on a gown, and lay on the bed. She was pleasant but spoke with an authority that Garrison knew better than to defy. After taking his vitals, she stepped away, pulling the room curtain closed behind her.

Garrison winced as he carefully slid his tattered denim pant leg off his swollen knee, then slipped into the gown and onto the bed. The sound of an inaudible country music song playing in the distance, and the muffled whispers of a conversation between, Garrison presumed, the nurse and the ER doctor permeated the otherwise quiet hospital. Then the curtain parted, and a tall, slender young man with short, jet-black hair combed straight back over a clean-shaven face entered the space.

"Good evening, Chief Garrison. I'm Ben Ackerman, the ER doctor on duty today," the physician announced with a firm handshake.

"John Garrison, Doc. Good to meet you."

Ackerman set his clipboard down on a stainless-steel bed table and looked at his patient's right knee, which was nearly twice the size of the left.

"Well, it's plain to see what brought you here this evening," Ackerman said.

"I thought it was just a bruise, but it just kept getting worse as the day wore on," Garrison admitted.

"How'd it happen?" Ackerman asked, sliding fingers from each hand under Garrison's knee and lifting lightly.

"Hit the pavement during a fight out at the Pumpjack," Garrison said flatly.

"This is gonna hurt," Ackerman systematically pressed on the swollen joint.

Garrison sucked in a quick breath through gritted teeth as the pain hit. "It sure does!" he hissed.

"Sorry, Chief. Despite the swelling, I'm going to order an x-ray. It's not to the point where it should affect the images. I'll also get you some pain medication. It won't take long to get the film, and then we'll see what's going on in there," Ackerman said before disappearing through the opening in the blue curtain.

Garrison leaned back and closed his eyes. Everything that had happened since he'd taken the oath of office—in what he'd thought would be a boring, dust-laden town—flooded his mind. Images of the bodies of Hardin and Dawson flashed through his mind, along with Officer Walker's wrecked patrol truck, the fight with the bikers, and a kaleidoscope of crime scene photos. On top of all that, a shots-fired domestic disturbance. His thoughts exploded at the jolting sound of his cell phone's ring.

Damn it! I really have to figure out how to change that! He picked up the call. "John Garrison, Bison Police."

"Hey, Chief, this is Jason Lee over at Ector County. How are things?"

"They've been better. Any news for me?" Garrison asked the detective.

"Unfortunately, no smoking gun, but Lieutenant Zimmermann granted the release of our evidence in the Dawson case to Sheriff Mitchell, who told us to send it to you first. Would you like to pick it up?" Lee asked.

"I appreciate that . . . the sooner, the better."

"I'm here all evening if you want to come and get it."

"I'll send one of my officers, if that's all right with you," Garrison said.

"Sure. I'm on duty until eleven."

"Excellent, thanks," and Garrison disconnected the call. Then he dialed Maria Fernandez, who was probably bored to death driving around Bison.

"Yes, Chief?" she answered in her songbird's voice.

"How's everything going?" Garrison asked, electing not to offer his whereabouts.

"Oh, you know, kicking ass and taking names."

"Okay, take a break from that. Run on over to Odessa and meet with Detective Jason Lee at the Ector County Sheriff's Department. They're releasing their evidence in the Dawson case to us."

"Will do. Thanks for the assignment. Are you here in town to take over my rigorous patrol duty?"

"Affirmative; I'll call the county dispatch and tell them to call me if we have anything," Garrison advised.

"Ten-four. On the way."

Thirty minutes later, Garrison's x-rays were complete, and he was back in his ER room surrounded by the familiar blue curtain. The pain medication Dr. Ackerman had provided was beginning to take effect. Garrison unsuccessfully tried to flex his knee. He leaned back, hoping his town would stay quiet until he could return to his office.

"Well, Chief, it looks a bit worse than I thought," Dr. Ackerman's voice broke the moment's tranquility.

Garrison sat up in bed. "Oh?"

The doctor snapped the x-ray image into the lighted panel on the wall. Removing a pen from his shirt pocket, Ackerman pointed to a thin, vertical line in the center of what Garrison figured was his kneecap.

"This line here represents a fracture of your patella. That's the bad news. The good news is it's vertical and only about an inch and a half long . . . and therefore, it shouldn't require surgery," Ackerman reported, then turned back to his patient. "I don't suppose there'd be any chance of you taking about three or four weeks off to let this heal?" he asked with a wince, indicating he knew that was damn near impossible but had to ask anyway.

"Doc, the reality is, I can't take three days off," Garrison admitted.

"I figured you'd say that. Okay. How about a compression brace and light duty for the next few weeks?"

"I'll do my best, Doc."

"I guess I'll have to accept that for now. Just know that if you take another significant hit to that knee . . . "

"I know, I know," Garrison answered with a slight grin and a wave of his hand. "Right now, I need to get back to my office as soon as possible."

"I'll order up that brace and a prescription for an anti-inflammatory. Baby it as much as you can," Ackerman advised before shaking Garrison's hand and disappearing through the slit in the blue curtain.

CHAPTER 35

MONDAY

Fernandez wheeled her new Ford Interceptor into the barren parking lot of the Ector County Sheriff's Office and sharply backed into a space marked "Police Parking Only." She'd not been inside the county building yet, only seeing it from the road weeks ago when she passed by on her way to pick up her uniforms. Garrison had spoken highly of Jason Lee and Bill Zimmermann, and she looked forward to meeting either or both. She scaled the five steps to the entrance and gracefully slipped through the single glass door adorned with a large gold star for the Ector County Sheriff's Office.

"Can I help you, Officer?" a uniformed deputy asked from behind a sprawling elevated desk that sat square in the middle of the expansive room. The man's uniform fitted crisply over his muscular body, and his high-and-tight, salt-and-pepper hair was neatly groomed.

Definitely a military man, she thought as she leaned against the front of the desk and flashed a flirty smile.

"Yes, sir. I'm here to see Detective Jason Lee," she announced.

The deputy smiled back and reached for the phone.

"There's a Bison PD officer here to see you," he announced into the handset before setting it back down on the receiver. "He's on his way. I didn't know Bison had a lady officer."

"I'm new. I think I'm the first one in the department's history. I retired from Houston PD and was talked into this job by the new chief, John Garrison. Used to work with him, back in the day."

The deputy leaned back in his chair. "I'm not trying to be cute, but you don't look old enough to be retired already," he muttered.

"Thank you, but unfortunately, I'm old enough to have done twenty-five with HPD. Now I'm pushing a patrol unit around in a one-horse town in the middle of nowhere." Fernandez couldn't help but chuckle. It all really did seem crazy, yet here she was.

"From what I hear, it's been anything but a one-horse town since your chief took office," the deputy stated.

"I guess that's true. We have this unsolved murder hanging over our heads with no real leads yet," she answered flatly.

A formidable wood door swung open, and a stocky man in his middle forties with short, strawberry-blond hair, a full but graying mustache, and a gold star clipped to his belt stepped through. Fernandez immediately noticed the detective's ephemeral pause, quick raise of his eyebrows, and gaping grin. Men had flashed that expression many times when they first laid their eyes on her. She stepped around the desk to greet the detective, who wore a tight, tan polo shirt, dark-brown khaki pants, and a pair of polished, brown cowboy boots glistening in the bright light.

"Detective Lee?" she asked with the same flirty smile she'd flashed to the deputy behind the desk.

Lee extended his right hand. "You must be Officer Fernandez."

"That's me. Chief Garrison sent me to collect the evidence from your Dawson homicide investigation," she stated as she accepted Lee's handshake.

"Yes, ma'am, come on back to my office. We really don't have much to offer, but it might be important later on if y'all or Sheriff Mitchell catch a lead," Lee stated.

He opened the russet door he'd just come through, then stepped aside, allowing Fernandez to enter first.

"Thank you," she said in a lilting tone as she passed him in the doorway.

Lee stepped around Maria and pointed down the hall and to the right. "I'm right down here," he reported before leading the way.

Fernandez followed the detective, glancing at the walls. Neatly framed photos of Ector County deputies engaged in various activities lined each side of the hallway. She stepped into Lee's cluttered but well-organized office. An eight-by-ten framed photograph of Lee receiving his detective badge from the sheriff hung on the wall behind his desk next to a framed Sherlock Holmes quote printed over a depiction of a dictionary page. A can of compressed air sat next to the computer keyboard and a Funko Pop figure of Jason, the masked killer from the *Friday the 13th* films, stood next to a stack of reports.

"Oh! I get it!" Fernandez laughed, pointing at the charismatic figurine.

Lee followed her finger and chuckled. "Yeah, that was a gift from Ziggy."

"Ziggy?"

Lee laughed. "Lieutenant Zimmermann. The whole Jason thing cracks him up, for some reason."

"Is he around? I'd like to meet him."

"No, he's strictly dayshift. When Sheriff Mitchell talked him out of retirement, he only agreed to join the department if he was permanently assigned to dayshift with weekends off."

"Where'd he retire from?" she asked, enjoying the small talk with the pleasant detective.

"Arlington, over where the Texas Rangers and Dallas Cowboys play."

"I'm an Astros and Texans fan myself," she announced.

"Oh, so close! I guess we can't be friends, then!" Lee laughed.

Maria balled her fists and jammed them into her hips, forcing a frown. "Well, then … do you get a dinner break around here?"

Lee paused and looked up from the evidence box on his desk. "Sure. You in a hurry to get back to the booming town of Bison?"

"Nope! And I haven't seen much of Odessa. Got a

favorite place you can show me?" she asked, tilting her head to the side and flashing the flirty grin again.

"Uh . . . yeah. Actually, I have several. Do you have a favorite food?" Lee asked.

"I'm partial to Tex-Mex, but I can put away a burger with the best of 'em."

"Perfect. We'll head over to El Buen Pollo on University Boulevard." Lee snatched a set of keys hanging from a hook on the wall beside the door. "Let's do this!" he bellowed with a wide grin.

Fernandez followed her guide down a short hallway and through the back door to several department vehicles parked neatly in a single row. Lee picked a silver Chevrolet Tahoe marked *SHERIFF* in large, yellow, block letters on each door and popped the electronic locks. Fernandez jumped into the passenger seat, leaving the door open to allow the immense heat to dissipate while Lee cranked up the air conditioner. Even in the evening as the sun's intensity weakened by the minute, the West Texas heat was brutal. After a brief respite, Lee spun the Tahoe around and headed for the restaurant, and Fernandez smiled as she picked up a bit of uneasiness in her presence. *Nothing unusual there,* she thought, and a smirk formed on her lips.

CHAPTER 36

MONDAY

Garrison leaned back in his office chair and propped his wounded leg onto a folding chair he'd confiscated from the lobby. His knee throbbed like a drummer keeping the beat of a wicked rock song. He hesitated to take another dose of the pain meds Dr. Ackerman had prescribed, primarily due to the warning that it could cause drowsiness. The last thing he wanted to do was nod off before Fernandez returned.

He flipped open the folder that contained the state police's final report on Walker's traffic-fatality pursuit. He scanned the narrative of facts, taking note of the criminal history of the deceased suspect. The investigation concluded that the deceased suspect had lost control of his vehicle while aggressively evading arrest from pursuing law enforcement officers. As a result of the intentional and reckless acts of the driver/suspect, the driver/suspect succumbed to fatal injuries sustained in the resulting single-vehicle crash . . .

Garrison's cell phone rang, startling him. The intrusion caused him to twist his damaged knee, sending bolts of sharp pain through his leg. Through a grimace, he managed to say, "Good evening, this is John Garrison."

"Hello, John, this is Billy Mitchell. Any chance you can meet me at my station as soon as possible?" the sheriff asked.

"Yes, sure can. What do you have?"

"We're searching for your secretary's husband. He's wanted for domestic assault. Amanda's being transported to the Bison Medical Center by ambulance," Mitchell reported grimly.

Trepidation washed over Garrison like he'd been doused with a bucket of dread. "How bad is it?" he asked.

"I think she'll be okay, but it's not good. Her husband beat her up pretty bad."

"I'll head to the hospital first, then out to your place when I can," Garrison advised.

"That'll work. I have all of my deputies looking for the asshole. Sorry to bring you bad news, John," Mitchell said before disconnecting the call.

As he rushed out of the station, Garrison tucked his radio into the back pocket of his Wranglers and tapped Fernandez's name on his speed dial.

"Hello, Chief. What now?" she asked, and he could hear her chewing and silverware clinking. He figured he must have caught her in the middle of her evening meal, and he found himself wondering where . . .

"I need you back here right now," Garrison began.

"What's wrong?"

"Amanda's on the way to the hospital. Her husband beat her up pretty bad."

"That son of a bitch! I'm on the way!"

Garrison wheeled out of the parking lot and headed

for the medical center. During the brief drive, he notified Dan Barber, who demanded an update on Amanda's condition as soon as Garrison had one. He then parked outside the emergency room entrance, blocked by the ambulance he presumed had transported Amanda. He knew she lived just north of the Bison city limits, near the medical center. He figured she'd been attacked at home.

Garrison dashed through the double doors and witnessed countless medical personnel scurrying around the ER. Was it because of Amanda?

Damn it! How bad is it?

Dr. Ackerman stepped out from behind a blue curtain shrouding Amanda.

"Hi, Chief. Please stay out here for the moment. The nurse is switching her IV, and they're changing her clothes," Ackerman advised.

"Can you tell me anything yet, Doc?"

"Only that she's conscious and reporting pain in her side, probably from cracked or broken ribs, and she has multiple lacerations on her face and neck. I won't know more until we can get the x-ray and CT scan results. She told us her husband attacked her. Is that right, Chief?" Ackerman asked.

"That's what Sheriff Mitchell told me. It's her estranged husband. They're going through a divorce," Garrison whispered, unsure if Amanda would want that information given to the doctor.

"I see. Has he been arrested?" the doctor asked, loud enough for everyone in the room to hear.

"Not yet. Mitchell's deputies are looking for him now,"

Garrison advised, keeping his eye on the blue curtain in case Amanda pulled it aside for him to enter.

"Well, I'm sure she'll authorize the release of her examination report for you. I'll be sure to be explicit in my description of injuries."

"Thanks, I appreciate that. We'll need it," Garrison answered with a pat on the doctor's back.

Garrison retrieved a chair from the registration area and set it next to Amanda's blue curtain. His right knee buckled as he began to sit down, causing him to miss the chair and tumble to the floor. He landed on his pistol, promptly sending lightning bolts of pain into his right hip. His radio catapulted out of his pocket like it had been slung from a slingshot.

"Ahhhhhh!" he cried out in pain.

Two nurses emerged from inside Amanda's curtained chamber as a young orderly rushed around the reception desk, sliding wildly on the slick, polished floor.

"What's going on out here?" the nurse who'd earlier assisted Dr. Ackerman with Garrison's knee injury demanded harshly.

"Sorry! Sorry! This damned knee gave out, and I missed the chair," Garrison growled, more embarrassed than anything else.

"Well, maybe if you wore the brace on it like the doctor ordered, that wouldn't happen!" she shrieked, obviously irritated with Bison's top cop.

"Yes, ma'am, as soon as I can," he assured her as he pulled himself off the floor and into the chair.

"Chief, can you come in here, please?" Amanda mur-mured.

Garrison carefully stood and limped through the parted blue curtain; each side held back by a nurse. He had seen many more mangled humans, death, and destruction than he cared to remember, but seeing friends, family, and coworkers in such a poor state was far worse. He peered down upon the woman who'd become much more than just his secretary and dispatcher in the few short weeks they'd been together. Her face looked like bruised hamburger, a sharp contrast to the pretty woman he'd seen this afternoon. Both eyes were nearly swollen shut; her customary made-up lips were bloodied, split in multiple places, and swollen three times their normal size. The distinct bruising on her neck indicated she'd been strangled, and a two-inch gash on her left collarbone was evidence of a wristwatch or some other metal object. She slowly turned her head and tried to look at Garrison. Tears began to seep from her damaged eyes. And heat crept up his neck as anger took hold.

"I'm sorry, Chief. I'm sorry you're here because of me," Amanda whispered.

Garrison didn't know if he was crossing boundaries, but he didn't care. He took her hand in his and squeezed gently.

"Don't you dare apologize for what that son-of-a-bitch did. I'm here for whatever you need," he assured her, then offered a gentle smile. "After all, you're the most important member of our team."

Amanda attempted to smile, only to grimace instead.

"I won't be doing that for a while," she murmured.

"Were you able to give a statement to the deputies?" Garrison asked, his cop instincts supplanting his aggrieved psyche.

Amanda nodded slightly. The remaining nurse scribbled something on a chart, then smiled and excused herself, closing the curtain behind her. He knew he should respect his employee's privacy and allow her to rest, but he decided he wouldn't battle the angry cop brewing inside of him. He only needed one answer.

"Why?" Garrison asked.

Amanda opened her eyes as best she could. Tears flooded the narrow slits she was forced to see through. "He was drunk and angry because I'd filed for divorce after I found out he cheated on me. He was hiding in the bedroom closet when I got home. He just kept hitting me and calling me . . . a-a-a fucking b-b-bitch," she cried.

"He strangled you, didn't he?" Garrison asked, wanting confirmation for what he already knew.

"Yes, sir. He choked me, then threw me down next to the bed. That's when I was able to call 911," Amanda explained.

"Do you have any idea where he is right now?"

"No, he ran out of the house when he heard me call the police."

"Mitchell's deputies are searching for him. We'll find him. He'll get what he deserves," Garrison said, uncertain his words were valid. "One more thing. Does he own a gun?"

"Yes, several. He goes out to his gravel yard and shoots beer cans sometimes. He might be there. Please . . . be careful."

Garrison smiled and carefully placed Amanda's hand at her side under the blanket. He then turned and headed for the door, determined to join the search for another piece of shit that gave men a bad name. A deputy carrying a metal clipboard met Garrison when the sliding glass doors parted.

"Hello, Chief Garrison. I'm here to check on Amanda and see what the doctor can tell me about her condition," Deputy Dave Bullard advised.

"Hello, Bull, good to see you again, though not under these circumstances," Garrison said, remembering him from the Hummer recovery scene.

"That's for damn sure. We haven't found Chuck yet, but we will," Bullard declared with confidence.

"That the guy's name? Her husband is Chuck?"

"Sure is."

"Well, I'm going to help y'all find that son of a bitch," Garrison said before limping past the deputy into the west Texas dusk.

Garrison didn't know much about Amanda's husband. He'd never met him but knew what he looked like from the picture Amanda used to keep on her desk. Amanda hadn't said much about him other than he drove a gravel truck for the Piper Sand and Gravel Company. Although he'd never been to the Piper Company, he knew it was an enormous operation west of town past Bison Lake. If Chuck Stewart were smart, he'd hightail it back to his casino-dealer girlfriend's place, wherever that was. Figuring he wasn't, Garrison called Billy Mitchell and confirmed Stewart's truck wasn't at the house when his deputies arrived. In that case, Garrison decided he'd head to the gravel pits and look for the bastard there. He chose not to tell Mitchell where he was going, after insisting he didn't need backup.

Fury rocked through his body like he'd been electrocuted. He always wanted to turn suspects into prisoners, but this was different. This was personal, and it felt like it. This time, he wanted more than mere justice. He wanted revenge. Garrison steered his Responder westbound on Coyote Road toward the Piper Sand and Gravel yard.

CHAPTER 37

MONDAY

The responder's tires hummed along the heated pavement. Garrison slipped into tunnel vision as he stared through the windshield into the last remnant of the day's light. Endless images of beaten, battered, and lifeless victims flashed through his mind. The bludgeoned face of Amanda swirled around all of the others. His surge of emotions wildly swung from immense anger to weariness. Beaten down from decades of the death and destruction so-called civilized humans laid upon each other, he'd suppressed the unspoken trauma his thirty-five years on the job had forced him to endure, but tonight was different. Amanda, his Amanda, had been brutally attacked by a man she once loved and trusted. For what? His indiscretion and too much booze? Not acceptable, never acceptable. Amanda was the sweetest woman he'd met in a long time and had been in his corner since he'd come to this dust-bowl town. He squeezed the steering wheel. His jaw ached from his clenched teeth.

Not this time. This son of a bitch wasn't going to hide behind the weak-ass criminal justice system.

Not this time, he thought as he turned the Responder into the entrance of the Piper Sand and Gravel Company.

The compound was vast, with enormous mounds of gravel, sand, and various-sized crushed rocks randomly dotting the area inside the entrance. Tall wooden poles connected with drooping thick black wires surrounded the business. Each timber had a flood lamp near the top, providing bright light for after-dark activities. The business was closed. The employees were gone. Only locked buildings, neatly parked trucks, and excavation equipment were present tonight.

He parked the Responder but kept the engine running, turned off the headlights, and rolled the windows down. The intense sound of crickets and frogs penetrated the thumping sound of his pounding heart. Closing his eyes, he took a few deep breaths, calming himself.

The crack of gunfire suddenly snapped the humming buzz of the critters. The echo of two shots bounced off the mounds of earth to his left.

Garrison slowly maneuvered his truck around a titanic mound of sand and parked, then thought, *It'll be safer to approach on foot.* Carefully closing the truck door so as to not to give away his position, Garrison slid his .45 revolver out of its holster and crept around piles of crushed rock and stone toward the back of the property where the gunshots had come from.

Two more shots erupted from the opposite side of a colossal gravel mound. Garrison took another deep breath and raised his gun to eye level. As he cleared the edge of the gravel, he saw Chuck Stewart standing in the center of a wide opening, pointing his pistol at a row of cans sitting on a split-rail fence.

"Drop the gun, Chuck! Garrison, Bison police! Drop the gun!" Garrison ordered.

Chuck froze and slowly turned his head toward Garrison. His face was bleeding, and Garrison figured those were courtesy of Amanda's nails as she fought for her life. Chuck held his black 9mm semi-automatic pistol up and ready, pointed at the cans while he peered at the Bison police chief.

Garrison noticed Chuck was swaying, either from too many beers or the adrenaline that was indeed pumping through him like a runaway pumpjack.

"Fuck you, Garrison! I ain't goin' to prison, you son of a bitch. It's because of you she's divorcing me! Everything was fucking fine until you got here!" Chuck shouted.

"Just drop the gun, and we'll talk it all over. It'll all work out if you just put the gun down," Garrison ordered again, this time in as calm a voice as he could muster.

Chuck glanced back at his pistol . . .

Then started to turn toward Garrison, yelling, "I ain't goin' to prison!"

"No, Chuck! No!" Garrison roared.

Chuck swung his pistol around and fired at Garrison, the 9mm bullet shattering a cinderblock next to Garrison. The muzzle flash lit Chuck up like a spotlight.

Crack! Crack! Garrison fired. The two bullets from his Long Colt hit Chuck in the center of his chest, knocking the six-three, two-hundred-fifty-pound assailant backward like he'd been hit with a sledgehammer. Like a slow-motion video, Chuck collapsed as his pistol flew into the air, seemingly taking minutes to fall to the ground.

Garrison no longer heard the buzz of the crickets or frogs. He'd not even heard the two shots he'd fired. He'd seen the muzzle flash and Chuck gradually crashing to the ground. He felt numb and hollow inside, as though he were only a shell. He lowered his gun and walked toward the unmoving Chuck. He knelt and placed his fingers on Chuck's neck, to see if he was alive. Garrison wasn't sure. His hand felt numb. He couldn't feel a pulse on Chuck's neck. He holstered his gun, reached for his phone. Forced several deep breaths. Slowly his senses returned, and he called Billy Mitchell.

"This is Sheriff Mitchell."

"Billy, it's Garrison. I'm out at the Piper Sand and Gravel yard. I found Chuck Stewart. I had to shoot him. I need an ambulance," he steadily reported.

"Okay, John, are you hit?"

"No, I don't think so," Garrison muttered before looking himself over.

"We'll be there right quick, John."

Garrison disconnected the call, then tapped the speed dial for Dan Barber.

"Hi, John, how's Amanda?" the mayor asked.

"I found Chuck Stweart out here at Piper's. He fired at me, Dan. I had no choice. I had no choice," Garrison stated flatly.

"Okay, John, are you hit? Are you all right?"

"I'm not hit. Mitchell is on his way."

"Is Chuck dead? Did you call an ambulance?" Barber asked, his officer-involved shooting training instinctively kicking in.

"Looks like he's dead. An ambulance is on the way," Garrison answered.

"All right, I'll get out there as soon as possible," Barber advised before disconnecting the call.

Garrison heard sirens in the distance. He looked around, then sat down on a nearby boulder. It was the size of those inflatable balls women used to exercise with. The name PIPER was painted on it in large, black letters. The excruciating pain returned to Garrison's knee. He looked at it and shook his head.

Never felt a damn thing after I left the hospital, he thought.

Three sheriff department Interceptors arrived, followed by the same ambulance that had transported Amanda to the medical center an hour earlier. Billy Mitchell quickly approached Garrison and looked him over for any wounds. Satisfied Garrison was okay, he joined the medics at Chuck's body. One of the medics looked at Mitchell and shook his head, confirming Chuck was dead.

"Bull, get crime scene tape around the whole area," Mitchell ordered, moving his arms in a wide arc. "Smitty, get the evidence markers out of my unit and start placing them, with number one being the pistol right here." He pointed to the Glock 9mm Chuck had fired.

Mitchell stepped over to Garrison, who hadn't moved or said anything, just leaned his elbows on his knees and watched and waited.

"What happened, John?" Mitchell asked.

"He was drunk when I arrived, shooting at cans on

the fence. I ordered him to drop the damn gun, but he refused. He started yelling, saying he wasn't going to prison, and I was responsible for Amanda divorcing him. I ordered him to drop the damn gun again, but he started firing at me," Garrison began. He paused and shook his head. "It was suicide by cop! Son of a bitch! I should've seen it coming! I didn't want to kill him, Billy, I didn't want to kill him . . ." He dropped his head, rubbing his broken knee.

Mitchell squeezed Garrison's shoulder. "Sounds like he gave you no choice. I'll need to call the Rangers to handle the investigation. I'll take care of it."

"His shot hit those stacked cinderblocks over there. I was standing next to them," Garrison advised.

"Bull, let's have a look," Mitchell called to Deputy Bullard.

"I don't know, Sheriff. I damn sure wouldn't want to be Garrison right now," Bullard exclaimed.

"Nor I," Mitchell agreed.

CHAPTER 38

TUESDAY

an Barber slammed his door shut and threw his Stetson onto a chair in the corner of his office. Opening the blinds, he stared out the window. He hadn't wanted to be mayor, trying to convince anyone who would listen that he wasn't a politician. He was a retired cop who just wanted to enjoy a little ranch life before his days were done. But no, he was too well-liked and far more educated than the two men who'd submitted their candidacy documents. The council members all had businesses they claimed prevented them from seeking the position, and his wife thought it would be something good to occupy his spare time.

Spare time? What spare time? There'd been more going on in their one-horse town than he could keep up with. First, the town wanted to expand and, thus, annexed the land on the south side. After that, the developers started coming in droves, wanting the exclusive rights to build apartments and houses on every square inch the town had purchased. Then the police chief decided to retire a week after his senior officer left for the Odessa PD. Throw in two murders, a high-speed, police-related death, the near-death of a dear town employee, and the new police chief killing his secretary's husband . . .

A light knock on the door interrupted Barber's thoughts.

"Come in, Connie, and close the door behind you," he said, anticipating the visit from his secretary.

"Good afternoon. Are you all right? I heard the door slam, which isn't like you," Connie said softly.

"I don't know, Connie. For the first time since I took this job, I'm beginning to think it was a mistake and I should move on," Barber admitted, keeping his attention out the window.

"I understand, but nothing that has happened has been your doing," Connie assured the mayor. "Can you imagine what it would be like right now if you'd just appointed Justin Walker as the police chief?"

Barber turned and forced a smile. "That's why you're the best, Connie. You always know what to say at the right time. Have you ever thought of running for mayor?"

"Oh, I think not!" Connie responded with a laugh.

"Were you able to contact Dale Finley?" Barber asked, returning to business.

"Yes. He said Chief Garrison could make his own appointment time. Here's his number if you'd like to talk to him personally," Connie advised, setting the note on Barber's desk.

"Thank you. Chief Garrison will be here shortly. Send him right in, please."

Boy, is John going to hate this, Barber thought, looking at Finley's name and number. Then he flipped through the messages on his desk. There were two from the radio station in town, two from the television station in Odessa, one from Natalie Hollingsworth, and four from Clayton Walker.

That's about right, Barber thought, looking at Walker's messages.

A loud rap on his door was immediately followed by John Garrison entering the office and closing the door behind him.

"How you doing, John?" Barber asked, waving Garrison toward a chair in front of his desk.

"About as well as expected, considering I had to turn over my gun to Mitchell and was instructed not to go to my office today," Garrison groused.

"Well, you know why Mitchell had to collect your gun, and my instructions to stay away from your office are just procedure."

Garrison frowned. "Procedure?"

"I know we're a small town and small police department, but I need you to see the psychologist before I return you to active duty," Barber advised.

"I don't need to see a damned psychologist, Dan. I've got a murder investigation to get back to."

"Look, if we don't follow proper procedure and something happens—"

"Nothing's going to happen!" Garrison interrupted.

"Think about what you just said, John."

Garrison paused, then sunk deep into the chair. Barber said nothing, letting the silence in the room do the talking. Garrison slowly nodded his head, realizing his boss was right. If one of his officers had killed Chuck Stewart, he'd insist on the standard three-day leave of absence and an examination by a qualified psychologist.

"You're right, Dan. I'm letting my emotions interfere with good judgment. I'm a chief now. I need to set a good example," Garrison admitted. "Who do I need to see?"

"Name's Dale Finley. He's a good guy. I interviewed him over lunch some time ago when I contracted him to be the town's shrink," Barber said, handing Finley's number to Garrison. "He said you can schedule an appointment at your convenience, which I assume will be as soon as possible, right?" He quirked an eyebrow.

"Yep, I'll call him immediately and see him as soon as he's available. Right now, though, I'm heading over to the hospital. I'm hoping Amanda will see me."

"Last night, when I told her what happened, she almost seemed relieved. She said she knew it wasn't your fault but Chuck's. I'm sure she'll see you, but don't you think it might be too soon?" Barber asked in a gentle tone.

"I don't know, but I have to talk to her. I need her to know I had no choice. He shot at me first," Garrison explained again.

"I know. I told Amanda that. Look, John, he damned near killed her. It'll be all right in time."

"Yep." Garrison rose to standing. "Thanks for everything, Dan. I'll let you know when I see Finley." He turned and limped out of the office.

Barber watched his friend go, then reluctantly picked up the phone and dialed Clayton Walker's number before tapping the speaker button and setting the receiver back down. After three rings, Councilman Walker answered the call.

"Took you long enough to get back with me," Walker snarled.

"Sorry about that, Clayton, but I was out at the scene until four this morning. I needed a little shuteye before I came into the office this afternoon. What can I do for you?"

"Well, Mayor, you can call a special council meeting so we can discuss the status of your police chief. You can't argue with the events that have occurred since Mr. Garrison took his position. Since we're not scheduled to meet for another week, I feel an emergency session is in order, possibly as soon as tomorrow. I've already spoken to Natalie and Hugh, and they're both available tomorrow evening," Walker advised.

Barber gazed at his phone and shook his head. "Okay, Clayton, since you've gone through all that trouble, I'll have Connie put it on the schedule for tomorrow at seven o'clock. That satisfactory?"

"Yes, that's fine. You know Dan, I'm not the kind to say I told you so, but ..."

"You're exactly the kind, Clayton," Barber announced before disconnecting the call.

He punched up Connie Maxwell's number next.

"Connie, please add a special council session to the schedule for tomorrow evening ... Yes, tomorrow at seven o'clock. Let everyone know. Thanks." He dropped the receiver into the cradle and let loose a long, loud sigh.

CHAPTER 39

TUESDAY

Garrison parked his truck in the visitor's lot, then slowly made his way to the front doors of the Bison Medical Center. His right knee was stiff as a board, but the pain medication Ackerman prescribed had dulled what felt like razor blades dancing through his knee. Now, the knee was just irritably sore as compared to breathtakingly painful. He'd checked in with Walker and Cooper before calling Fernandez, who'd advised she was already at the medical center visiting Amanda.

Garrison passed through the emergency room, waving to Dr. Ackerman as he limped down the hallway to the elevator, which promptly carried him up to the third floor. Fernandez had given him Amanda's room number. After he passed the nurse's station on his right, he limped through the open door of room 309.

He hesitated when he saw Amanda. Her face and neck looked worse than they had yesterday, and she remained connected to various monitors. An oxygen tube was also clipped to her swollen, crimson nose. A nurse was replacing an IV bag and checking the monitors while Fernandez stood on the opposite side of the bed. Garrison slowly limped his way inside the room and stopped at Fernandez's side.

"How's she doing?" Garrison whispered into her ear.

"Doctor said she has two broken ribs, a fractured right orbital bone, and lacerations and contusions. Fortunately, the strangulation didn't permanently damage her organs," she reported. "How are you holding up?" She gave him a once-over, looking doubtful that he was anything but miserable.

"I'm all right, just worried about her," Garrison responded.

"I'm sorry I didn't come out to the scene last night, but Barber ordered all three of us to stay away from the area."

"I know. Dan told me. It was for the best. There wasn't much of a scene. By the time the two Rangers arrived, Mitchell had everything taken care of. We gave statements to them, and they took a few photos. That was it," Garrison advised.

"What were the Rangers doing there?" Maria asked.

"Out here in the country, the Rangers work most police shootings. They have the resources small-town police and sheriff departments don't have. Mitchell has his department well equipped so the Rangers will work the investigation with him."

"Damn. It is a different world out here, isn't it?" Fernandez said.

"Chief? Is that you?" Amanda asked, attempting to see through her swollen eyes.

"Yes, it's me. Maria Fernandez is here too. Are you in

much pain?" Garrison asked, knowing better than to ask how she was doing.

"No, not much pain. They've got some good stuff here for that." Amanda sighed and attempted to smile but wasn't successful.

"She's out of it for now. Doc says she'll be okay," Fernandez cut in. "He's concerned about her vision, but they won't know until the damn swelling goes down. Poor thing can't even open her eyes, as you just witnessed. Also, the doctor gave me his report. Amanda signed off on the papers last night before her eyes swelled completely shut. It's just the preliminary, but now we won't need it for trial, so it doesn't matter anyway."

"She's probably going to sleep for the rest of the day," the nurse announced before leaving the room.

"Let's go get something to eat, and I can tell you about the evidence I picked up," Fernandez suggested.

"Sounds good. The mayor just said to stay away from the office. He never said to stop working. I have to make a call first," Garrison said.

"Okay, I'll meet you at Clyde's for a burger," and she left the room.

Garrison paused and gazed at Amanda. Despite her injuries, she looked at peace. A tinge of satisfaction rushed over his body, thankful Chuck Stewart would never have the opportunity to harm her again. He shook off the feeling as best he could.

I better not tell Finley about that, he thought.

After returning to his truck, Garrison rolled down

the windows to allow the oppressive heat to escape, then turned the A/C knob one more click toward Max. He punched in Dale Finley's number and waited. The phone rang through his speakers, his dash screen depicting the doctor's number.

"Dale Finley," the doctor's voice resonated loud and clear.

"Hello, Doc, this is John Garrison, Bison police chief."

"Hi there, Chief. Good to hear from you. Dan Barber told me you'd be calling."

"I need to come see you. I'm sure you know what it's about. When can we meet?" Garrison asked.

"I do. How about tomorrow morning at ten?" Finley offered.

"Could we make it nine? I want to get into my office tomorrow, assuming you clear me,"

"Nine, it is. Let's see how it goes."

"Thanks, Doc. See you then," Garrison said before disconnecting the call.

It would only be two days, not the customary three, but Garrison didn't have time to sit around and dwell on his encounter with Chuck Stewart. He put his truck into Drive and headed to Clyde's, looking forward to another great burger and discussing the evidence Ector County had put together.

When he stepped through the front door of the burger joint, Clyde himself greeted him with a "Howdy, Chief!" He was working his magic behind the massive grill separating the kitchen from the small dining area encased on three sides by large windows.

Garrison waved and slid into a chair opposite Fernandez, who was reading a report while guzzling what looked like iced tea from a huge half-empty plastic glass.

"What's Ector County have for us?" Garrison asked.

Fernandez set her glass down on a folded napkin—a futile attempt to keep the steady stream of condensation from soaking the table. "These are the biggest damn cups I've ever seen!" She chuckled, then got serious. "Well, there's not much more than what we already knew. The gun found on Dawson was the gun he was killed with. Detective Lee talked to a few oil field employees who work at the drill site where Dawson was found, but they didn't offer anything useful. He also talked to an attorney from Rockland's legal department. They, of course, offered nothing more than an acknowledgment of Dawson's body being found on their land . . . and I already ordered for you," Fernandez reported.

"Thanks. If anyone from Rockland were involved, I wouldn't think they'd dump Dawson on their land," Garrison speculated.

"Agreed, unless they hired someone from out of town, say El Paso and the killer didn't know where the hell the boundaries were," she surmised. "When do you see the doc?"

"Tomorrow morning at nine. I want Finley to clear me so I can come into the office right after," Garrison admitted.

"John, that's only two days. Don't you think—"

"No, I don't," he interrupted her. "You know this isn't my first time around; I just need to move on and get back on this case. You know that." Garrison waved a hand in her direction.

"Having to shoot a street thug in a gunfight is one thing, but killing our secretary's husband?" Fernandez said with a wince.

Garrison looked out the window at Center Street and watched a few trucks drive by. "You notice there aren't many cars coming through this town?" he asked, more of a rhetorical question than anything.

Just then, Clyde set plates of burgers and fries on the table, then hurried back to the grill. Neither law officer spoke as they plunged into their meals.

CHAPTER 40

WEDNESDAY
DALE FINLEY, PHD

Dale Finley earned his doctorate in psychology from Texas Tech University many years ago, far more than he would admit. The son of an oil field geologist and a Midland Texas native, he opted to distance himself as far from the oil and gas industry as possible. After years of practice in Dallas, he'd returned to Odessa and opened a small practice focusing on therapy and counseling. He was the contracted psychologist for several of the smaller police and fire agencies in and around Ector County, which made him an easy choice for Dan Barber after Barber had been elected mayor of Bison.

Finley unlocked his office at eight o'clock and opted to turn on the two table lamps instead of the bright recessed bulbs in the ceiling. The office was warm and comfortable, with framed pictures of horses adorning three dark-brown walls. Decorated more like a den than a counseling office, the room contained two chairs opposite each other, one upholstered in a brown and tan print fabric, the other a chocolate-brown leather recliner. Each chair was accompanied by a side table of dark wood. A long narrow glass-top table, lined with assorted green ivy-like plants, sat against the wall opposite the door. The setting encouraged friendly conversation rather than the clinical examination-type analysis most people envisioned.

Finley set a steaming cup of coffee on the table next to his chair and settled in to read the report about John Garrison's fatal shooting of Charles Dean Stewart at the Piper Sand and Gravel yard. Despite the fact the official investigations remained open for both the Kutseena County Sheriff's Office and the Department of Public Safety Texas Rangers, Dan Barber had provided Finley with significantly more than just the pertinent facts of the incident. Background information on Chuck Stewart and his estranged wife, Amanda, was included in the file. Finley skipped the documents on the Stewarts and focused on his client, Garrison.

John Gregory Garrison joined the Houston Police Department two years after graduating high school. He completed a handful of criminal justice classes at the community college, earning a perfect 4.0 grade point average before Houston hired him at age twenty. A top-five finisher in his cadet class, he flew through the field training program in the minimal amount of time and was immediately assigned to the night shift of the south-central patrol division. After a whirlwind five years of major crimes and high-speed chases, he was promoted to sergeant and remained in the patrol division. Five years later, he moved on to the burglary and theft unit as a detective sergeant. Two years later, he moved into the robbery-homicide unit and remained there until his retirement earlier this year after a brief stint as the unit's acting lieutenant.

Finley scanned the list of awards and commendations, forty-three in all, and examined the Critical Incident section of the summary. The report confirmed Garrison's involvement in four on-duty officer-involved shootings, the first as a patrol officer during a 1988 traffic stop. The second, a fatal incident while serving a felony arrest warrant in 1995. Five years later, another deadly incident occurred during a shoot-out with several suspects wanted for various drug-related crimes. During a murder investigation in 2017, an armed suspect ambushed him and his partner, Detective Sergeant Maria Fernandez, resulting in Garrison being wounded.

This is a hell of a resume, Finley thought before turning the page.

The sound of the front door prompted Finley to close the file and check his watch. His Tag Heuer Formula One timepiece confirmed the time to be 8:55 AM. Finley stood and greeted his client.

"Good morning, Chief Garrison. Good to meet you," Finley said with a firm handshake. "I'm sorry I don't have the coffeepot going. I've been engrossed in your file. Please get comfortable," he added, waving toward the leather chair.

"That's fine. I've already had my one-cup limit for the day," Garrison advised, settling into the recliner, before propping his hat on his left knee and casually glancing around the room. "I would think my file would be pretty boring," he added.

"On the contrary, you seem to have had an action-filled career."

The chief grimaced. "Well, unfortunately, I've added another chapter."

"Before we get into that, let's get acquainted a little. Would that be okay?" Finley asked, leaning back and propping his left foot on his right knee.

"Sure, Doc, whatever you'd like to know," Garrison responded gruffly, rubbing the crown of his hat.

After a forty-five-minute inquiry into Garrison's career and the subsequent haunting effects of thirty-five years in law enforcement, Finley addressed the topic of the visit.

"So, Chief, officers always come in here and tell me they don't need my services. They don't need to talk about the incident," Finley began.

"That's right. It's better to just put it behind us and move on," Garrison retorted with a wave of his right hand.

"You might believe that's the best way to handle it, but we've found opening up about these types of traumatic incidents is far more effective in dealing with them."

Garrison offered no response and just looked at Finley.

"Let me ask you this," Finley said, "how are you handling this? Honestly, please."

"I'll admit, Doc, this one's different. I had no choice, but I feel guilty, like I have some mark on me now, and I fear I've destroyed my relationship with Amanda," Garrison admitted, squeezing the crown of his mist-gray Stetson.

"That's understandable; you were forced to shoot her husband. That was quite traumatic for both you and her."

"Well, they were estranged, and after the way he beat her . . . I think that made the situation a little easier. I hope everything will be fine, and it'll be business as usual."

Finley leaned forward in his chair and looked carefully at his patient. "A little easier for you . . . or her?" he asked.

"I damn sure didn't want it to happen that way! I had no choice!" Garrison shouted, obviously agitated with the direction of the conversation.

Finley leaned back in his chair, steepling his fingers. "Yes, I understand. It's just that a couple of the other things we've discussed here today have me a bit concerned."

"Yeah, I know . . . the nightmares and inability to sleep much."

"Yes, that and a couple of other issues. We'll get to them, but I'd say that's enough for today." Finley stood and came around the desk to shake the chief's hand. "Thank you for coming in and for your honesty about your situation."

"Enough for today? You want me to come back?" Garrison asked.

"I believe it would be best if you came back at least once more. Is that all right with you?"

"Well, Doc, I don't have much choice, but of course. Whatever you feel is best," Garrison stated.

"Perfect. I'll be in touch with a couple of dates and times. You pick which one works best for you," Finley said.

Garrison stood, paused at the door, and looked back at Finley. "Honestly, I'm not a fan of this process, but I'm the chief now. I need to set a precedent. I can't ask my officers to do something I wouldn't do myself. I'll be seeing you, then. Thanks for your time." And with that, he turned and let himself out of Finley's office, leaving the good doctor to ponder what their next discussion might bring.

CHAPTER 41

WEDNESDAY

Garrison drove through the small parking lot of the Coffee Mug Café and decided to pass on the one available narrow space. Instead, he parked his F-150 on an adjacent patch of dirt that had once hosted what passed for West Texas grass. The usual line of heavy-duty pickup trucks occupied Bison's favorite morning landmark. Garrison passed through the front door doing his best to hide his knee injury. When Callie saw him, she brightened and waved him to a table she'd just finished cleaning.

"How's that knee, Chief?"

"It's okay. I'm doing my best to ignore it," Garrison responded with a faint grin.

She chuckled. "How's that working for ya?"

"Not very well," Garrison said with a laugh of his own.

"Kind of late for coffee, isn't it?"

"Yes, ma'am. I figured I'd indulge in one of your pastries and a glass of ice water," He looked past Callie at the glass case of sweets.

"One cinnamon roll and water coming right up, Chief," Callie announced before she walked over to the counter and selected a gooey treat.

He rubbed his aching knee and flexed it as best he could. He couldn't tell if the pain had subsided or if he was simply growing more tolerant of it. Scanning the faces in the café, he recognized most of the patrons, even though he hadn't been around long. Soon he'd be able to match faces with names.

Callie returned to the table with a warm cinnamon roll the size of a salad plate and a crystal-clear glass of ice water.

"That ought to take care of you, Chief," she announced with a canyon-wide smile.

"You're the best, Callie!"

The sharp ring of his cell phone caught Garrison with a mouthful of pastry. Seeing it was Billy Mitchell, he swallowed hard and tapped the screen. "Morning, Billy. Any update?'

"Good morning, John. How are you doing?"

"I'm good. Solving these damn cases would make me much better, though," Garrison admitted.

"I wanted to let you know I'm meeting with Clayton Walker and his attorney this morning," Mitchell advised.

"Oh?"

"Yep. I told Walker an attorney wasn't necessary, but you know how that went. I'll call you as soon as possible after the interview, assuming his attorney will let him answer questions about the Dawson land offer."

"I wish I could join you, but—" Garrison began.

Mitchell cut him off. "I know. It's better this way, though. I'll call you around noon." Without waiting for a response from the chief, he disconnected the call.

Garrison set his phone down and stared at his cinnamon roll. He'd always heard of small-town police chiefs and sheriffs having to investigate their bosses, but he'd not given that scenario much thought when he agreed to take the Bison job. He didn't like Clayton Walker but didn't believe his councilman was involved in land fraud and murder. The Hardin and Dawson murders were professional hits, which seemed a bit of a stretch for his councilman nemesis.

Garrison's phone interrupted his thoughts. He checked the screen. The name Dale Finley appeared front and center.

"Hi, Doc. Anything wrong?" Garrison asked in a muted voice.

"Not at all, Chief. I just wanted to let you know I called Mayor Barber and told him that you'd agreed to meet with me again and that I saw no reason to keep you from your work any longer," Finley reported.

"Thanks, Doc. I appreciate that. I'll get back to you about the next visit," Garrison promised before cutting the call short and hurrying for the door.

He waved at Callie as he headed out the door, then hopped into his truck and drove across the street to the station. Officers Walker and Fernandez were at their desks punching away at their keyboards. The chief paused at Amanda's desk, noticing everything was perfectly set in its place. A pink sweater hung lazily over the back of her chair.

"Hey, Chief! Good to see you!" Walker called out to his boss.

Garrison returned from his thoughts and limped over to his senior officer for a quick handshake. Fernandez stopped typing and looked at Garrison without a word, flashing her solid-gold smile.

"What are y'all up to this morning?" Garrison asked.

"I'm finishing a minor wreck report," Walker announced before looking at his fellow officer with an impish grin.

She sighed. "Someone painted another penis on the side of Hollingsworth's feed store," she mumbled. "What the hell is the infatuation with penises out here?"

The chief and Walker burst out in laughter.

"Walker, can't you use your connections around here and find out who's infatuated with penises?" Garrison managed to say.

"Yes, sir. I'll dig around a bit. It shouldn't be too hard to figure out," Walker snickered as he stood and started for the door. "I'm going to head out on patrol unless you need me for something else."

The chief waved him on. "No, nothing right now. Go ahead."

"Did Mitchell call you about Justin's uncle this morning?" Fernandez asked when they were alone.

"Yep. Walker's bringing his attorney, so I figure Mitchell won't get much, though."

She nodded. "Agreed."

"Do me a favor and call the county dispatcher. Have our calls routed to my phone. Finley authorized me to return to duty," Garrison said before disappearing into his office.

He noticed the message light on his desk phone was blinking and two handwritten messages were on his desk—the last two messages Amanda had taken before leaving the office two days ago. One of the written messages was from V. Vessey, the ME. Garrison quickly dialed him up.

"Medical Examiner, Vessey."

"Hi, Doc, It's John Garrison from Bison PD returning your call."

"Hello, Chief. Hey, you doing all right? I heard about your secretary and what followed."

"I'm fine. It might take a while, but I hope things will return to normal around here. Do you have anything on Hardin or Dawson?" Garrison asked.

"As a matter of fact, I do. I got the toxicology report back for Hardin. He had traces of tetrahydrocannabinol and methamphetamine in his system, along with enough alcohol to make him DWI had you stopped him driving. Other than that, nothing out of the ordinary."

"Okay, then. Thanks for the update."

"Sure thing. I'll fax over the report today," Vessey advised.

Garrison hung the phone up, sunk back in his chair, and glanced at the clock, wishing he was sitting in on the Clayton Walker interview. Fernandez appeared in the doorway.

"Did you see the doc this morning?" she asked.

He nodded but said nothing. Before she could prod him further, his phone rang. Deputy Morrison greeted him.

Garrison got right to the point. "Whaddya got for me, Morrison?"

"I'm out here at the county administration building north of town. It looks like we may have a burglary, but this is odd. Nothing's been stolen or disturbed, it seems. Sheriff Mitchell is in an interview, so I thought you might want to come out and look."

"You bet I do. I'm on the way." Garrison dropped the receiver into its cradle and stood, giving his desk one more glance. Everything else could wait, he decided, pleased to have something new to investigate. It would keep his mind off the Amanda situation.

"What is it?" Fernandez asked.

"The county has a burglary at the administration building, but it doesn't look like anything was stolen. You wanna join me?"

"You know I do," she said, hustling to catch up.

CHAPTER 42

WEDNESDAY

Garrison jumped into the passenger seat of the new Interceptor he'd assigned to Fernandez and looked around the interior. The F-150 Responders were nice, but he felt he'd significantly upgraded his patrol fleet with the Explorer Interceptors.

"How do you like this?" Garrison asked as Fernandez turned the ignition.

"Nice, and they sure do fly!" she shouted before stepping on the accelerator and squealing the tires as they exited the parking lot.

"Well, let's not wreck it before the paint's dry!" Garrison hollered back with a laugh.

Unfazed by his words of caution, she sped north on Center Street past the medical center, which caused Garrison to wonder how Amanda was doing. Two turns on numbered county roads brought the Bison officers to the entrance of the Kutseena County Administration Building. The single-story structure was wrapped in brown brick with modern sliding windows framed in white trim. The concrete of the parking lot was still a bright white, indicating the place was fresh out of construction, probably less than two years ago. The flagpole, equipped with the United States and State of Texas flags, stood fifty feet in front of the main entrance. On the front door was an image of a howling coyote outlined in the shape of Texas—the seal of Kutseena County. Fernandez parked next to a sheriff's department Explorer near the front door.

"Very nice out here," she announced.

"Isn't your apartment building in the distance?" Garrison asked, pointing north past the government structure.

"Yep. You should come to see it sometime," Fernandez suggested with a sly grin.

"If I keep my job, I should see if an apartment is available over there. I can't stay with Barber forever, and I canceled that real estate agent who was going to show me rental houses," Garrison flatly stated before exiting the Interceptor.

Deputy Morrison met the two of them in the lobby, then led them toward the back, through a locked door into a large area occupied by three gray-steel office desks, each equipped with a desk phone and computer. There was a long counter up front, protected by thick plexiglass from the top of the counter to the ceiling. Two rows of four-drawer black metal filing cabinets lined the back wall, which contained one elevated window. Gray carpet squares covered the floor. Everything looked neat and orderly.

"Chief, this is Colleen Trask," Morrison said, indicating the woman seated at the counter. "She's the county clerk in charge of all the legal documents filed here in Kutseena."

Colleen Trask was a short, curvy woman with long, strawberry-blond hair and a pleasant face dotted with freckles.

Introductions were made all around, then Morrisons said, "Colleen, go on and tell the chief why you called us out today."

"Well, earlier today, our maintenance man came by and asked if there had been anything unusual in the office the past few days. I hadn't noticed anything, but he said the padlock on the alarm system box didn't match his key. After he cut the lock off, he discovered the alarm wires had been cut or broken. Well, then, all of us started looking around more carefully, and I found our back window over there had been broken near the locks. That's when I called the sheriff," Trask explained.

"Check this out, Chief." Morrison walked over to the rear window. Using his ink pen, he pointed to the two small holes in the glass just above the latches.

Garrison and Fernandez stepped up to take a look. Sure enough, there were tiny slits visible, punched through the window. Hardly noticeable behind the wide rotating latches.

"Any idea how long these holes have been in the window?" Fernandez asked.

"No, ma'am. With the summer heat, we haven't opened it for a couple of months, and nobody noticed them until today," Trask confirmed.

"Is the alarm set every night?" Garrison asked.

"I don't know. I'm usually not the last person out the door. I don't know who is responsible for setting the alarm."

Garrison looked at Morrison.

"I've asked around, Chief," he said. "I don't think anyone has set that alarm for quite a while. Also, there's nothing missing or damaged other than the window itself. Weird." He scratched his head.

Garrison nodded. "Definitely strange. So, Colleen, what files do you keep in this office?"

"Well, mainly we keep property deeds, marriage licenses, and death certificates as well as several other lesser filed legal instruments," she advised.

"Have you checked the files? Anything missing or suspicious?"

"No, sir, nothing I've noticed, and no one has reported anything suspicious."

"Someone goes through the trouble of disabling the alarm system, locking it back up, then covering up the forced entry so discovery would be delayed, then doesn't take any of the office equipment or computers," Garrison thought aloud.

"This is a professional job, Chief. I think documents were the target," Fernandez offered.

"Colleen, aren't your files electronic these days? Would you keep hard copies of the documents?" Garrison asked.

"Yes, sir. We scan and enter the documents into the

computer, but we also keep the original signed documents."

"Please check on the Hank Dawson file."

Trask opened a drawer and flipped through several files before locating the Henry Lucas Dawson file. She flipped it open and said, "Only a few pages in here." "Take a look at the documents and see if they look authentic or altered in any way," Garrison suggested.

Trask set the file on a desk and began examining the contents. She spread the pages on the desk and looked at each intently. After several moments, she picked up one record in particular and looked at Garrison and company.

"Something's wrong here," she announced.

"What is it?" Garrison asked.

"It's the General Warranty Deed on Hank Dawson's land. It reads that Hank sold his land to the Rockland Oil Company on the first of June this year. I would've remembered that transaction, and Hanks's signature doesn't look right compared to the other signatures in the file," Trask advised.

"Please put the deed down on the desk," Morrison instructed her, and she quickly obliged. He then removed a pair of latex gloves from his belt and put them on. "I'll have Colleen go through each document again, and I'll collect the questionable ones. She touched this one, but we can still check for prints. If we find any, we'll eliminate Colleen's prints and go from there. That sound good to you, Chief?' Morrison asked.

"That'll be great, and I'm sure your boss would agree,"

he said, then looked at Colleen. "I don't believe we'll need a search warrant since these are public records, and Hank Dawson is deceased with no known relatives."

"That's fine, Chief. We're all sick about what happened to Hank. Anything I can do to help find his killer . . . " she assured the officers.

Garrison stood over the Warranty Deed and noted Sutton Land Management had allegedly facilitated the transaction of Dawson's property.

"Colleen, if I understand this, it indicates Sutton Land Management brokered the sale between Dawson and Rockland Oil. Correct?' Garrison asked.

Trask looked over the deed again and nodded. "Yes, sir, that's correct. I don't know why Rockland would use a management company. They have their own legal team that handles all real estate transactions with their company."

"You have other land deals with Rockland Oil on file?" Garrison asked.

"Oh, yes. Rockland owns several hundred acres on the east side of the county where Hanks's place is," Trask confirmed.

Garrison paused to shake hands with Trask, who smiled brightly at him. "Thank you for your assistance, Colleen." He gave her hand a light squeeze. "Thanks for calling me, Deputy Morrison. It looks like we finally have a good lead in our cases." After quick goodbyes, he then led Fernandez out of the building.

"Oh my God, I'm gonna be sick!" Fernandez exclaimed before breaking out in loud laughter.

"What?" Garrison asked.

"*Thank you for your assistance, Colleen.* Really? You're smitten with the county clerk?" Fernandez teased.

"I'm not smitten! I'm too damned old to be smitten! Besides, she's too young for me. And why do you care, anyway? You jealous?" Garrison bellowed, followed by a fit of laughter. "First, I suspect she's older than you might think, and second, I've got nothing to be jealous about. If I wanted to snatch you up, I could have done it years ago!" she scoffed, but Garrison noted the twinkle in her eye.

"That's probably true," he said, trying to hold back another snicker, "but right now, let's get back to the station and dig up everything we can on this Sutton Land Management Company and Rockland Oil. And that's an order!" He slid into the passenger's seat as she took the wheel.

"Don't you start acting like my boss now, mister! You're lucky we have a couple of homicides to clear up, or I'd set you straight!" Fernandez retorted in between boisterous laughs.

CHAPTER 43

WEDNESDAY

Fernandez wheeled the Interceptor into the Bison PD parking lot, pleased she had kept Garrison laughing on the way back from the county building. She'd been with the man through a handful of difficult situations and always seemed to keep him steady. She pulled the key from her pocket, then reached for the front door of their building and noticed it was unlocked, which was odd since Walker was out on patrol and Cooper was off. She slowly opened the door.

"Something wrong?" Garrison asked from behind her.

"Door's unlocked," Fernandez flatly announced.

After a cautious entry, they found Dan Barber sitting at Amanda's desk, scrolling through his cell phone.

Fernandez greeted him first. "Hello, Mayor Barber; what can we do for you?"

"Stop with the formality, Detective Fernandez," Barber chuckled.

"Something wrong, Dan?" Garrison asked.

Barber stood and locked eyes with each of them in turn. "I might as well tell you both. Clayton Walker requested a special council session to discuss your position as police chief," Barber stated, pointing at Garrison. "I had no grounds to deny the request, so we're meeting tonight at seven o'clock."

"Has that dumbass thought this through?" Fernandez blurted.

"Doubt it," Garrison cut in before the mayor could respond. "But Walker's right to call the council together to discuss what's happened since I took over,"

"The good news is I've had the opportunity to talk with the other council members and explain how real police investigations are handled and that Amanda's husband nearly killed her and tried to kill you," Barber declared. "I don't believe Walker will get the support he needs to suspend you."

Garrison stood silent, nodding his head ever so slightly.

Fernandez felt numb. Her concerns about following Garrison out here were being validated. They were big-city cops with no tolerance for small-town bullshit. And this was nothing but a personal vendetta from a small-town jackass with an axe to grind.

Barber clutched Garrison's shoulder and squeezed it. "I'll look for you both about six forty-five. This meeting is just a formality, mind you. Everything'll work out fine. Just keep up the good work," the mayor said before leaving the station.

Garrison looked at Fernandez. "He's testing me. Wants to see if I'll roll over and resign."

"He doesn't know you very well," she quipped before striding over to her desk.

"Damn sure doesn't," Garrison agreed.

She signed on to her computer and began her search for the Sutton Land Management company. The lone entry listed an address on Texas Avenue in El Paso and a telephone number.

"This doesn't look good," she told Garrison as she punched the telephone number into her cell phone.

The call was answered after just one ring. "Sutton Land Management, can I help you?" a woman asked in a monotone voice.

"This is Detective Maria Fernandez with the Bison PD. I'm attempting to reach someone who can help me with information on a land purchase."

"I'm sorry, this is the answering service. I can forward a message if you'd like," the woman offered.

"Is this a virtual office, ma'am?"

"Yes, ma'am, it is," came the expected response.

Maria confirmed the answering service's address to be the one she'd found in the search. "Is there anyone there who has ever met with a Sutton Land Management representative?"

"I can only speak for myself, but I've never seen anyone from that company. We just accept messages, and then someone calls us, and we pass the messages on," the woman explained.

"Do you have a contact number for anyone connected to Sutton?"

"No, ma'am. They call us."

"One last question. Does your office receive mail for Sutton Land Management?"

"Not usually. We shred any Sutton mail delivered to this office," the woman clarified.

Fernandez thanked her for her time and hung up.

Fernandez spun in her chair to face her boss. "Well, that confirms Sutton Land Management is a dummy company." She gave him the rundown of the brief conversation.

He screwed up his lips as he listened, then she paused to allow him to respond. When he didn't, she continued.

"Okay. So, we know the sales documents for the Dawson purchase are counterfeit. I figure the only fingerprints on those papers will be the clerk's. No sur-prise there, which means our next move is to pay a visit to Rockland Oil and see what they have to say about all of this."

Garrison looked at his watch, grunted, then frowned.

"Unfortunately, we won't be able to do that today since I have to be next door in a couple of hours," he muttered.

"I'm sure their legal department shuts down at five, if not earlier," Fernandez said. "I'll look into Rockland and see what I can find out. Why don't you head out to the ranch and get cleaned up for your appearance?"

"Thanks, but they'll get me the way I am. You want to call it a day and head home or work a little overtime?" Garrison asked.

"I'm not going anywhere but with you to the council meeting, so I might as well get a little OT for my loyalty." She chuckled.

"Very well. Your overtime is approved. That might be the last order I ever give as Bison's police chief," Garrison said, forcing a thin grin.

"I doubt it, but if acting like a victim makes you feel better . . ." Fernandez quipped.

He shot her a half smile and said, "Have I told you how grateful I am that you're here?"

"No, but you don't have to. I know how you feel—" she nudged him as she brushed past him on the way to the door "—I've always known."

The front door burst open, and Officer Walker rumbled through like a bull charging out of a rodeo gate.

"What is it? Something wrong?" Garrison asked his senior officer, whose contorted face resembled one of those caricature drawings one might get at a carnival.

"Chief, I just heard about tonight's council meeting. I had nothing to do with that. I need you to know—"

Garrison held up a hand. "It's no problem. I didn't think for a minute you had anything to say about that."

"I'll be there, and I called Cooper. He'll be there too."

"I appreciate the support, but are you sure you want to be there? I don't want this to create turmoil in the family," Garrison offered.

Walker waved his hand in disgust. "My uncle already called me, bitching about Sheriff Mitchell interviewing him about the Dawson murder. I told him not to call me about police investigations. He got pissed and hung up on me." He shook his head and laughed but only briefly. That smile quickly fell into a somber droop. "Oh, and . . . I just came from visiting Amanda at the hospital."

"How is she doing?" Fernandez beat Garrison to the question.

"She still looks bad, but she can see now. She asked how y'all were doing. I didn't tell her about the council meeting, but she knows. Word's out all over town, and I guess a couple of folks stopped by to visit her and told her about it," Walker advised.

Garrison said, "I better go see her, then."

"I'll stay here and start on Rockland Oil," Fernandez offered, returning to her desk. "Tell her I said hello, and I'll stop by tomorrow."

Garrison hurried out of the station.

"What about Rockland Oil?" Walker asked.

"Someone broke into the county building and planted a forged deed in Hank Dawson's file. The deed claims Dawson's land was sold to Rockland Oil just before we found him dead," Fernandez reported.

"Damn. I know a couple of guys who work for Rockland. That company's been around a long time. You think somebody over there had Hank killed?"

"I'm not sure what to think yet, but it doesn't look good. Who do you know over there? Anyone in management?"

"Not in the office. I know two roughneck supervisors on the team that drill on new land. They might know if Hanks land is on the list," Justin suggested.

"You know them well enough to call and see?"

"Sure can." And he pulled his phone from his pocket and scrolled through his contact list.

Fernandez found the Rockland website and began to peruse the section titled "About." Founded in 1968 by Walter P. Rockland, the company held ownership and leases on over 14,000 acres of oil-producing land. Only Occidental Petroleum and Chevron owned more land in the Permian Basin than Rockland Oil. She noted the phone number and address for headquarters was in Odessa.

"I got ahold of one of the guys," Justin said, drawing her attention away from the computer screen. "He says they haven't been told anything about Dawson's land." His phone rang, and he glanced at the screen. "It's the chief."

"Already? He just left," Maria said. "What the hell . . . ?"

He answered the call, and she heard just one side of the conversation, which was brief. "Yes, sir . . . Okay, on the way," He disconnected and, as he headed toward the front door, said to her, "There's a wreck out in front of the Pumpjack Bar. Chief wants me to take care of it. I should be done in time to get to the meeting." He waved over his shoulder as he left the building.

Fernandez paused and listened to the silence in the station. Other than the low hum of her computer, there was nothing.

The Detective Bureau back in Houston was never this quiet, she thought.

CHAPTER 44

WEDNESDAY

Garrison parked his truck behind the station, shut off the engine, and reviewed the highlights of the Hardin and Dawson murders. The motive for killing Hank Dawson was now evident, and even though there still wasn't any concrete evidence connecting the Hardin murder to Dawson's, Garrison was sure they were. With Hardin's criminal history, including theft and burglary, it made sense that Hardin broke into the county building and planted the counterfeit sales documents in Dawson's file. Garrison figured Hardin was then eliminated to tie up that loose end. El Paso was also a factor. The stolen Hummer, Hardin, and the fake Sutton Land Management company had connections to the town.

The chief switched his thoughts to evidence they'd found at Dawson's ranch. The only oddity there was the Clayton Walker entry in Dawson's ledger. Garrison checked his watch, then tapped Billy Mitchell's phone number into his cell.

"I was wondering when you'd get around to calling," Mitchell answered, skipping the obligatory greetings.

"I know, I've been a little preoccupied over here," Garrison admitted.

"I heard. Big council meeting this evening," the sheriff said with a chuckle. "Welcome to small-town policing, Chief."

"Thanks. What can you tell me about your interview with Councilman Walker?" Garrison asked bluntly.

"There's not much to share, other than one bombshell. Walker's attorney was quite cooperative in letting Walker answer my questions. Walker admitted to making the purchase offer to Dawson, adding that, like many other investors, he'd made several previous purchase offers. Walker said, unlike the previous offers, Dawson said he would consider selling to Walker but wanted to think about it for a while. Walker said Dawson had never even considered selling before," Mitchell reported.

"If Dawson told Walker he'd consider selling to him, there'd be no need to risk a murder," Garrison mused.

"Agreed. Based on my interview with him, I'm comfortable clearing Walker from being involved. But get this, Walker stated he contacted Rockland Oil about the possibility of contracting them to do the drilling on Dawson's land after the sale was completed."

"Then Rockland knew Dawson was considering selling to Walker. That would ramp up their efforts to beat him to it!" Garrison exclaimed.

"Exactly," Mitchell agreed.

"Thanks, Billy. Good to know before I head into this meeting. I'll let you know how it turns out."

"Before you go . . . how's Amanda?" the sheriff asked.

"I just left the hospital. She's getting better. She said she may get to go home tomorrow."

"Good news. Talk to you soon."

Just as Garrison had ended the call, Officer Cooper pulled into the parking space right next to Garrison. Garrison stepped out of his truck and pressed the lock button on his key fob.

"Good to see you, Coop. Thanks for coming to see the show," he said with a grin.

"No worries, Chief. Since you arrived, I haven't enjoyed my days off much. I like to be where the action is nowadays."

"Well, let's see if I'll still be your chief tomorrow."

"No doubt in my mind, sir." Cooper slapped him on the shoulder as they headed for the meeting room.

Garrison entered first to find Dan Barber and the council members were already seated behind the dais. Connie Maxwell was typing on a laptop; the sound of the keyboard permeated the room. Bob Crawford of Crawford's Farm and Ranch store and Callie Johnson from the Coffee Mug were sitting in the front row of perfectly lined chairs. Callie caught his gaze and greeted him with an extended right hand. He nodded in her direction and offered what felt like an awkward smile. She beamed brightly back at him.

Bob Crawford stood, and they shook hands, then Garrison looked toward the side door that led to the police station where Fernandez and Cooper stood with two of Billy Mitchell's deputies. Garrison met Fernandez in the middle of the room.

"Walker's gonna be a while," she said. "He said there was a serious injury, so he was going to take measurements. The vehicles are off the road, so he didn't need backup."

"Please be seated, everyone, and we'll get started here," the mayor announced. After a moment, he continued, "We'll dispense with the customary formalities, as this is a special meeting called for by Councilman Walker. This will go on record as an official meeting. The purpose of this gathering, as stated in Councilman Walker's written request, is the official review of Police Chief John Garrison's performance since he took office on the sixth of June through today's date. All members of the council are present, as is Chief Garrison. Councilman Walker, please proceed with your concerns."

"Thank you, Mayor Barber. Before I proceed, I'd like to state for the record that I have no ill feelings toward Chief Garrison, nor do I wish to challenge his integrity. Several community members, including myself, are concerned about the undeniable increase in criminal activity and police actions since Chief Garrison took over the Bison Police Department."

He paused to clear his throat, then, "To quickly review, our town has seen its first murder in thirty years, a traffic crash death due to a high-speed police pursuit that seriously injured one of the department's officers, another member of the department brutally beaten, and the chief himself fatally shooting the suspect in that investigation—which, might I add, is the first fatal police shooting in the history of the Bison PD. These incidents don't include another murder being investigated by the sheriff's department, which appears to be connected to the murder in our town.

"Now, I'm certainly not placing responsibility for all of these terrible incidents on Chief Garrison. Still, his decisions were paramount in the results of at least two of the aforementioned tragedies—the deadly police pursuit and the killing of Charles Stewart. And to my knowledge, the chief is no closer to solving the murder today than when the victim was discovered. Based on these facts, I believe it's this council's responsibility to revisit Chief Garrison's capability to lead the Bison Police Department and thus consider his removal," Walker declared.

"Thank you, Councilman Walker. I'll open the proceedings for discussion. Councilwoman Hollingsworth, do you have anything to add?" Barber asked.

"Yes, thank you, Mayor Barber. While I agree that our quiet town has recently seen its share of shocking events and tragedy, I find no reason to blame Chief Garrison for any of it. On the contrary, every contact I have had with Chief Garrison and his officers has been prompt and professional. Furthermore, from what I've heard, Chief Garrison had no choice but to defend himself from Charles Stewart, and I believe if anyone can solve our town's murder, Chief Garrison and his officers can and will. I find no reason to question the chief's capabilities," Hollingsworth stated.

"Councilman Giddings," Barber prompted.

"I also share Mrs. Hollingsworth's thoughts on the matter. To blame Chief Garrison for our town's recent chaos is ridiculous. I also find no reason to question Chief Garrison's capabilities," Giddings said.

"Very well. For the record, Chief Garrison has my full support and confidence. As each council member has expressed their view on the subject, no individual vote is necessary. The matter is considered closed. This meeting is adjourned," Barber quickly declared.

Garrison joined his officers and the deputies near the front door and thanked each of them for their time and support. He did the same with Callie and Bob Crawford as they left the building. He then sent his officers to the station before he briefly met with Hugh Giddings and Natalie Hollingsworth individually. Clayton Walker stood silent near the front door waiting for everyone else to leave before approaching Garrison.

"Chief Garrison, I meant what I said about no ill feelings toward you. I hope you understand. I felt it was my responsibility as senior council member to call this meeting and put everyone's thoughts on the record. I hope there are no hard feelings," Walker stated.

Garrison offered him a handshake, which Walker accepted.

"Next time, meet with me before you feel you need to call a formal meeting," Garrison requested.

"I'll do that," Walker answered with a hint of a grin.

CHAPTER 45

THURSDAY

Garrison and his three officers nervously wandered around the discharge counter at the Bison Medical Center, awaiting Amanda's arrival. Fernandez fidgeted with the bouquet of roses they'd collectively purchased for the occasion while Walker and Cooper scrolled through their cell phones.

Garrison's phone buzzed as they waited, and a glance confirmed it was the sheriff's department dispatcher. He hustled through the automatic doors and outside, sending a dash of sizzling West Texas air into the modest lobby.

"Garrison," he announced, then listened to the status update. "Was there forced entry? . . . Mm-hmm . . . Okay, I'll send an officer as soon as possible," he advised before disconnecting the call.

Garrison stepped back into the lobby just in time to see a nurse pushing a wheelchair occupied by a smiling Amanda. Garrison paused as his officers surrounded their friend and coworker. A feeling of relief washed over him like an early morning rain. Despite the dark shadows of healing contusions painted across her face and neck, she still had that charming look about her. Her battered lips caused a crooked smile, which Garrison found both adorable and unsettling.

"Well, are you just going to stand there?" Amanda asked.

Garrison snapped to attention, leaned down, and gently grasped Amanda's hands. "I've arranged a police escort for you, ma'am. May I help you to your feet?"

"Yes, you may, and you'd better have arranged for a police escort, if you know what's good for you!" Amanda declared, igniting boisterous laughter from the group.

"Unfortunately, Fernandez and I must go to Odessa this morning," Garrison explained, "so Coop will drive you home. Are you sure you'll be all right by yourself?"

"I'll be fine. Connie's going to stay with me for a day or two," Amanda assured everyone. "Other than my ribs, I feel pretty good. What's in Odessa?"

"We're going to meet Billy Mitchell at the Rockland Oil company regarding Hank Dawson's murder," Garrison advised. "Walker, I need you to go over to the bait shop. Milt called in a burglary."

They parted ways, Fernandez riding shotgun in Garrison's F-150 as he drove eastbound on Highway 302. She was flipping through her notes on Rockland Oil.

"It will be interesting to hear how this transaction played out. In their haste to buy Dawson's ranch, I'm guessing Rockland didn't do their normal due diligence," she offered.

"That wouldn't surprise me either. Billy and I talked about that this morning. How in the hell do you secure a multimillion-dollar deal with a fake company in El Paso?"

He pulled into the Rockland Oil visitor's parking lot and noted Billy Mitchell hadn't arrived yet. The four-story Rockland building was modest compared to the massive skyscrapers back in Houston. With mirrored glass on all four sides, the double-wide entryway held two revolving doors centered between tall chrome statutes of a pumpjack and derrick. Garrison located the security cameras mounted on each corner of the building and directly over the rotating doorways.

"I wonder how long they keep their security video?" he mused.

Fernandez added, "The real question is will they allow us to view it?"

Billy Mitchell arrived, parking his Kutseena County Interceptor next to Garrisons' truck. The three investigators met before entering the building.

"Have you ever been here before, Billy?" Garrison asked.

"Nope. I've dealt with their legal department a couple of times when their trucks were involved in wrecks, but never in person," the sheriff explained.

Sheriff Mitchell, in full uniform, led them into the building's lobby, its walls adorned with numerous expansive photographs of oil field activity, including a massive, framed image of an oil well fire blazing into the night sky. The picture was positioned directly behind a curved security desk occupied by a single uniformed guard. Garrison observed cameras were mounted high on the wall behind the desk.

"Good morning, Sheriff. Can I help you?" the guard asked.

"Yes, sir. I'm here with Bison Police Chief John Garrison and Detective Maria Fernandez. We don't have an appointment, but we want to speak with someone in your legal department, please," Mitchell explained.

The guard nodded, picked up a telephone, and punched in a four-digit number.

"I have the Kutseena County sheriff and Bison police chief here to speak with someone," the guard announced into the phone. After just seconds, he said, "I'll send them right up." He cradled the phone and said to the officers, "The elevator is around to the left. Take it to the fourth floor. Someone will meet you there."

The ding of the elevator's bell announced its arrival to the fourth floor and opened into a large area furnished with a black leather sofa and two matching chairs surrounded by tall green plants and an eight-foot-tall indoor waterfall that methodically changed colors as the water splashed into a bed of red river rock at its base. A young-looking woman was waiting near a glass door that led to a long hallway. Short and slender, her dark brown hair was pulled back into a large bun. Her impeccably manicured eyebrows sat atop beautiful green eyes, and her navy-blue business suit appeared perfectly tailored.

"Good morning, I'm Joann Krumbach, one of the staff attorneys."

"Good morning. I'm Sheriff Billy Mitchell. This is Chief John Garrison and Detective Maria Fernandez. We were hoping to speak with someone regarding the Hank Dawson ranch purchase," Mitchell announced.

"I see. Please follow me to my office, and I'll see what I can do for you," Krumbach answered before opening the glass door and proceeding down the hallway.

Once seated, Garrison looked around the attorney's office and figured it was ten times the size of his office back in Bison. A young woman carrying three clear glasses and a pitcher of iced water balanced on a tray entered the office. She set the tray on the corner of the desk before disappearing without a word. Garrison noticed the glasses and pitcher were adorned with the Rockland Oil Company logo etched in the drinkware.

"Please help yourselves. We may need to wait a few minutes before our records clerk retrieves the file," Krumbach advised.

Garrison looked at the elegantly framed law degree from Duke University hanging on the wall behind Krumbach's desk. "So, Ms. Krumbach, what's a law grad from Duke doing in Odessa, Texas?" he asked.

"I'm originally from Dallas. After graduation, Rockland recruited me, so I packed up and moved here," she explained.

The ping of the desk phone interrupted Garrison's attempt at small talk. Krumbach answered the call and listened but said nothing before hanging up. Her face grew dark, and a frown crept across her red-painted lips.

"Excuse me, please. I have to attend a meeting," she said as she lifted from her chair. "Mr. Jordan will be here in a moment."

"Is there a problem?" Mitchell asked.

"I'm sorry … Here's Mr. Jordan now," Krumbach stated before hurrying to open her office door. In walked a tall, heavyset man with gray hair and a short beard to match.

"Thank you, Ms. Krumbach. I'll take care of this," the man muttered.

Joann Krumbach hastily exited the office and disappeared down the hallway. Mitchell, Garrison, and Fernandez all stood.

"I apologize for any misunderstanding. I'm Frank Jordan, Vice President of Exploration and Procurement. All land acquisitions come through my department. I understand you are here about the Hank Dawson transaction?"

"Yes, sir, we have some questions about the transaction and about Sutton Land Management," Mitchell stated.

"It's our policy not to discuss any of our transactions. I'm sure y'all know the purchase and deed transfer are public information on file with your county clerk. Unless you have a search warrant or other court order, I'll not be authorizing the release of any information," Jordan clarified then added firmly. "Leslie will see you out." He spun on his heel and left the office without another word.

After a few seconds of shocked silence between the

three of them, Mitchell said, "That didn't go quite as I thought it would." They walked back toward the elevator.

"I'm not completely surprised that he didn't share the details of the transaction, but to cut us off and leave as he did leads me to believe he's hiding something," Garrison said.

"He damn sure just became suspect number one," Fernandez sneered.

CHAPTER 46

Garrison and Fernandez returned to their station and found Walker at his desk, typing a report. After Frank Jordan's suspicious lack of cooperation, Fernandez immediately sat down behind her computer and began a background investigation on the man.

"Anything to that burglary out at Milt's place?" Garrison asked Walker.

"Not really. There was forced entry on his storage room door, but Milt said nothing was disturbed or missing. Didn't even look like anyone entered the room. I'm just listing the damage to the door frame unless you want me to note something else," Walker reported.

"No, sounds like you have it covered."

"How'd the visit to Rockland go?"

"Damn poor!" Fernandez scoffed.

"Oh?"

"It looked like we were going to get some information from the staff attorney, then all of a sudden, she's called away, and some jackass vice president comes in and tells us we need a warrant and throws us out," Fernandez explained, wrapping up the high points of the failed visit.

"It was obvious he wanted nothing to do with us," Garrison added, "and I'm guessing he's covering up a quick no-questions-asked deal for the Dawson ranch. Sheriff Mitchell is going to work on a search warrant for the file. We all agree we have enough probable cause to get the warrant."

"My buddy at Rockland called me back a while ago and said they just got the order to start mapping Dawson's land so they can start drill prep," Walker advised.

"I'll call the DA's office and see if we can get a temporary restraining order to halt any work out there," Garrison said before disappearing into his office.

Fernandez clicked through several possible names in the search engine, looking for the right Frank Jordan. She had approximate age and employment data, but there were plenty of Frank Jordans to work through.

"You think somebody over at Rockland killed Dawson?" Walker asked.

Her eyes never left the screen. "That's a damn good possibility, especially if they somehow got word that Dawson was considering selling to your uncle."

"Selling to my uncle?"

"Yep. Your uncle told Mitchell that he offered to buy Dawson's land again, and for the first time, Dawson said he'd think about it. If somebody at Rockland found out about that, they'd damn sure have the resources to make this bullshit purchase happen double quick," Maria said, finally looking up to catch Walker's bewildered expression.

"Damn. I knew my uncle had money, but I didn't know he had the kind of cash it'd take to buy Dawson's ranch."

"Apparently, he does, and like everyone else around here, he's been trying to buy it for years."

The sound of boot heels tapping the asphalt preceded Officer Cooper coming through the door with white paper bags of food from Clyde's burger joint clutched in each fist.

"I figured none of you took the time to get lunch, so I made a command decision," Cooper proudly announced.

"You. Are. The. Best," Fernandez declared, holding out a grateful hand. "I'm starving."

"Plain or cheeseburger?"

"Cheeseburger, my friend."

"American or Swiss?"

"Damn, boy! You are the man! Swiss!" And she snagged the bag that Cooper offered.

"Okay! Okay, brownnoser," Walker teased, then wiggled his fingers at Cooper. "You have one for me or just your girlfriend?"

"Hey, he brings me cheeseburgers without me even asking, and he can call me his girlfriend anytime!" Fernandez exclaimed.

Cooper blushed and handed Walker the other bag. "I know you're an American man."

"Damn right, I am!" Walker proclaimed, eagerly rummaging through the sack of food.

Cooper then spun around and headed for Garrison's office with the last paper bag.

Taking a big bite of her burger, Fernandez got back to work at her computer and clicked on another name.

"Boom!" she said, the word slightly muffled by a mouthful of cheeseburger. "Frank Alan Jordan, born on the twenty-eighth of February 1970, age fifty-two. Lives on Crested Butte Court in Midland. Let's see what the value of his house is . . . " She snapped her mouse several times before landing on the sought-after data. "Not bad, 1.2 million. Being vice president of exploration at Rockland Oil pays damn well." She looked over at Walker, who was inhaling some fries. He shot her a thumbs-up.

Garrison poked his head out of his office. "Did I hear you right?"

"You did," Fernandez assured him. "There's nothing listed here in the criminal history section, but I'll run a check through NCIC to be sure."

"Good. The DA thinks they can get a judge to sign a temporary injunction based on the counterfeit deed on file. He's going to call Mitchell since it's his case," Garrison announced.

Fernandez snickered. "Oooh, when ole VP Jordan finds out there's a temporary injunction, he'll be pissed!"

"He'll wish he'd cooperated with us . . . or maybe not. The motive for both murders is now square on Rockland Oil," Garrison speculated.

Billy Mitchell's name flashed on Garrison's cell phone screen as an old-fashioned ringing bell, his ringtone, filled the room. Garrison answered and tapped the speaker icon.

"Go ahead, Billy, you're on speaker. We're all here," he informed the sheriff.

"Good. I've got my detectives working on the search warrant for the Dawson file. We're also submitting the documentation to the DA to secure the injunction to stop all activity on the Dawson property. I'll let y'all know when we get these signed. Oh, and John, I meet with the Rangers on Monday morning at nine o'clock in regard to your shooting. Their investigation is complete. I was informed you're required to attend, but I don't anticipate any problems."

"Very good. I'll be there. Thanks, Billy."

"Talk soon," Mitchell said before disconnecting the call.

Garrison's phone rang again, and this time it was the county dispatcher. Garrison listened and nodded.

"On the way!" he advised, then looked to his officers. "Bob Crawford's fighting with a shoplifter out at his store..."

Walker, with half a burger dangling from his mouth, and Cooper were running out the door before Garrison finished his announcement.

"Stay here and listen in. I'll follow the guys out there," he told Fernandez before limping out the door.

She fought the urge to join everyone. She turned her radio on to monitor the action and then ran a criminal history check on Frank Jordan.

Just moments later, Cooper had keyed his mic, the sound of his siren flooded over his announcement that he and Walker were arriving. Maria stopped typing and listened to the silence on the radio. Even after all these years, these silent moments when she knew her fellow officers were in harm's way were brutal. Maria fought the urge to get on the radio and ask for an update, despite knowing that she'd hear it when one was available. That didn't make the silence any more bearable.

Finally, Garrison's voice broke the excruciating hush. "Fernandez, call for an ambulance. Suspect is in custody, but Bob Crawford's a little banged up."

She wasted no time in calling for the ambulance, then took a deep breath. She wanted nothing to do with uniformed patrol anymore but hated not being involved when something like this was happening. She sighed and took a bite of a cold french fry, the constant conflict of a cop's life rattling through her.

CHAPTER 47

THURSDAY

Garrison parked his truck behind the station and took a couple of deep breaths. The pulse of his heartbeat thundered through his right knee while he did his best to calm the painful storm. The knee had responded well to the combination of his pain tolerance and the medication Ackerman had prescribed. Now, after twisting the hell out of it while assisting Walker in handcuffing the dumbass thief at Crawford's store, Garrison knew he'd need more than pills to quell this pain. He pulled his keys from the ignition and pushed the truck door open with his left foot. Sweltering heat banged against him like a rowdy fan at a Blake Shelton concert. He carefully stepped down and hobbled his way to the front door.

He made his way inside, surprised to find Dan Barber seated at Fernandez's desk, helping himself to a fry. Fernandez was intently studying something on her computer screen.

"Well, John, that doesn't look good. What the hell is going on now?" Barber asked, standing to shake his police chief's hand.

"I twisted the damn thing handcuffing that jackass out at Bob Crawford's place," Garrison answered.

"What happened out there?"

"Some meth-head from Odessa tried walking out with high-end bits and harnesses, figuring Bob wouldn't stop him. He was wrong," Garrison declared with a satisfied smirk.

"Bob, okay?"

"He's fine. A couple of scrapes is all. Walker and Coop are en route to the county jail with the thief. He'll get a robbery charge for his efforts," Garrison explained. "What can we do for you?"

Leaning back in his chair, the mayor popped a fry into his mouth, chewed, then said, "Just looking for an update on the homicide."

"Oh? I wondered what happened to the hourly update requests." Garrison chuckled.

"Well, ever since Councilman Walker became involved in the investigation, he's been rather quiet on the matter," Barber said with a laugh.

Garrison sat down and stretched out his wounded leg, then filled in the missing blanks of the investigation for the mayor.

"Are you going to ask DPS for assistance?" Barber asked.

"Mitchell and I talked about that, but for now, we decided to keep the state police out of it. If it looks like something we need help with, we'll ask them to join us."

"I don't know, John. Messing with a company like Rockland Oil could get a little dicey."

"I'm sure Frank Jordan has already finished his research on the chief," Fernandez chimed in. "He knows he's not dealing with a small-town cop."

"I'm certain you're right about that, but their reach extends far beyond its office doors. You two be careful," Barber demanded before excusing himself.

After the mayor had left the building, Fernandez said, "That's interesting. Dan's demeanor changed dramatically when you mentioned Rockland."

"Agreed." Garrison rubbed his whisker-infested chin, then gingerly touched his aching knee, wincing as he did so.

"You need to go to the hospital for that?"

"No. I'm convinced the only relief I'll get for this knee will come from a few weeks of rest, or surgery, and I don't have time for either right now," Garrison admitted. "Find anything on Jordan?"

"Just a drunk driving arrest from thirty years ago. I got interrupted by our mayor," she explained with a wide grin. "John, you look beat down. Why don't you take tomorrow off? Sleep in, take one of Dan's horses for a long ride. We're in waiting mode until the sheriff gets those search warrants executed anyway."

Garrison took a deep breath and closed his eyes for a few moments. The thought of taking a long ride after sleeping late was mighty appealing. He envisioned the clear blue sky and miles of West Texas terrain he'd planned to explore when he agreed to take the Bison job.

"I'm not gonna lie," he started. "I feel like a worn-out wash rag, but I don't know how I'll relax with everything that's going on."

His thoughts were interrupted by the bell ringer on his cell phone.

"If you don't change that back to the quiet buzz sound you had before, I'll put a bullet through it!" Fernandez exclaimed.

Garrison laughed and tapped the speaker icon on his phone. "Go ahead, Walker. We're here."

"Hey, Chief, just wanted to let you know the deputies found a bag of meth shoved up this guy's ass when they strip-searched him."

"Well, hell, can we get a delivery charge on him?" Garrison asked, unable to control his boisterous laughter, which Fernandez matched. "Thanks, Walker. Y'all get back here ASAP."

After hanging up, he slowly rose from the chair and limped to his office, where he relished the idea of devouring his cold burger and fries.

"Keep up the good work, Detective!" Garrison called out to Fernandez before closing his office door.

After finishing his burger in what he calculated to be his personal record time, he tapped the favorites list on his phone and stared at Amanda's name and number. Despite the limited space in his head and everything that was swirling around in it, he'd constantly thought of her from the moment he'd taken Billy Mitchell's call the night she was assaulted. He'd held a special place in his heart for her right from the beginning, but he was surprised at the thoughts and feelings he'd been wrestling with since her assault. It was true—he found her attractive and more desirable with every kind gesture and favor she did for him. And he found himself wanting to return those favors, to protect her. He'd worked with and for several women in his career, but except for Fernandez, he'd never allowed himself to become smitten . . . until he arrived in Bison.

Why now? Why here? And for God's sake, why a married woman?

Widowed because of me, he corrected himself. Any relationship with her outside the office was now out of the question. Their relationship would be taboo in a city the size of Houston, let alone the trappings of a small town like Bison. They'd run him out of town on a rail.

Maybe that wouldn't be so bad.

He tapped the phone icon and waited.

"Hi, Chief. Everything all right?" Amanda asked in a surprisingly upbeat tone.

"Well, no. You're not back to work yet, but other than that, everything's fine. How are you feeling?" Garrison asked.

"Actually, pretty good. I'm glad to be out of the hospital, and it doesn't hurt as bad when I breathe. Say . . . what's happening at the station? How's the murder investigation going? I've heard all kinds of rumors. I don't think I'll be able to stay home very long," she teased, giggling.

"Well, most of what you've heard is probably true.

Sheriff Mitchell interviewed Councilman Walker, Rockland Oil may be involved, and we found forged documents at the county records office."

"This is all very thrilling! Bison's never had intrigue like this before! I'm just sorry you have to deal with it all."

"That's okay. As long as it's entertaining for the community." Garrison chuckled. "Amanda, I know it's soon, but about Chuck—"

"Please don't blame yourself for what happened. Chuck hadn't really been my husband for a long time, and the man who attacked me wasn't the one I used to know. He'd been violent and unfaithful before, but I was too stupid to do anything about it. I told you . . . you saved me, and I mean it. So, no more about that, okay?"

Garrison sat silent for several moments, angry with himself for having such a critical discussion on the phone instead of in person. He felt like a teenager having one of those sappy telephone talks with his girlfriend.

"Chief, are you still there?" Amanda asked. Her soft voice had a hint of an apology in it.

"Yes, I am. I'm sorry. I feel like we should be having this conversation in person and not on the damn phone," Garrison admitted.

"Naw, that's not necessary. You don't have to prove anything to me. I know you're a good guy, not hiding behind a phone."

Garrison laughed with Amanda.

"I'm not so sure that's true. I could get used to this hiding behind the phone stuff," he joked.

"Well, I won't let you off the hook that easily. I'll give you a pass this one time only."

"Yes, ma'am, I'm sure you won't! All right, now ... You take care, and if you need anything at all, you call me. Understand? I'm still the boss!"

"Don't you threaten me with that boss stuff, Chief Garrison!"

Her laughter lasted until the call disconnected—and probably long after, he suspected. He smiled to himself and sat back in his chair.

Don't even think about it, John!

CHAPTER 48

MONDAY

Garrison took a long swig from his coffee cup and set it next to the biggest, stickiest, best-smelling cinnamon roll he'd ever seen, smelled, or eaten. The chatter at the Coffee Mug was exponentially loud for an early Monday morning. Callie Johnson, clad in a bright-green dress masked with a white apron, whisked her way through the labyrinth of tables with a pot of hot coffee in each hand, stopping at Garrison's table just long enough to fill his cup before moving on in her quest to make every customer happy. The weekend had passed in near silence. Besides a loud noise complaint in the varmint neighborhood and a drunk biker who needed encouragement to leave the Pumpjack bar Saturday night, Bison police had three quiet days peeled off the calendar.

Garrison had notified everyone the day before that Officer Walker would be in charge until he returned from the meeting with Sheriff Mitchell and the Texas Rangers. After finishing his roll and coffee, he waved at Calie on his way out the door, disappointed he'd not been able to visit longer with the beautiful coffeeshop proprietor.

He climbed into his truck, assisting his right leg with both hands. One thing that wasn't quiet over the weekend was his blasted aching right knee. It felt like a rusted door hinge desperate for an oil bath. The pain pills doctor Ackerman had prescribed were not helping much anymore.

The sun lazily crept up behind the eastern horizon as Garrison piloted his F-150 along County Road 1610 toward the Kutseena County Sheriff's Office. Oil tankers and large and small work trucks displaying oil and gas company logos pockmarked the otherwise forlorn highway. He cruised down the road attempting to stay clear of the big rigs that intermittently clogged his path. The drive allowed him to review his answers to the questions both Billy and the Ranger had asked him during the Chuck Stewart shooting. He knew that the fact he was meeting with Billy and the Rangers meant he was not being indicted or disciplined. Otherwise, he'd be with a lawyer on his way to the District Attorney's office. Still, these meetings were distressing, and cops just had to deal with the anxiety these situations created.

Garrison decided to drive past the Dawson ranch and take a look at what, if any, activity had begun. As he approached the main gate where Callie Johnson's food bin had once been, he noted a large No Trespassing sign above the fence. The gate was reinforced with tall vertical I-beam posts reminiscence of the massive timbers the natives used on Skull Island to keep Kong out of their village. The former cattle pastures were marred with a gaggle of deep ruts caused by the enormous tires of Rockland's earth-moving machines. The machines were parked in neat rows in front of the Dawson house. A white pickup truck, equipped with an amber light mounted on the roof and a Rockland Oil security logo affixed to the door, was parked on the side of the house.

Pulling up to the gate, he paused, looking around. This caused the lone security guard to poke his head out of his truck window. Garrison snickered under his breath, figuring he would be the only action the guard would enter into his otherwise useless report. Backing out onto Soaring Eagle Road, he headed for his rendezvous with Mitchell.

Standing in the lobby was Deputy Morrison, who smiled when Garrison walked into the sheriff's building.

"Hello, Chief Garrison! Good to see you again!" Morrison exclaimed, his voice bouncing off the marbled walls.

"Hi, Deputy Morrison. I'm here—"

"Yes, sir, I've been waiting. Sheriff Mitchell is in the conference room with a couple of Rangers. I'll take you back." He gestured for the chief to follow him down the glistening hallway, then said, "The word is that Rockland Oil is involved in Dawson's murder."

"Keep a lid on that. We're not sure yet," Garrison whispered.

"Will do, Chief. Here we are." He stopped and opened the conference room door.

Garrison stepped inside and noted two Rangers seated beside Billy Mitchell on the far side of an oblong, highly polished, dark-wood table. A single chair sat on the opposite side of the table. The three men stood as Garrison stepped toward the vacant chair.

"Good morning, John," Mitchell cheerfully greeted Garrison with a firm handshake from across the table. "This is Ranger Jeff Franklin and Ranger Curt Wagner," gesturing toward each man as he spoke their names.

Both Rangers shook Garrison's hand before Ranger Franklin waved toward the vacant chair.

"Glad to meet you in person, Chief Garrison; I believe you've already spoken to Curt about the incident. Please take a seat," Franklin said.

Garrison eased into his chair, taking care of his knee. "Yes, sir, that's right."

"I don't think I've ever seen you in uniform, John," Mitchell said with a chuckle.

Garrison grinned. "No, you probably haven't. I only wear it when I have to."

"Well, Chief, you didn't have to get all dressed up for us," Franklin joked.

"Now you tell me!"

Mitchell leaned in, taking on a more serious posture. "John, as you know, my office began the initial investigation of your deadly force incident, then I turned over everything I had gathered to the Rangers. It's customary that the Rangers handle most, if not all, deadly force encounters involving officers out here."

Garrison said nothing, just nodded in agreement.

"With that, I'll turn this meeting over to Ranger Franklin."

"Chief Garrison, with you being a veteran officer, I'm sure you know there were no findings that warranted criminal action or official discipline. Otherwise, you'd be meeting with the District Attorney," Franklin began.

Garrison nodded.

"The purpose of this meeting is to formally advise you of that fact and answer any questions you may have afterward. I'll skip the particulars and move to the incident itself. The investigation confirmed that Sheriff Mitchell informed you of the aggravated assault slash serious bodily injury to your employee Amanda Stewart by her estranged husband, Charles Edward Stewart. Afterward, you personally verified the victim's injuries at the hospital, then gained information from the victim as to the possible whereabouts of the suspect. Upon arriving at Piper Sand and Gravel, you encountered Stewart armed with a handgun. You confronted Stewart in an attempt to make a legal felony arrest. Upon being confronted, Stewart raised his weapon in a threatening manner and fired a single shot either directly at you or in your direction. In order to protect yourself and stop the threat, you returned fire twice, striking Stewart twice in the chest. As a result, Stewart suffered fatal wounds and died at the scene," Franklin reported, then paused, flipping the page of report.

"Following standard practice and law enforcement protocol, you immediately reported the incident and requested life support for Stewart. Based on the confirmation of these facts and other physical and forensic evidence collected at the scene by Kutseena County Sheriff deputies and members of the Texas

Rangers, this deadly force encounter was deemed justified self-defense. Thus, no further action is required, and the investigation is closed," Franklin concluded. "Do you have any questions, Chief Garrison?"

"No sir," Garrison answered.

"Very good. Sheriff Mitchell received a copy of this investigation, and a copy will be provided to Bison Mayor Daniel Barber," Franklin added.

"Thank you for your work on this. I'm sorry you had to deal with it at all." Garrison stood and shook each Ranger's hand.

"It's no problem, Chief. It's what we do. We appreciate your actions, and you walked away from a deadly situation," Ranger Wagner answered.

"Sheriff Mitchell, we'll be on our way. We'll find our way out," Franklin announced before he and Ranger Wagner left the room.

Garrison waited for the door to close.

"I'm glad that's over with," he admitted, exhaling a deep breath.

"I know. No matter how justified we are, you never really know anymore," Mitchell said.

Garrison let that sit for a second before changing the topic and jumping in with a question of his own. "So, how are we looking on those search warrants and injunction orders?"

CHAPTER 49

MONDAY

The clicking sound of the keyboard echoed off the walls encroaching on the otherwise silent Bison police station. Cooper pecked away at the suspicious person report Milt wanted on file in case of trouble near the boat launch. Since Milt found his storage shed door kicked in at the bait shop, he'd seen ghosts every night by the lake.

"Bison unit three, come in, Cooper."

The crack of the radio startled Bison's lone on-duty officer.

Kutseena County dispatcher Darci Lynn's voice sang loud and clear through the mic.

"Unit three, go ahead, Darci."

"We have a report of a dark-colored SUV racing up and down East Bison Boulevard—possible drunk driver. Last seen out near the Pumpjack Bar."

"Bison three on the way," Cooper advised.

"Bison three on the way at 2213 hours," Darci announced.

He hustled to his Interceptor and quickly sped out of the police parking lot north on Center Street, then banked a right turn on Bison Boulevard toward the Pumpjack.

Bison Boulevard was a long, flat, two-lane blacktop highway that allowed a driver to see several miles down the road. Up ahead, Cooper saw headlights crossing the road, then appearing to turn in a circle and crossing again.

Really? Doing donuts on the highway in the dark? Gotta be drunk, Cooper thought.

As he approached the erratic vehicle, he confirmed it was a dark-colored SUV moving in circles on the highway.

"Bison three," Cooper called into his radio mic.

"Bison three, go ahead," Darci answered.

"This looks like a drunk. Send a county unit my way for backup."

"KSO unit five, I'll be en route to his location," Deputy Bullard advised.

Darci made the confirmation. "KSO five en route at 2216 hours."

"I'll be there in five or six, Coop," Bullard added.

"Thanks, Bull, stopping now, eastbound, just west of the Pumpjack," Cooper reported.

Cooper activated his overhead red and blue emergency lights and popped the Yelp siren twice. The SUV slowed down, completed its last circle on the highway, and pulled over onto the gravel shoulder on the south side of the roadway. He pulled behind the SUV and noticed there wasn't a rear license plate mounted on the rear bumper or displayed in the back window.

"Bison three, I have the vehicle stopped. A Black Cadillac Escalade, no license plate visible."

"Ten-four," Darci answered.

Cooper grabbed his flashlight from the seat and slowly

exited his Interceptor, lighting the SUV with his spotlight. He walked to the vehicle's left rear and looked into the rear window. His efforts to see inside the vehicle were futile due to the dark-tinted windows. As he approached the driver's-side door, the driver lowered the window.

Before Cooper reached the back door, an explosion of muzzle flash blinded him, followed by three gunshots. The three bullets hit him in the chest, violently forcing him backward onto his heels. He dropped his flashlight and stumbled, his right boot heel catching a rock before he fell backward, slamming the back of his head on the Interceptor's front bumper. Nothing but black silence followed.

"Coop! Coop! Can you hear me? Can you hear me, buddy?" Deputy Bullard frantically bellowed, carefully squeezing Cooper's right shoulder. "Coop! Are you with me?"

Cooper slowly opened his eyes, seeing nothing but a pitch-black wall. He forcefully closed and opened his eyes again to no avail. He heard sirens in the distance and someone yelling his name.

"Coop! You're gonna be okay! The ambulance is coming! We called Chief Garrison. He's on his way. Can you hear me? It's Bull!"

Cooper recognized Bullard's voice.

"Yeah, Bull, I hear you? Am I dying?" Cooper murmured.

"No, man, your vest stopped the bullets. You'll be

okay. The medics are here," Bullard announced as the ambulance came to a screeching halt next to Bullard's patrol vehicle.

Cooper's vision failed him, but he heard Bullard telling the medics it looked like his body armor had stopped the bullets, but his head was bleeding. Cooper reached up and felt his face, then around to the back of his head. His fingers slid into a mass of warm sticky goop. A sharp pain danced through his head. No doubt, it was saturated in blood.

"Officer Cooper, can you hear me?" the medic asked.

He tried to nod, but the excruciating pain resonated through his head like a lightning bolt. "Y-yes."

"We're going to lift you onto the gurney and take care of you, okay?" the medic advised.

Cooper felt himself being lifted onto the gurney, then hands unsnapping and removing his gun belt. A soft and thick pad was placed under his head before the medics loaded him into the ambulance. Points of bright light began to attack his eyes like flies to a barnyard. Gradually his vision began to return. He saw the blurred images of the medics' light-blue shirts. Leaning forward, he saw a blurry image of Bullard standing at the back of the ambulance, his face pale, and eyes wide open like he'd been electrocuted.

Cooper felt the sting of the IV needle puncturing the vein in his left arm. He forced a grin and held up his right thumb. "I'm okay, Bull. Thanks, pal."

Bullard managed to crack a thin smile. "The chief is pulling up now."

Garrison, Fernandez, and Walker all appeared at the back of the ambulance. After sighs of relief, Maria and Walker walked toward Cooper's Interceptor, the beams of their flashlights roaming through the air like searchlights during an air raid.

"How is he fellas?" Garrison asked the medics.

"Got a nasty cut on the back of his head and blunt-force trauma to his chest. His vest stopped the bullets," one of the medics reported.

Garrison allowed a smile to cross his face. "Coop, you're the only one of us who wears his vest, and I'm damn glad you do!" he gushed in relief. "I've got your weapon and gun belt. Did you return fire?"

"No, sir. I didn't have time. Ambush. They opened fire from inside the SUV."

"Okay, I'm going to look around with Fernandez and Walker, then I'll be over to the hospital as soon as possible," Garrison assured his officer.

"Yes sir, no problem. I'm fine."

Garrison asked the medic to remove the front panel of Cooper's vest in order to secure it as evidence. The medic did as asked, handing it to the chief, who closely examined the cluster of bullets lodged in the front panel.

"Damn. Three rounds inside a three-inch diameter. That's pretty damn good shooting," Garrison muttered. Cooper couldn't believe what he'd just heard his chief say.

"Are you kidding—" he started before Trimble interrupted with an announcement that it was time to hit the road. The medic jumped out of the back of the ambulance and slammed the doors shut.

Cooper looked at the medic who'd remained with him in the ambulance. "I still can't see very well. It's like I'm looking through a dirty window or something."

"Your vision will come back. It's tunnel vision. Happens to all of us when we're traumatized," the medic said.

"Oh, yeah. That's right," Cooper mumbled, laying his head back down. The siren blared as they finally took off for the medical center.

He tried to take a deep breath, then realized his chest felt heavy. Pain crept outward from the center of his chest like a spiderweb. He reached for his chest and felt his breastbone. The reality of what had happened started to sink in. His head began to swirl. He felt dizzy, then nauseous. Before he could warn the medic, he vomited on the man's right arm and the gurney.

"Sorry," Cooper whispered, his throat burned from bile and stomach acid.

He closed his eyes and listened to the wail of the siren.

CHAPTER 50

MONDAY

Garrison had Fernandez and Walker position their vehicles toward the area in front of Cooper's Interceptor. The bright headlights worked adequately to provide as clear a view of the scene as possible at midnight in the middle of nowhere. Fernandez snapped several photos of blood smears on the left-front corner of the Interceptor's front bumper. She also photographed the boot markings in the gravel directly in front of the bloody bumper.

"Looks like he stumbled and fell backward, hitting his head right there," Fernandez surmised, pointing at the bumper.

"Make sure we swab that blood just in case it's not his," Garrison directed, and she nodded.

Garrison followed the beam of his flashlight along the ground from where Cooper had stumbled to the two shallow ruts caused by the suspect vehicle's tires. Based on the spin marks in the dirt and scattered gravel, Garrison figured the driver buried the accelerator into the floorboard to flee.

He and Walker searched the ground looking for spent bullet casings. Despite the interference of rock, gravel, and intermittent weeds along the shoulder of the highway, a freshly spent brass casing shouldn't be too difficult to find. After straining his eyes for twenty minutes, Garrison stood up and told Walker to disregard.

"Either the casings stayed inside the vehicle, or more likely, the shooter used a revolver to prevent evidence from spewing out the window. I'll check the rounds in Cooper's vest and confirm, but my guess is they'll be .38s or .357s." Garrison speculated.

"Thinking ahead not to leave casings. You think this was a hit?" Walker asked.

"That's exactly what it was," Fernandez retorted. "And that son of a bitch over at Rockland ordered it."

Deputy Bullard approached Garrison, cell phone in hand.

"Chief, Sheriff Mitchell wants to talk to you. They shot up our station," Bullard reported.

"This is Garrison. Damn, what happened, Billy?"

"I heard your officer is okay. Glad to hear it, John. They did a drive-by at my station. Shot the shit out of our front door and one of my Interceptors out front."

"Anyone get a vehicle description?"

"Not really. By the time my deputies got out of the building, all they saw were taillights hauling ass down the road. They think it was a black pickup or SUV, but they don't know. Bullard says your shooter was in a black SUV, is that right?" Mitchell asked.

"Yep. Coop called out a black Cadillac Escalade, no plate," Garrison confirmed.

"Probably the same vehicle, John. It looks like we have a real problem here. This was no coincidence."

"Agreed. They baited us. This was definitely a hit on my officer."

"I know you'll be busy the rest of the night and tomorrow, but I'd like to come over to your station and meet with you about this."

"I'll call you later and give you a time," Garrison said before disconnecting the call, then he turned toward his officers. "Do everything you can here. I'm heading over to the hospital. I'll see you both back at the station."

Garrison sped down Bison Boulevard, thoughts racing through his mind like cars on a NASCAR track. He knew he'd been lucky. Cooper was the only one of them who wore his body armor. That would change now that they were being attacked. The shootings looked like the work of hired gunmen, and Rockland Oil seemed the logical employer. However, there was no evidence and cops' hunches meant nothing to judges for warrant purposes.

Garrison wheeled his truck into the Bison Medical Center parking lot and stopped in his usual space in the horseshoe driveway in front of the ER. Turning on the dome light, he looked closely at Cooper's vest. He pried one of the chunks of lead out of the Kevlar layers and noted the bullet was surprisingly intact. The tip of the hollow point was crushed and had started to "mushroom" out, but it looked like a .38 round to him.

He tucked the bullet into his pocket, hopped out of the truck, and walked through the familiar automatic doors that led into the triage area of the hospital. A young man wearing dark-blue scrubs and an identification badge that read "Orderly" rushed up to him.

"Hello, Chief, right this way. Your officer is back here," he advised waving his hand toward the same curtain-enclosed area that Amanda had occupied weeks earlier.

Garrison slipped between the opening of the divider curtain. Dr. Ackerman was lightly pressing on Cooper's bare chest with hands covered in opaque latex gloves.

"Hi, Chief. Did you find anything out there at the scene? Cooper asked.

"Only your blood smeared on the bumper of your Interceptor." Garrison was relieved to find his officer alert enough to ask relevant questions.

"My head hurts worse than my chest," Cooper admitted.

"That's because you have a significant laceration and a concussion, Officer Cooper," Ackerman announced. "I don't know what I'm going to do with you and your department, Chief. You all seem to take turns getting injured."

"The stakes are rising, Doc," Garrison answered somberly.

"Yes, sir, I agree. May I see Officer Cooper's vest, please? It will help with my examination."

"Damn it. Of course. I should have known to bring it in," Garrison grunted before quickly leaving to retrieve the vest.

Upon his return, he held the vest up for Ackerman and Cooper to view. Ackerman looked at the area surrounding the bullet hits, then turned the vest over and looked briefly at the back. The indentations were minor, considering three bullets had hit the armor at a relatively close range.

"These appear to be reasonably effective," Ackerman said, looking at Garrison, as if waiting for any additional information or opinion he could offer.

"Yes, sir. They can work like this against these types of ammunition, but we never really know," Garrison said. "We were damn lucky this time." He glanced at Cooper, who was still staring at the vest.

"My main concern at the moment is the trauma to the chest. We'll know more after x-rays, and I'll also order an MRI," Ackerman said.

"Coop, were you able to notify your parents?" Garrison asked, realizing he hadn't made the notification yet.

"No, sir, I didn't want them called this time of night."

"Okay. They need to be notified, and if you're up to it, I'd like you to call. They'd be alarmed if they heard my voice. They might panic before I can say you're okay."

"Yes, sir. I have my phone. I'll call now if that's okay?" Cooper addressed that question to the doctor, who was busy writing notes on the chart.

"Certainly. We'll get you back to x-ray in a couple of minutes," Ackerman clarified.

"I'll be here until Dr. Ackerman reads your x-rays," Garrison said.

"Are Walker and Fernandez out at the scene?" Cooper asked.

"Yes. They're finishing up out there. Cooper, did you see the shooter?" Garrison asked.

"No, sir. I was getting close to the driver's door when I saw the flash, then heard the shots. It knocked me back. I never saw the gun or anyone inside the vehicle. The windows had dark tinting on them. Sorry."

"No apologies, pal. I'm just damn glad you wore your vest, and it worked," Garrison said. "Go ahead and call your parents. I want to be here when they arrive. I'll just wait outside here until then." He ducked out of the examination area and took a seat in the hallway, thinking about recent events and how they might all converge . . . or not.

CHAPTER 51

TUESDAY

Garrison turned his truck into his parking space behind the station, parked, and sat back. He noted both Fernandez and Walker had returned from the ambush scene. He also saw Dan Barber's truck parked in the lot. He took a few minutes to run through as many highlights of the two murder cases as he could remember. He thought about the visit to Rockland and the poor attempt to cover the fraudulent purchase of Dawson's ranch with counterfeit documents. That was what bothered him the most.

If Rockland Oil is behind the fraud purchase and subsequent murders, why would the cover-up in the county be so blatant? They had to know me, or Billy would eventually look at the records, he thought.

Garrison walked into the station and found Fernandez and Walker at their desks, typing away on their computers. The clatter of the keyboards filled the room with life before ceasing and bringing a pall of silence. Dan Barber was seated at Amanda's desk, scrolling through his cell phone, before looking up and seeing his weary police chief stroll into the room.

"How's Coop doing?" Barber asked.

"He's doing remarkedly well for an officer who was just shot three times," Garrison gloomily responded.

"I was headed to the hospital but figured I'd just be in the way. Nobody needed the mayor around asking inane questions."

"That's fine. I stayed until Ackerman read his x-rays and his parents arrived," Garrison announced before setting Cooper's front body armor panel on Fernandez's desk and sitting down.

"How'd that go?" Walker asked.

"About as expected. They were pretty shaken up, and his mother was already telling hm that he was quitting the police job effective immediately."

"That's normal," Fernandez chimed in.

"It is. I'm not sure it's a bad idea anymore," Garrison remarked, looking back at Barber.

The mayor nodded but remained quiet. Garrison knew his boss had been in his shoes more times than he could remember back in Houston. He also knew that his officers would need to process what had happened and deal with it in their own way at their own pace. He felt confident he knew how Fernandez would handle the shooting, having worked with her before, but Walker was an unknown entity. Cooper . . . well, nobody knew how he'd handle it once the adrenalin rush subsided.

"Did y'all find anything out there after I left?' Garrison asked.

"Nothing we could connect to the suspects," Fernandez said. "We'll go out after sunrise and look around in the daylight." She looked at Walker, who gave a thumbs-up, confirming her summary.

Garrison nodded and stared off into the distance, feeling hollow inside. Other than the constant pangs of pain in his damaged knee, he felt numb. The fact that an inexperienced kid under his command had nearly been killed brought a plethora of emotions swirling within him.

"Do you want me to send the blood from the bumper to the lab?" Fernandez asked.

"No, hold off on that. I'm sure you're right that it's Cooper's." He paused, then added, "Also, I talked to Billy Mitchell. He had a drive-by at the Sheriff's Department shortly after Cooper was shot. They're probably the same suspects. They shot the shit out of the front of the building and a patrol vehicle. While I'm thinking about it, body armor is now mandatory for both of you when you're on duty." He pointed at Fernandez, who was about to say something—probably a retort—and he shut it down. "I don't want any arguments either."

"Any idea who did this?" Barber asked.

"That son of a bitch at Rockland Oil," Fernandez said in a near-growl. She was clearly hot under the collar . . . and with good reason. Garrison didn't blame her one bit.

"I'm going to meet with Mitchell as soon as I can," he said. "It looks like Rockland, but that's just cop instinct. We need a lot more before we start pointing fingers."

"Thank you all for everything you've done," Barber said before standing. "John, let me know if there's anything you need that will assist in this investigation."

"Yes, sir," Garrison answered before shaking the man's hand.

Garrison waited for him to leave, then turned toward Fernandez and Walker. "I fully agree someone connected to Rockland did this tonight. I'll talk to Billy and see what he wants to do, but I'm up for another visit to that VP at Rockland," he said.

Both officers expressed their eagerness to participate, but Garrison waved them off.

"Nope. Not this time," he said with some steel behind his words. "I don't want either of you to go with me. I can't let all of us get fired if things go sideways."

"Well, that makes sense for Walker, but—" Fernandez began.

"No! Not this time!" Garrison barked.

Fernandez stood, slammed her fist on the desk, then headed for the ladies' room, her heels beating on the floor as she marched away.

"Ooh, boy, that didn't go well" Walker said with a chuckle.

"I knew it wouldn't," Garrison admitted. "By the way. Billy offered to have his deputies handle our calls for service tonight, so I let dispatch know. We'll pick it up again at noon."

"That'll give us time to finish checking the scene, but what about sleep?" Fernandez asked, returning from her brief pouting session.

"You and I will go back out to the scene. Walker, I want you to head home and get some shut-eye. That's an order," Garrison added before Walker could protest. "I need you to handle the department business while I'm out of touch."

As Walker began to speak, the front door flew open, and Amanda marched into the room, stopping just inside the door.

"Can somebody tell me why I had to hear about Cooper from someone other than any of you?" she shrieked, fists buried into each hip.

Garrison slowly stood and forced a grin. "Uh, It's three o'clock in the morning. Shouldn't you be home asleep?"

Amanda didn't respond, just smiled before receiving gregarious hugs from everyone.

"I'm back at work as of right now, and I don't want to hear any crap from anyone, especially you, John Garrison!" Amanda declared.

Garrison gave her a hard glare, frowning. "I don't know . . ."

"I'm doing just fine. My ribs are sore, but the doctor told me they'd be sore for six to eight weeks, so I might as well be here. Besides, I don't want to return to the house," Amanda explained, pausing only for a second before adding, "Now, I'll get the coffee going, and y'all can bring me up to date on what' s been happening around here since I've been gone."

"The Sheriff's Department is handling our calls until noon today," Garrison informed her, and she nodded as she walked to her desk.

"Chief, I'll head home and get back before noon if that's all right," Walker said.

"Perfect. Try and get some sleep if you can. Fernandez,

I'll pack these bullets for delivery to the DPS lab. Maybe we'll get lucky on the ballistics test."

"It's a long shot, but we're due for some good luck. I'm ready for some of that fresh coffee," Fernandez announced.

"Coming right up," Amanda stated as she organized her desk.

Garrison carried a chair over to Amanda's desk and sat down. He figured it would take him the entire three hours before daybreak to bring her up to speed on what had transpired since the night Chuck nearly killed her.

CHAPTER 52

TUESDAY

Garrison and Fernandez finished their whirlwind report to Amanda, then headed back to Cooper's ambush scene along Bison Boulevard. Garrison was both pleased and surprised when he and Fernandez arrived at the scene to find a deputy parked on the side of the road near the shooting location. The deputy explained that Sheriff Mitchell wanted to keep the scene as secure and protected as possible until Garrison could return.

The place appeared tranquil and unassuming in the daylight. The darkness of night had a way of making everything more sinister. Garrison and Fernandez combed the ground, sweeping the area well off the highway into the tall weeds and thicket that lined the road. After searching for ninety minutes, Garrison gestured toward Fernandez, directing her to join him back at their Interceptor. He was convinced they'd not overlooked any potential evidence.

"There's not a damn thing out here," Garrison stated, feeling something akin to despair. They needed a break.

"I agree. We'd have found whatever evidence there was," Fernandez agreed. "Not like back in Houston where we could search for camera images."

"Those were the days. Now it's just coyote crap and rabbit pellets every twenty feet," Garrison lamented.

The hum of Garrison's cell phone interrupted the banter. Billy Mitchell's name appeared on the screen. He tapped the screen and put the call on speaker. "Morning, Billy. You have anything for me?"

"Well, I can tell you that the barrage of gunfire I had here last night did not include any .38 weapons," Mitchell advised.

"Not a surprise."

"On a more interesting note, I received a call at seven this morning from Vice President Frank Jordan."

Garrison's interest was immediately piqued. "Oh? What did he want that early?"

"He is not very happy with our injunction prohibiting further activity on the Dawson property. He claims Rockland will lose five grand for each day they're delayed, and that's only if they don't find oil."

"It sucks to be him," Fernandez chimed in.

Mitchell chuckled and said, "I agree, Detective, and that's what I told him before he hung up on me."

"Billy, wouldn't it be more appropriate for someone from Rockland's legal department to contact you?" Garrison asked. "Seems odd that the vice president of procurement would call and bitch at you."

"Good point, John. I planned on calling the legal department later this morning anyway. I'll ask them about Jordan."

Garrison's cell phone vibrated, indicating he had another call waiting—from Dan Barber.

"Billy, the mayor's calling. I better take it. I'll talk to you soon," Garrison said before tapping his phone to accept his boss's call. "Yes, sir?"

"John, Coop is being released from the hospital this morning. You might want to head over there or call him," Barber suggested.

"Yes, sir, good news. We'll head over there right away."

"You find anything else out there?"

"Nope. Nothing helpful, unfortunately."

"Okay, keep me posted," and with that, Barber hung up.

"They're sending Coop home. Let's head over to the hospital and see if we can catch him before he leaves," Garrison told Fernandez.

At the ER, he parked in what he was starting to think of as his personal spot, then followed Fernandez through the automatic double doors. The gust of cold air sent a brief shiver through Garrison. Since he hadn't taken any pain medication for the past several hours, his knee felt awful, and the pain had intensified, causing him to limp more noticeably. They met Cooper's parents, who were waiting in the lounge near the nurses station.

"Hello again, Chief Garrison," Cooper's father greeted him with a handshake.

"Good morning, Mr. Cooper. I understand your son is being released." Garrison offered up a smile.

"Yes, the doctor says he has nine stitches in the back of his head, a mild concussion, and his chest will be sore for a while, but otherwise, he's in good shape."

"I'm pleased to hear that," Garrison said in honest relief.

Cooper's mother, Maddie, a short, thin woman with sharp angular features and long, brown hair tied back in a ponytail, pushed around her husband and confronted Garrison.

"I know you're happy about my son, and I apologize for my behavior last night, insisting that Coop quit the force, but I'm sure you understand how I feel about what happened," Maddie Cooper began.

"Yes, ma'am—"

"And I still feel the same way. I might as well tell you right now that I will do everything in my power to convince Cooper to leave the police and look for other work."

"Now, Maddie, you're just upset," Mr. Cooper stated.

"You're damn right. I'm upset. Cooper's our only child, and I will not stand by and see him killed . . . and for what? A dead drug addict. Is that worth our son's life, Chief?" She shot a menacing glare at Garrison.

"No, ma'am. Nothing is worth your son's life. Nothing a police officer does is worth losing their life over, but—" Garrison paused, wanting to choose his words carefully. "Your son will decide if he wants to continue, and I will support whatever he decides. I'll have him speak with Dr. Finley, and we will go from there."

"Who's Dr. Finley?" Maddie asked.

"He's the psychologist my department uses in these types of situations. He'll see how Cooper handles the shooting and make a recommendation based on his analysis," Garrison explained.

"What if Cooper doesn't want to see this Dr. Finley?"

"I would highly recommend at least one visit, but if your son decides he wants to return to the police department, he'll be required to attend as many sessions as Dr. Finley feels are appropriate."

The conversation ended when Fernandez escorted Cooper into the waiting area. Garrison was relieved when he saw the big smiles on both of their faces. He was also grateful his conversation with the parents was over. Talking with parents and spouses regarding officer-involved shootings or any other life-threatening event was nearly as brutal as delivering a death notice.

"Here he is, a little bruised and bloodied but otherwise in good shape!" Fernandez cheerfully declared.

She tucked her arm under Cooper's, giving him much-needed stability and causing him to blush.

"Why aren't you in a wheelchair?' Maddie Cooper yelped.

"He refused a chair. I think he just wanted to be close to me," Fernandez jested.

"Well . . ." Cooper said with a wide grin.

Mr. Cooper chuckled. "All right, let's get him to the truck."

"I'll be back in a few days, Chief," Cooper assured Garrison.

"We'll discuss your return in a few days," Garrison said. "Just get some rest. We'll let you know how the investigation is going."

Garrison and Fernandez watched the Coopers help their son up into their truck. Mr. Cooper waved before he drove his family away.

"You think he'll come back?" Fernandez asked.

"Despite what his mother wants, I think he'll be clamoring to get back in uniform, even before Finley says it's okay," Garrison said with a sigh.

CHAPTER 53

TUESDAY

The clock on Garrison's dashboard read 4 PM. After grabbing a couple hours of sleep in his office, then intentionally not responding to Billy Mitchell's late afternoon phone call, Garrison decided it was time to pay Frank Jordan another visit. Despite Amanda and Fernandez pleading their cases for him not to go alone, he'd worn down Amanda and threatened Fernandez with suspension if she followed him. He didn't want Billy Mitchell to have any knowledge of his actions, either. Plausible deniability was always the preferred means of keeping fellow officers out of trouble. He figured he'd arrive just before five o'clock when most of the management staff would leave for the day or already be gone. He wanted as few witnesses to his visit as possible.

His phone buzzed. He checked the screen and blew out a long, loud sigh. The local newspaper reporter had finally grown tired of avoidance tactics used by Mayor Barber and was now blowing up Garrison's phone. Garrison was both relieved and shocked at how long Barber had been able to keep the media at bay—and away from him and his officers. It had been far longer than any big city politician could have done.

He sent the call to voicemail and continued his mission, dodging a litany of customary oil field trucks, trailers, and tankers that littered the highways throughout the surface of the Permian Basin.

The shale basin measuring 250 miles wide and 300 miles long spanned the better part of western Texas and extended into southeastern New Mexico. In 1920, when the first oil well was drilled, the basin had produced over 30 billion barrels of crude oil, with some geologists predicting that another 20 billion barrels remained untapped. With Occidental Petroleum and Chevron owning the bulk of the land, any patch of ground appropriated by a smaller company such as Rockland would be a multi-million-dollar victory. Indeed, a surfeit of motivation to commit murder.

Reaching the Rockland complex a few minutes earlier than expected, Garrison parked across the street and watched the exodus of employees through Viper HD binoculars. Retailing at nearly 500 dollars, the Vortex Optics field glasses were his retirement gift from the homicide squad at HPD. He'd wanted the high-end gear for scanning his livestock and horses on what he thought would be his retirement ranch. Instead, here he was, eavesdropping on an oil company's workforce amid what many people would consider an improper investigation.

Garrison waited until five o'clock before parking his F-150 near the front entrance. The security guard intermittently opened the door for the last few employees making their workday escape. Garrison casually approached the entrance and attempted to walk through the door before the guard stopped him.

"I'm sorry, sir, we're closed for today's business," the guard announced.

Garrison flipped his wallet open, revealing his badge. "I have an appointment with Mr. Jordan.

"I'll need to check on—"

"Don't bother. It looks like you're needed here at the moment," Garrison offered as more employees prepared to exit the building. He scooted quickly to the elevator.

The guard started after Garrison, then stopped and returned to unlock the front door to allow a group of women to exit. Garrison pushed the button, looked back at the exasperated guard, and smiled. The elevator door slid aside, and Garrison found himself face-to-face with Frank Jordan.

Jordan's deadpan face immediately changed into a crumpled, angry mess. Garrison stepped inside the elevator, blocking Jordan's path.

"What the hell are you doing here?" Jordan barked.

"We have a meeting, remember?" Garrison said, matching Jordan's glower.

"I have nothing to say to you, Officer. My lead attorney will be speaking with Sheriff Mitchell tomorrow. Since you were not invited, and it is after closing time, I suggest you leave, or I'll have security escort you out."

Unfazed, Garrison pushed the button for the fourth floor. "I believe your office is on four, correct?'

Jordan said nothing other than an inaudible grunt.

The bell rang, and the door slid open. Garrison stepped aside, then followed Jordan past the waterfall and exotic plants, down the narrow hallway, past a series of vacant offices to a tall, dark-stained wooden door emblazoned with the name *Frank Jordan* in gold script. Jordan entered a four-digit code into an alarm panel, opened the door, and stepped inside.

"You must be a critical man to have an alarm on his office," Garrison quipped.

"I'm late for an appointment. What is it you want?" Jordan asked before falling back in his broad leather chair.

"I want to know who tried to kill my officer last night, then shot up the Sheriff's Department building," Garrison stated, his tone stone-cold.

Jordan leaned farther back and snorted. Garrison let the silence hang in the air like a prairie fog on a summer morning. The VP then shot forward in his chair, his eyes narrowing into snake-like slits.

"You think I had something to do with all that?' he yelled. "I'm a respected businessman with nearly forty years in the oil industry. I make ten times your salary and couldn't care less about your trivial police department." He stood and pushed his hands flat against the top of his polished rosewood desk. "Furthermore, if I wanted you or any of your officers dead, I wouldn't just *try*."

Garrison stepped forward, pounded his fists onto the surface of Jordan's desk, and leaned within a few inches of Jordan's patrician nose. "Understand this, you pompous son of a bitch. *When*, not *if*, I find out you put a hit on my officer, I'm not going to the county prosecutor, DPS, Texas Rangers, or the FBI. I'm coming to see you. And no amount of money or corporate bullshit will stop me. You understand?" He then pushed himself away from the desk and headed for the door.

"Calling the FBI office in Midland is an excellent idea, Officer. I believe I'll make that call first thing in the morning to report your illegal intrusion, harassment, and abuse of power," Jordan growled.

Garrison opened the door and paused before turning and facing Jordan. "You haven't seen the abuse of power I'm prepared to wield on you and your company," he calmly replied before stepping out of the office.

Garrison pushed the elevator button, then watched the hallway to see if Jordan dared to follow him. He didn't. The ding of the bell sounded before the doors slid open. Garrison stepped inside and pushed the button for the first floor. The doors quietly closed as he worked to calm himself after his encounter with Mr. Jackass.

CHAPTER 54

TUESDAY

Fernandez wheeled her Charger out of the station parking lot and headed north on Center Street past the closed Coffee Mug café and busy medical center before crossing Coyote Highway, leaving Bison behind. She stepped on the accelerator, then rolled her window down, allowing the fiery West Texas air to blast into the car. Her long, raven-black hair exploded in every direction, including across her face. She smiled as she pushed the locks out of her eyes, playfully annoyed she'd not pulled them back into a ponytail.

"Well, you didn't think that one through, Fernandez," she said to herself, laughing.

She pushed her speed up to seventy-five and cruised down the lonely highway. One of the things she liked most about Bison and Kutseena County was the freedom from gridlock traffic that she'd endured her whole life in Houston. Back there, driving home at four thirty in the afternoon was a commuter's nightmare. Here, she was lucky to see an oil tanker or another car on the highway leading to her new apartment. The ten-mile drive took less than ten minutes.

Despite enjoying her stay at the Barber ranch, she

was both relieved and anxious to have secured her place. It was nice to have her privacy back, but she was anxious about the six-month lease she had signed. Initially facing a mandatory twelve-month contract, she'd successfully negotiated a shorter commitment with the manager after offering to pay a higher monthly rent. She wanted nothing to do with a one-year lease. Her future in West Texas was cloudy at best. Then again, she could be wrong.

She parked in front of the black-iron staircase that led to her one-bedroom unit on the second floor. She exited her car and glanced at the half-dozen late-model trucks scattered across the small parking lot.

Doesn't anyone drive a car in this part of the country? she thought before pressing the lock button on her control fob. The Charger's alarm chirped, and the locks clicked.

When she stepped into her home, she took a moment to scan the nearly empty space. The newly built apartment had an open kitchen with black cabinets, gray stone countertops, and stainless appliances. The floor was gray faux wood, and the walls the standard off-white paint. The manager confirmed Fernandez was the unit's first tenant, thus its new smell. After locking the front door, she tossed her keys onto the counter and kicked off her shoes. She hadn't had time to have her furniture and possessions shipped from the storage unit in Houston, thus no sofa or comfortable chair to plop into. She'd purchased a card table, two matching chairs, a folding bed, and a small shelf unit that passed for a dresser.

Retrieving a bottle of Ozarka water from the fridge,

she twisted the top off before stepping to the sliding patio door and gazing out upon acres of pasture, chock full of grazing cows. The manager had provided a brief history of the complex—its builder had purchased the patch of land from a cattle rancher who needed the money to augment the considerable loss of cattle due to the past year's drought and intense heat. Ranchers from Texas to Kansas had lost millions in revenue due to cattle deaths from the heat. Having grown up on a ranch, Fernandez was irritated that she'd not known about the recent plight of the cattle ranchers. She watched the cows for several minutes, surprised at the ease she felt.

That's some cheap therapy.

Her cell phone buzzed, interrupting her reflections. She glanced down at the screen and saw it was the mayor. She pulled up the call. "Hello, Mayor. Everything all right?"

"Well, I hope so. How are you holding up these days?" Barber asked in a cheerful tone.

"I'm good. A little tired, but no complaints."

"Glad to hear that. I hope I'm not interrupting anything important, but I need to talk to you about your chief," Barber said, his tone now serious.

"No interruption." She plopped down into a chair, took a sip of water. "What'd you want to know?"

"You know I'm not one of those bosses who like to constantly look over my people's shoulders, but this mayor thing is a bit different. I've asked John how he's doing, but I'm not sure I'm getting the true answer. I've called him several times this afternoon, but he hasn't answered. That's the first since he became chief. Any idea what he's up to this evening?"

Fernandez paused, uncomfortable that she was about to lie to her longtime friend. "Well, he was going to Coop's shooting scene for another look. After that, I'm not sure what his plans were," she fibbed.

"How's he handling Coop's shooting? It hasn't been that long since his own,"

"Oh, you know John. He's far more focused on Coop than his own issues. It's a little awkward around the office since Amanda came back, but that'll fade soon enough."

"What do you mean by awkward?" Barber pressed.

"John's been quieter than usual . . . and her vacant desk. You know, just not as comfortable as it was before the shooting," Maria offered.

"Hm-hmm. So, how's the investigation going?" Barber continued to probe.

She stood and meandered into the kitchen area. "Hard to say right now. We're short on evidence, but we believe Rockland Oil is behind our case and Mitchell's Dawson murder."

She looked out the front window, expecting nothing in particular, but the hair on her neck prickled when she saw a black SUV with dark-tinted windows pull into the parking lot and back into a parking spot next to the garbage dumpster. No one exited the vehicle.

"Thanks for the update. Sorry to bother you while off duty," Barber was saying.

"No problem. Thanks for calling." I'll be in touch." She disconnected, her eyes never leaving the SUV. She hadn't previously seen it in the few times she'd been in the apartment, and it certainly didn't fit in with her new neighbors' truck rodeo. The SUV also lacked a front license plate. She figured there were only three reasons for the SUV's presence. One, they were waiting to make a dope deal. Two, they were looking to rob the leasing office, which made no sense since everyone knew apartment offices didn't collect cash anymore. Or three, they were there watching her.

Only Garrison and Barber knew she'd moved into the apartment. She hadn't even told Walker or Cooper yet. She stepped back from the window a tad but continued to watch. After five minutes, the SUV pulled out of the parking space and sped out of the parking lot. She rushed closer to the window and saw a temporary paper registration tag affixed to the rear bumper.

Same as the SUV in Coop's shooting.

She tapped the contacts icon on her phone, then touched Garrison's name. He answered on the first ring.

"Yes, ma'am," Garrison said.

"I just received a visit from a black SUV with temp tags," Fernandez reported.

"You get a look at anyone?"

"Nope. Never got out of the vehicle."

"I'm on the way," Garrison stated, and the line clicked dead.

CHAPTER 55

TUESDAY

Garrison pulled into the apartment complex parking lot and parked two spaces away from Fernandez's Charger. He carefully scanned the area before exiting his truck. She met him at the top of the stairwell, nodding toward the corner of the parking lot where the green dumpster sat.

"Parked over there next to the dumpster for about five minutes, then left in a hurry," Fernandez said.

Garrison glanced that way, then back to her. "You can't stay here."

"I figured you'd say that. But no way…This is a perfect opportunity to catch these assholes," she insisted. "We'll sit here and wait for them to return, then—"

"And risk your life? No chance in hell. As it is, I nearly got a nice kid killed," Garrison said.

"I'm no kid," Fernandez calmly said with a grin. "If we were back in Houston, you'd agree with me."

"Well, we're not back in Houston. I'm the chief now, and I can't recklessly expose my officers," he said as they walked to her apartment.

Fernandez locked the door behind them, then waved toward her folding chairs.

"Please, make yourself comfortable," she snickered.

Garrison sat down and looked at the card table "Three more chairs, and this would be a perfect poker joint," he said, trying to lighten the mood.

Fernandez set a bottle of water in front of him and took the other seat. "How'd your visit with Jordan go?"

"About as expected. He denied knowing anything, boasted he'd not just *try* to kill my officer, and he threatened me with an FBI complaint for abuse of power," Garrison reported, then took a long pull on the water bottle.

Fernandez laughed. A lock of black hair dropped over her left eye. She quickly flipped her head, tossing the tress away from her face.

Garrison felt his expression soften as he watched her, remembering times when they'd go out for margaritas.

"I haven't seen you look at me like that in quite some time." She sighed and peeked at him beneath her lashes.

Garrison looked down at his bottle of water. "Well, I'm sorry if I made you uncomfortable. It's just that it's funny when things hit you. With everything going on, I suddenly stopped seeing you as my detective," he stammered.

"And you see me as what instead?"

He looked up briefly before dropping his gaze again. "You know. We've been down this road before."

"Yes, but not when you're sober." She giggled, and he couldn't help but join in.

He held up his bottled water. "Is this all you have here?"

"Yep. Sorry, but you'll have to talk your way out of this without any liquid courage."

"We both know I'll just stick my boot in my mouth!"

"It wouldn't be the first time," Fernandez agreed. "Now, do you want to spend the night with me and see if our friends in the SUV come back?"

The seduction had begun, he thought.

He held up his hands in surrender. "All right, all right, you win. I'll spend the night with you."

"I don't know how I should take that." Smirking, she crossed her arms in front of her.

Garrison's phone buzzed, interrupting the jocularity. It was Billy Mitchell again. This time, he answered the sheriff's call. "Hello, Billy."

His jovial expression vanished as he listened to what the sheriff had to say. His brows furrowed, and his eyes narrowed—everything tightening, including his gut. He hung his head as he took in the words.

". . . Neighbors found her in her driveway after work today. She was shot once in the head," Mitchell reported.

"Okay. Fernandez and I will head your way. Text me the address," he said before dropping the phone from his ear.

She reached a hand across the table. "What is it?"

"They found Colleen Trask dead in her driveway this afternoon. Shot once in the head. Neighbors heard the gunshot and a vehicle speeding away."

"She's the county clerk who found the forged documents," Fernandez said.

"Yep. Our one possible witness who could dispute Hank Dawson's signatures," he confirmed. "Billy's still at the scene. Let's go."

Fernandez stepped into her shoes, grabbed her keys off the counter, and followed Garrison to his truck. When his phone lit up with the address of Kutseena County's latest murder, he handed her his cell phone. He said, "Punch this into Google Maps for me. I know where FM 2171 is, but that's about it."

He spun his tires as he rocketed out of the parking lot and headed west. Twenty minutes after weaving around countless oil tankers, box trucks, and panel vans, they arrived at the somber scene.

Colleen Trask lived in a well-kept white and green double-wide mobile home about two hundred feet from the road. The gravel driveway led from the edge of FM 2171 to a white metal canopy suited to accommodate a single parked vehicle, positioned next to the home. Colleen Trask's blue 2015 Jeep Wrangler was stopped halfway up the driveway. Yellow police tape was stretched around the vehicle.

Sheriff Mitchell was talking to one of his deputies, who appeared to be charged with taking photographs of the scene. As Garrison and Fernandez approached the area, Garrison noticed Colleen Trask's body was already gone. A crimson blood stain marked the driveway's gravel surface where Kutseena County's clerk had died.

Mitchell nodded at them. "Thanks for coming."

"What've you got so far, Billy?" Garrison asked.

"It looks like she stopped short of where she usually

parks. She was shot outside of the Jeep. There's no sign of a struggle or an attempt to run."

Fernandez walked around the Jeep, and Garrison knew she was scanning the area for anything that could possibly be construed as evidence. She stopped and looked at the open carport approximately a hundred feet from where the Jeep had stopped.

Mitchell called out to her, "We can't tell if there was another vehicle in the driveway, but it looks like a set of wide tires crossed over the grass on the passenger side of the Jeep. With the tire size on her Jeep, we're not sure the tracks were hers or from another vehicle. I think the killer was parked under the carport, waiting for her to arrive. When she started up the driveway, they met her vehicle here, and she got out to see what the killer wanted."

"Makes sense to me," Garrison said. "There'd be no other reason for her to stop halfway up the drive and get out of her Jeep."

Mitchell pointed in an easterly direction. "The one neighbor close enough to see or hear anything said she heard what sounded like a gunshot, then tires spinning in the gravel. By the time she came out to look, the vehicle was gone. She walked over and found Colleen lying next to her Jeep."

"What time did the neighbor hear the shot?' Fernandez asked, returning from her perimeter check.

"About quarter to five. Colleen left the office at four thirty, which would put her here at that time," Mitchell confirmed.

Garrison ran through the sequence of events. The

Trask killing and the SUV at Fernandez's apartment had to be connected. "Fernandez, what time did that SUV get to your place?"

"I can tell you exactly," she said before pulling her phone from her back pocket.

She checked her call list. "Called me at 4:48 on the dot. We talked for about five minutes before I saw the SUV pull into the parking lot."

"That would've given them enough time to leave here and go directly to your place," Garrison said.

"What SUV?" Mitchell asked.

"Black Escalade, no front plate. It looked like a paper temp tag on the rear bumper. Parked by the dumpster, waited a few minutes, then left," Fernandez explained.

"Where was this?"

"Coyote Crossing Apartments north of the county buildings. I just moved in a few days ago."

"Same vehicle description as the one involved in your officer shooting?" Mitchell questioned Garrison.

Garrison nodded. "What bothers me is she only moved in a few days ago, and they already knew about it. They've obviously been watching us. Did you find a gun near Colleen's body?"

"No. I don't know if she carried a gun or not. We haven't searched her Jeep yet. Want to stick around while we do?"

"No. We'll get out of your way. I'll call you tomorrow." After just a few steps toward his truck, Garrison turned back to Mitchell. "Oh, by the way, I paid Jordan another visit today."

"Ya did, now, huh? You get anything out of him?"

"He didn't admit to anything, but he didn't have to. Threatened me with an FBI investigation. Talk soon," Garrison said before turning and heading back to his truck.

He and Fernandez got into the truck and sat silently for a moment.

"Why did Barber call you?" Garrison asked.

"Just wanted to know how we were doing."

"He wants to know if I'm losing it, doesn't he?" He shook his head and chuckled.

She smirked. "Something like that."

"Times sure have changed," Garrison said with a sigh.

Fernandez popped him on the shoulder. "Come on. Let's go see if those jackasses have the nerve to come back to my place."

He flipped the ignition and steered back toward the apartment complex.

CHAPTER 56

TUESDAY

Garrison pulled his truck into the small parking lot of a diner across the road from the Kutseena County administration building. The fieldstone structure had been many things over the years, including an antique shop, before an entrepreneur took advantage of the new development across the road and turned it into a diner. Garrison parked as far from the front door as possible, then glanced at Fernandez.

"I'm guessing you don't have any real food at your place," he said in monotone.

"You'd be correct, sir." She snickered.

"I've lost my appetite, but how about we get something to go?"

She didn't answer, just opened the door, and stepped out into the radiant heat. Swinging the door closed, she cautiously looked around the area. The parking lot was empty, but for an old Chevrolet Silverado pickup truck parked on the side of the building. Years of abuse from the unrelenting sun had devoured the Silverado's blue paint, and the windshield had a crack from the mid-roof of the passenger side to the bottom of the driver's side.

Garrison led the way to the front door, which he

opened, allowing Fernandez to enter before he stepped inside and looked around. He'd driven past the diner a couple of times without stopping. The small, single room had red ceramic-tile flooring, white walls, and red and white checkered Gingham farmhouse curtains hanging on the windows. A large black chalkboard, mounted behind a white counter, displayed the day's sandwiches, sides, and soft drink options. A teenage girl with long, dark hair twisted up in a ball on her head, wearing a white apron and a broad smile, stood erect behind the counter.

"Welcome to Hiller's," the girl greeted them cheerily.

"Good afternoon, young lady," Garrison responded.

"What can I get for you?"

Garrison and Fernandez paused and looked over the chalkboard menu.

"First time in, not sure," Fernandez advised.

The girl explained each item on the board, then recommended a couple of diner specialties. They placed their orders and grabbed two chairs at a small table in front of the window. The view from the diner captured the entire county campus, which included the administration building where Colleen Trask had worked. After a moment, Garrison walked back to the counter where the girl was busy wrapping up two sandwiches.

"Excuse me. Have there been any strangers in here recently?"

She immediately stopped and nodded. "Yes, sir. The same two guys were in here earlier today and a couple of days ago."

"What'd they look like?" Garrison prodded.

"They were both big and mean-looking white guys," was her matter-of-fact response.

"Mean looking?" Garrison asked.

"Ya, they were taller than you with short beards, big muscles."

"Do you recall what they were wearing, and did you see their car?'

The girl paused, chewing on her lip, and staring down at the polished countertop, apparently thinking hard about it. "Black pants like the police wear sometimes. You know, the kind with lots of pockets and zippers. And tan vests."

"Did you see their vehicle?" Garrison nudged.

"I'm pretty sure it was a one of them big ole' black SUVs, like a Tahoe or Escalade."

Fernandez had joined them just then. "Did they ask you any questions about the people who work across the road?" she asked.

"No, but they didn't order anything to eat. Just a couple of cokes and sat at the same table you are." A man in a greasy apron brought their bag of food to the counter, and the girl snatched it and gave it to Fernandez.

"Thank you very much for the information," Garrison said.

"Aren't you the Bison police chief?" the girl asked.

"Yes, I am. Have we met?"

The girl smiled, her ashen face blushing a light crimson. "Yes, sir. I was one of the gang who found the dead guy at the old gas station," she replied.

"That's right . . . now I remember. How are you doing?"

"Ya. I'm okay. It freaked me out at first, but I'm all right now," she said.

"I'm glad to hear that," Garrison offered, then turned to leave.

"You catch who did it yet?"

"Not yet," Fernandez answered before following Garrison out of the diner.

Once inside the privacy of Garrison's truck, Fernandez snapped her seat belt on and said,

"Pretty obvious, isn't it?'

"Yep. It sounds like two ex-soldiers or some half-ass militia types turned assassins. The question is, who hired them? Also, where are they now?"

"We know who hired them, and I figure they'll show up at my place sometime tonight," Fernandez answered. "Let's go wait for them."

Garrison sat quietly for a moment, pondering his next move. He still wasn't certain using Fernandez as bait was the best plan, but he knew it was probably the best way to catch the bastards. In his mind, he scanned the parking lot and area surrounding Fernandez's apartment complex. He recalled a cluster of trees near a stock tank in the pasture on the east side of the building. He could hide his truck in the trees, and they could watch Fernandez's apartment from there. If and when her visitors arrived, they could monitor their movements, then tactically approach in the dark.

He turned to Fernandez. "Okay, here's what we'll do ..."

He described his plan, then put the truck in gear and

headed for the pasture. Halfway to their destination, Amanda called.

"Everything all right?" Garrison skipped the salutations and went right to business.

"Well, yes and no. I'm fine, but Walker fought with a drunk at the Pumpjack and cut his hand. He turned the suspect over to the deputies, then went to the medical center for stitches. He told me not to bother you, but I figured you should know since we don't have Coop available," Amanda reported.

"Okay. Thanks for letting me know. I'll call Mitchell and have his deputies cover our calls for the rest of the night. Also, go home, and that's an order."

"Yes, sir! On my way out the door," Amanda promised her boss, then said goodbye.

"I need at least two more officers if we're supposed to handle investigations and these dumb-ass calls," Garrison groused.

He dialed Walker and checked on his condition, which Walker assured was no problem, then parked his truck inside the tree shroud that would conceal their position. Garrison handed Fernandez a sandwich, then adjusted his binoculars. The front door to Fernandez's apartment went from a blurred mess to a crystal-clear vision where he could read the number on the door.

"It's scary how well these things work," Garrison mumbled.

"Now, I just hope those assholes show up," Fernandez chimed in before taking a bite out of her dinner.

CHAPTER 57

WEDNESDAY

Garrison clicked the ignition off. The engine stopped, bringing the sound of silence into the truck's cab. He lowered his window just a smidge, and Fernandez did the same, allowing an entourage of endless insect chatter to fill their tomb of silence.

"I figure I'll qualify for hazard pay once the heat takes over here," Fernandez said through a mouthful of sandwich.

"Not to mention the mosquitos," Garrison said flatly.

"I didn't think there were mosquitos out here in West Texas."

Garrison kept his binoculars fixed on the apartment complex. "Me neither, but I was sadly mistaken."

"You think they'll have the guts to come back in the daylight?"

"Daylight didn't stop them from killing Trask," Garrison solemnly quipped before setting the binoculars on the dashboard.

Fernandez held out Garrison's sandwich. He looked at it, then halfheartedly accepted the roast beef and Swiss cheese wrapped in thin white paper. He unwrapped the top half, folding the rest underneath to keep the mustard from dripping onto his lap.

"That's not bad," he admitted after swallowing the first bite. "I don't remember the last time I ate something. The only thing that would improve it would be an ice-cold beer."

Fernandez laughed. "Yeah, well, I like you better when you're drinking frozen margaritas."

"That's because those damn things are like drinking truth serum."

"Yep. They get you telling the truth, all right!" She continued laughing, even as she attacked her sandwich.

"What? I'm no liar," Garrison insisted.

"That's not what I mean, and you know it. You only let people get to know you after you've had a few."

"Now you sound like my ex-wife."

"Don't you dare compare me to your former spouse, John Garrison!" Fernandez shot back.

After a few more jabs back and forth, they finished their meal and settled into their seats, preparing for what they believed would be a long night.

Garrison peered through his binoculars for the umpteenth time in an hour and watched a cowboy park his truck near Maria's Charger. The man then stepped out and closed the door while finishing off a can of beer, which he tossed into the truck bed. Then he straightened his cowboy hat and headed to apartment 106, not bothering to lock the doors of his battered twenty-year-old Dodge Ram.

"Looks like the only neighbors you have are cowboys and oilfield roughnecks."

Maria snorted. "I'm sure. There are ten trucks to every car in the lot every night."

He checked his watch. "Two thirty-five in the morning. Damn."

"Well, everyone who was going to make it home after the bars closed should be there by now," Fernandez surmised. "Now would be the time for our visitors to show up."

Garrison nodded. "Agreed."

Another thirty minutes of sweating and incessant cricket chirping passed before Garrison saw a dark-colored vehicle slowly turning into the parking lot. Its lights were out as it maneuvered through the parked trucks and occasional cars. He kept the lenses on the big SUV as it backed into a space near the dumpster.

"I think our wait is over."

Fernandez scooted forward, closer to the windshield. "I see it."

"Let's see what they do," Garrison muttered.

After several minutes, both front doors slowly opened. One figure dressed in black, including a hood, exited from each side of the SUV. Garrison handed the glasses to Fernandez, who quickly adjusted the focus and watched as the two figures moved quickly from the parking lot to the side of the building, where the dark shadows cloaked their presence.

"They both have pistols strapped to their thighs. Both right-handed," Fernandez reported. "They're in the shadows now. I can't see them very well."

"My guess is they're moving along the side of the building toward your apartment. I'll wait until they get to the second floor, then drive up."

"Well . . ." she started, and they took a few minutes to analyze their options. They decided to wait until the suspects breached Fernandez's apartment door before they'd bolt to the scene, ideally catching both inside the apartment. That would eliminate a foot chase that Garrison knew his wounded knee would not allow.

"They're going up the staircase now," Fernandez said, and Garrison started the engine.

"Let me know when they're in." He put his truck in Drive and waited, his heart pounding, the adrenaline rush exacerbating the sweat pouring from his body.

"One of them just kicked at the door," Fernandez hissed. A few more beats, and she yelled, "Now!" tossing the binoculars onto the front seat and adjusting her holster.

Garrison stomped on the accelerator, pushing the F-150 through the thicket, low-hanging branches, and waist-high weeds. The deep-cleated tires churned up the pasture surface, sending clods of dirt and rock in every direction. In what seemed like an instant, he hit the brakes, sliding sideways onto the grass near the staircase leading to Fernandez's apartment.

Before the truck came to a stop, Fernandez jumped outside the passenger door, gun in hand, running up the iron steps. Garrison bailed out the driver's door on the heels of his partner, doing his best to ignore the biting pain shooting through his knee with every step.

As Fernandez reached the top of the stairway, she instinctively stopped and lay flat against the iron edges of the stairs. A flash broke the dark rectangle of the doorway, followed by the crack of a gunshot. *Crack! Crack! Crack!* Fernandez returned fire, sending three shots into the empty opening.

"Get back down!" Garrison yelled, pulling at her left foot.

Crash! The sound of shattering glass erupted into the night air. Shards of broken glass sailed through the air, glistening in the beam of the building's light towers. In the middle of the explosion, the first black-clad suspect leaped from the second-floor balcony, followed by the second would-be assassin, soaring through the air like a hawk descending on its prey. Both killers hit the ground with a thud, the second screaming in pain as his leg snapped beneath him. The first assassin rolled over and fired toward the staircase. *Crack! Crack! Crack!* Bullets pinged against the iron stairwell, piercing sparks marking the sudden impacts.

Garrison and Fernandez pressed against the stairs, using every inch of cover they could find. Both assassins scrambled to their feet and sprinted to their SUV, the second screaming out in pain with each lunge across the parking lot.

Garrison and Fernandez ran down the stairs and jumped into his truck as the SUV sped past, bullets shattering the back window of the F-150. Garrison started the engine and stomped on the accelerator, making a hard right turn. The rear of his truck swung across the grass and smashed into the iron stairwell, caving in the left rear quarter panel.

"Are you okay!" he yelled as he sped out of the parking lot.

Fernandez rolled across the console, slamming into Garrison's side before she could grasp the dashboard.

"I'm good! Go! Go! Go!" she yelled before pulling herself up and jumping into the passenger seat.

Garrison activated the emergency lights and siren he'd had installed, then flipped on his bright headlights. With the shattered rear window, the siren's deafening yelp pierced the truck's interior, forcing them to scream out to each other. Garrison snatched the radio mike from its dashboard clip and tried to speak calmly—a near impossible task.

"This is Bison PD, unit one. We're pursuing murder suspects westbound on Murphy Road from the Coyote Crossing Apartments. The suspect vehicle is a black Cadillac Escalade, no plate," he reported before handing the mike to Fernandez.

The radio barked with responses from the sheriff's deputies.

"K-C unit 19. I'm en route!"

"K-C unit 29, en route!"

"Bison unit one, I have two units heading your way. We'll notify Sheriff Mitchell. What's your location now?" the Kutseena County dispatcher asked.

"Bison one, still westbound on Murphy Road. Not sure what this turns into," Fernandez announced into the mike.

"That'll be Jackrabbit Road!" K-C unit 29 advised.

"Is every damn road named after a desert animal around here?" Fernandez shouted.

"At least they know where we're at!" Garrison called back.

His F-150 was slowly closing the gap on the big SUV. The suspects were swerving back and forth, crossing over into the eastbound lane, a common tactic to get the police to back off. With no traffic, Garrison decided to chase them until their wheels fell off if necessary. Suddenly, the SUV veered to the right, leaving the pavement, and hitting an open field void of fences. A massive cloud of dust and dirt erupted as the black car rocked and lurched over the uneven terrain.

"Bison one, the suspects have left the road and are heading cross country into an open field. Not sure of our location!" Fernandez reported over the radio.

The suspect's ill-advised tactical move allowed Garrison to catch up to the fleeing SUV. He was now less than two car lengths behind the Escalade, still doing eighty miles an hour. Dirt and rocks pummeled the front of Garrison's truck.

"Hang on!" he yelled to Fernandez, who grabbed the door handle to brace for an impact.

He then sped up and smashed into the rear of the Escalade, causing both vehicles to swerve back and forth. He knew this tactic wasn't the best, but he figured he couldn't maneuver his truck into position to "PIT" the Escalade.

"Bison one, what's your location?" the dispatcher asked.

"Still moving across open land, heading northwest," Fernandez reported, failing to keep her head from banging against the truck's roof. "We're coming up to a dirt road."

The Escalade hit a depression and then bounced up onto the dirt road. The driver kept the rear end from spinning around, straightened out, and sped forward on the road. Garrison followed, nearly losing control of his truck. He turned into the slide and kept the chase alive, keeping the SUV's taillights in view.

"We're northbound on a dirt road," Fernandez advised the dispatcher and sheriff's deputies, whom she hoped were closing in.

The dispatcher responded with, "Ten-four, Bison one, you're on Kemper Farm Road heading toward County Line Road. We've notified Winkler County you're heading their way."

"K-C unit 29, I've got Bison one in sight. I'm secondary unit," the deputy advised.

"K-C unit 29, engaged in the pursuit. Bison one, unit 29 will call the pursuit," the dispatcher advised.

Garrison looked in his rearview mirror and saw the red and blue strobe lights approaching quickly.

"A county unit with us," he called to Fernandez. "When I get close enough, shoot out the tires!"

Fernandez said nothing. She hooked the mike over

the rearview mirror and rolled down her window before drawing her pistol. Garrison accelerated, catching up to the lumbering SUV. He pulled over to the driver's side of the SUV, giving Fernandez as much room as the narrow farm road would allow. *Crack! Crack! Crack!* Her third shot blew out the SUV's left rear tire, sending its rear end into an uncontrollable serpentine. Garrison backed off two car lengths as the SUV's driver lost control. The SUV's front end dipped hard, then abruptly turned right, forcing the car sideways. Then it launched off the ground, its driver's side smashing into the rock-hard West Texas clay. It tumbled forward, rolling over multiple times, sending glass, side-view mirrors, and other debris in every direction. Garrison hit the brakes as the SUV came to a rest upside down on its crushed roof.

"Unit 29, the suspect vehicle has wrecked out just south of County Line Road. Get an ambulance en route!" the deputy advised.

Garrison and Fernandez approached the wreckage, Fernandez on the passenger side. Garrison waved at Deputy John Morrison to follow her, then he looked over the sights of his .45 Long Colt revolver into the shattered driver's-side window. A quick assessment confirmed the driver was dead. Most facial bones had been crushed, and his right eyeball protruded halfway out of its socket.

"Dead," Garrison announced.

"This one's moving," Fernandez responded.

"Keep your gun on him," Morrison said before reaching into the wreckage and grabbing a handful of tactical vests. Morrison leaned back and gradually pulled the passenger from the vehicle. Fernandez scanned the interior of the SUV and confirmed there were no other occupants. Deep lacerations shredded the passenger's face, and he was missing numerous teeth inside a bloody mouth. His complexion had a greyish pallor. Garrison and Fernandez exchanged looks. They had seen this more times than each cared to remember. Garrison knelt next to the dying suspect.

"Who hired you? Who do you work for?" Garrison demanded.

The suspect looked up at him. His dilated pupils fixed on Garrison's gaze. A siren sounded in the distance.

"An ambulance is on the way. Tell me who hired you," Garrison pressed.

The suspect reached up and clutched Garrison's arm. Garrison leaned down closer to the suspect's mutilated face.

"Sawyer. Barret Sawyer at Rockland."

Garrison stayed in that position, thinking there might be more, but . . . the suspect was dead.

Another deputy arrived along with a Winkler County ambulance.

"Did he say anything?" Fernandez asked.

"Morrison, let them know both are dead. We'll need the medical examiner out here," Garrison advised the deputy, who nodded and headed for the ambulance and his partner.

"I'm pretty sure he said Barret Sawyer at Rockland. We've not seen that name, have we?"

Fernandez thought for a moment, then shook her head. "Nope, that's a new one."

CHAPTER 58

WEDNESDAY

The air-conditioning unit in the DPS Interceptor was no match for the West Texas sun's heat penetrating the windshield. Garrison sat quietly in the front seat of the state trooper's vehicle. At the same time, a group of troopers and investigators from the Texas Rangers milled about the wreckage of Bison PD's latest entanglement. The Rangers had separated him and Fernandez, who was occupying another trooper's cruiser behind his.

While displeased with the "suspect" treatment he and Fernandez were receiving, he understood its necessity. He'd have done the same—standard operating procedure if he were in charge. Law enforcement shots were fired, and suspects were dead. These investigations always superseded those of criminal activity. He watched Billy Mitchell's arrival and subsequent encounter with one of the Rangers before strolling toward Garrison, who lowered the window and nodded toward the sheriff.

"Hello, Billy," Garrison offered up.

"Raise your right hand," Mitchell said.

Garrison paused, somewhat confused.

"Raise your right hand," Mitchell repeated, his tone firm.

Garrison said nothing, but raised his right hand as ordered.

"Do you promise to uphold the law in the County of Kutseena, State of Texas?" Mitchell asked.

"I do," came Garrison's simple response.

"You're now a Kutseena County special deputy, retroactive to last week," Mitchell advised.

Garrison lowered his hand. "Thanks."

"That'll cover your actions here," Mitchell explained through a frown. "Now, why didn't you advise me about your surveillance?"

Garrison felt what little energy he had left drain from his body. He hadn't even considered that his investigation was outside his jurisdiction and without the sheriff's knowledge or involvement.

"Damn it, I'm sorry, Billy. I didn't think of the consequences. Guess I'm not thinking straight."

Mitchell let the weak explanation pass, saying, "Morrison told me what happened out here. It looks like you got our trigger men."

"Looks like it."

"Were you able to get anything out of the passenger?" Mitchell asked. "Morrison said you talked to him before he bought it."

"He dropped the name 'Barret Sawyer.' Apparently from Rockland," Garrison advised. "I'll have Walker work on it this morning,"

"Hmm. Barret Sawyer. I don't know that name. Probably best to call over to Jason Lee in Ector and see if he knows him," Mitchell suggested.

"We need to get over to Rockland ASAP before this Sawyer disappears," Garrison said.

Mitchell looked back toward the DPS cruiser that held Fernandez, then back at Garrison. "Think you two are up to it?"

"We've been down this road plenty of times, Billy. As soon as the Rangers release us—"

Mitchell interrupted Garrison. "Let me find out what's happening first."

Garrison got out of the vehicle and walked back to Fernandez as Mitchell walked away.

"What the hell's going on? I finished my statement an hour ago!" Fernandez fussed.

"Me too. Billy's finding out now. I just called Walker and gave him the Barrett Sawyer name. I'm waiting to hear back. Mitchell had never heard of him. He suggested we call Detective Lee in Ector. You have his number?"

"Yep. I'll call him right now," Fernandez said, bringing up the contact list on her phone.

"Of course you do!" Garrison chuckled.

She tapped Lee's name and put the phone up to her ear. "Jealous?" she asked through a mischievous grin.

Garrison walked over to Billy Mitchell, who was engaged in an animated discussion with a Ranger.

"Sheriff Mitchell here advised he previously deputized

you. That's convenient," the Ranger spouted. "It's also rather helpful, all things considered."

"I explained our need to get over to Rockland Oil ASAP," Mitchell said to Garrison.

"I'd like to go with you," the Ranger cut in, "but I won't be finished here for another hour or so, and if someone at Rockland hired these two, there's no time to waste. Get going, and that's an order."

"I'll follow you!" Garrison called to Mitchell as he waved at Fernandez, indicating she should follow him, then hurried to his crumpled truck. Its front end was smashed in, its windshield broken, and the left rear quarter panel looked like a rhino had rammed it.

Garrison and Fernandez jumped into the gnarled F-150 and took a final look at the scene.

"In all the chases I've been in, I've never seen one end quite like that," Fernandez muttered.

"Nope," Garrison agreed. "You get ahold of Lee?"

"Yep. He's checking on the guy now. He said he'd meet us at the Whataburger across the street from Rockland."

"Damn! That sounds good right about now!" Garrison blurted.

He started the engine, which, other than a brief, high-pitched squeal of the fanbelt, sounded remarkably good considering what it had been through. He then pulled behind Mitchell, who sped off for what Garrison hoped would be the final piece of their homicide puzzle.

CHAPTER 59

WEDNESDAY

Garrison followed Billy Mitchell's Interceptor into the Whataburger parking lot. A silver Chevrolet Tahoe was backed into a parking space in the far corner. Despite its lack of markings, the Tahoe's essential wheels and spotlight protruding from the left windshield brace screamed government issue. Detective Jason Lee sat behind the wheel, draining an orange-striped, white Styrofoam cup through a clear straw. Garrison parked next to Lee's Tahoe, with Mitchell stopping in front of the Ector County detective. Lee lowered the driver's door window. A wide smile cut through his short, salt-and-pepper beard.

"Good afternoon!" Lee bellowed, his eyes widening when he saw Fernandez hurry around Garrison's truck and approach him.

"Hi, Jason! Thanks for your assistance!" she gushed, rubbing on his exposed left arm.

Lee blushed like a schoolboy. "No problem! Glad to help."

Garrison scrunched his face and peered at Billy with a look of disgust. Billy caught the gaze and laughed, shaking his head.

"That's enough out of you two!" Fernandez scolded the men.

"I miss something?" Lee asked.

Fernandez waved a hand. "Oh, nothing worth mentioning. So, what did you find out about this Sawyer dude?"

"Well, he's an assistant vice president of field operations for Rockland Oil. It looks like he's moved up the food chain pretty quickly. He's only been with the company for two years. He joined Rockland from rival Single Star Exploration and Fuels."

"Any criminal history?" Garrison asked.

"Not much, other than the fact he likes to speed. My source told me he left Single Star under suspicious circumstances, but they didn't know what those were. Stuff like that wasn't always well documented during the pandemic."

"Okay. Since we don't have a warrant, we'll look for the field operations department and go from there. Any better suggestions?" Garrison asked the trio of law officers.

"Actually, we do have a warrant, Chief," Lee grinned. "Two of Sawyer's speeding tickets went to warrant. I have them with me. I also have a copy of his driver's license photo."

Garrison grinned. "Nice work, Detective. Now, let's see if Mr. Sawyer's in the mood to talk."

Although Mitchell was the only official in uniform, he, Garrison, and Fernandez followed Lee into the Rockland

Oil lobby. Lee, whose badge hung in clear view from his neck, identified himself to the guard seated at the information desk.

"Can you direct me to the Field Operations office?" Lee asked the guard.

"I'll be happy to call their office for you," the guard offered, reaching for the telephone.

Lee placed his hand on top of the phone. "No need. Just directions, please."

The guard frowned, then glanced up at one of the security cameras. All four officers followed the guard's gaze to the camera mounted on the wall, then back to the guard.

"Field Operations is on the second floor," the guard said.

"Thank you," Lee responded, then led the group to the elevators.

The bell dinged as the door opened into a large reception area, decorated similar to the one on the fourth floor, where Frank Jordan's office was.

A young woman wearing a dark-green polo shirt with the Rockland Oil logo embroidered in white on the left front was seated at a desk behind a tall sheet of protective glass.

She greeted the foursome with a bright smile framed in satiny, blood-orange lipstick. "May I help you?"

Lee stepped up. "Yes, ma'am. We want to speak with Mr. Barret Sawyer, please. We don't have an appointment, but as you might guess, it's important."

"Yes sir, who should I say is asking?" the woman asked, her smile fading.

"The Ector County and Kutseena County sheriff's and the Bison police," Lee advised.

The woman pressed a button on her phone and paused. "Mr. Sawyer, there are police officers here to see you—" the woman abruptly stopped speaking before hanging up. She looked behind her.

Garrison and the other officers followed her gaze.

Barret Sawyer appeared down the hallway, briefcase in his left hand and a semi-automatic pistol in his right. He fired shots at the officers. *Crack! Crack! Crack!* A hail of bullets smashed into the wall. The glass at the reception desk shattered. One of the bullets hit Lee in the left thigh, knocking him down before he could return fire. Another bullet struck Mitchell in the shoulder, spinning the sheriff around and sending him to the floor.

Fernandez and Garrison dropped to the floor and returned fire down the hallway. *Boom! Boom!* Garrison's .45 Long Colt sent thunderous explosions throughout the floor. The young woman screamed and dove under her desk. Fernandez pumped four 9mm rounds down the hall. *Pop! Pop! Pop! Pop!* The brass pinged off the wall.

Sawyer turned and ran toward a door at the end of the hallway. A man stepped out, frantically looking around. Garrison and Fernandez ceased their fire.

"Get the hell out of the way!" Garrison shouted as Fernandez rushed past him after Sawyer.

Garrison checked on Lee and Mitchell, who shouted "Go! Go! Go!" in unison.

Garrison went. He could hear Lee on the radio, advising that officers were down, then asking for an ambulance and backup. He scampered after Fernandez, ignoring the pain in his knee. Fernandez disappeared through the doorway at the end of the hall—it led to a stairwell. He pushed through the door and descended the stairs, skipping three steps at a time. When he turned on the landing, his damaged knee buckled, and he rolled headfirst down the second flight of stairs. A piercing pain shot through his forehead and left ribcage as his body smashed into the stairs.

Fernandez cleared the first-floor door, which slammed shut in Garrison's face. He jumped to his feet and pushed the door open into the main lobby, where people were screaming and running in every direction.

Sawyer ran through the glass front doors of the building and between the full-sized pumpjack and derrick towers. Sawyer spun around and crouched behind the pumpjack, firing back into the front doors, shattering massive panes of glass in the process. Fernandez slid on the polished floor behind the rotund concrete base of a tall Ficus tree in the center of the lobby. Sawyer shot out of his hiding place and ran into the parking lot. Fernandez quickly gave chase.

Garrison felt nothing now as the adrenaline dump masked his pain. He kept pace behind Fernandez, keeping an eye on Sawyer, who refused to drop the briefcase or gun. Sawyer darted between parked cars in the lot, then turned toward an open patio with picnic tables occupied by Rockland employees who were still oblivious to the gun battle playing out in their building. Sawyer turned toward Fernandez and fired again. *Crack! Crack!* The shots punched two holes in the door of a red Dodge Charger that Fernandez had crouched behind.

Garrison dropped to a knee and raised his .45 revolver up to eye level. *Boom!* His .45 bullet hit Sawyer in the pelvis, knocking him to the ground like a linebacker had drilled him on the gridiron. Sawyer's pistol clanked to the pavement, followed by the briefcase, which cracked open upon impact. Bundles of cash fell all around the man, who thrashed in pain, clutching his gut.

Fernandez rushed forward and quickly cuffed Sawyer's hands behind his back amidst screams, sirens, and shouts from dozens of spectators in the Rockland parking lot. Garrison limped that way as police units from Odessa PD and Ector County pulled into the lot. Fernandez and Garrison held their badges up so as not to be shot by fellow officers.

"Bison PD! Lee and Sheriff Mitchell are inside on the second floor!" Fernandez called out to the arriving officers.

"No, we're not!" Billy Mitchell shouted from the pumpjack.

Garrison and Fernandez looked back to see Mitchell and Lee holding onto each other against the old oil field machinery.

"Sir, are you all right?" an Odessa EMS medic asked Garrison.

"Damn, John, the left side of your face is covered in blood!" Fernandez shrieked.

Garrison looked at her and realized he could only see with his right eye. He touched his forehead and felt a huge gash in his flesh. "Apparently, I'm not," he calmly answered the medic.

Sharp bites of pain made their way back into Garrison's consciousness. His head, ribs, and knee sounded off like soldiers in roll call.

"Can you make it to the ambulance?" the medic asked.

"We can make it," Fernandez answered, pulling Garrison's arm over her shoulder, and grabbing the back of his belt.

"Follow me!" the medic ordered.

Garrison looked back to ensure Mitchell and Lee were being attended to, then limped to one of the three ambulances on the scene.

Fernandez recognized Ector County Lieutenant Bill Zimmerman as he spoke to Lee and Mitchell, who were being loaded onto gurneys. A glance in the other direction confirmed the Odessa officers had secured a perimeter around Sawyer, the briefcase, cash, and pistol.

She left Garrison in the good hands of the medics and walked over to Zimmerman and her wounded comrades. "You fellas gonna make it?"

"I don't know. I may need some serious homecare," Lee answered with a grimace.

Mitchell laughed, then moaned, grasping at his injured shoulder.

"Jason filled me in on what the hell happened

out here. All this for a couple of traffic warrants?" Zimmerman asked with a mischievous grin.

"What can I say, LT? You know us Bison cops," Fernandez countered.

"I'm learning, that's for sure!" Zimmerman said. "OPD will handle the initial report on this, but DPS and the Rangers have already been called."

Fernandez shook her head and sighed. "DPS and the Rangers are still at our crash site," she informed him.

"There's more where they came from, Detective," he uttered with a smile.

CHAPTER 60

MONDAY
(FIVE DAYS AFTER THE ROCKLAND
SHOOTOUT)

The steel door's electronic lock buzzed loudly for a moment, followed by the hammering sound of the lock releasing. The excessive weight of the door resisted Garrison's effort to pull it open. Taking a step back, he leaned back and slowly tugged the door toward him, allowing Billy Mitchell to walk ahead. The two men waited for the door to close and lock behind them before a jail deputy flipped the switch of the automatic interior door. The steel entry door, coated with a thick layer of tan paint, slowly slid open, allowing Garrison and Mitchell to enter the command center of the Ector County Detention Facility. The area contained observation windows and temporary holding rooms, each with a steel door, a waiting bench, and a long stainless-steel counter for what Garrison figured was the booking station. The air smelled of bleach and disinfectant spray. Previously providing their credentials at the facility's exterior security desk, a deputy emerged from the control room and returned ID cards to Garrison and Mitchell before proceeding.

"Right this way, gentlemen," the deputy said as he stepped down the hall. "We have the interview room set up for you already. Once you close the door, the video will begin. The camera faces the single chair opposite the officers' chairs."

Garrison and Mitchell had previously agreed to Garrison conducting the interview since his experience far exceeded Mitchell's in that arena. They entered the modest cinderblock room, which contained a narrow table in the center and three chairs. The room was surprisingly clean and painted the same tan color as the walls in the entrance.

Garrison slowly sat down, favoring his knee and ribs as best he could. Mitchell, left arm secured in a tight sling, occupied the chair next to Garrison.

A moment later, a tall deputy filled the room's doorway. Dressed in a command officer's uniform, he wore captain's bars on the collar of his neatly pressed khaki shirt.

"Good afternoon, men. I'm James Reeves, detention center commander. Barret Sawyer will be here in a moment. His hands are secured in the front. He doesn't have ankle chains since he's having trouble walking."

"That's fine, Captain. We don't expect any problems," Garrison assured the commander.

"He's already signed the appropriate documents and agreed to be interviewed," Reeves added.

"Yes, sir. The Rangers made us aware of that," Mitchell said.

"Surprising, considering what he's in here for," Reeves said before stepping aside to allow two deputies to escort Sawyer into the room and help him sit down.

At five feet, ten inches and one hundred eighty-five pounds, Sawyer had a muscular build, short black hair, brown eyes, and a narrow black goatee. His dark blue prisoner jumper was reminiscent of a doctor's scrubs.

"I'll be right outside," the deputy advised before closing the door.

Sawyer leaned back and stared at Garrison and Mitchell.

"Before we get into this," Garrison began, "I need to read you your legal warning and have you sign my document. I know you've already been through this when the Rangers interviewed you, but I need to make sure you've waived your right to counsel and have agreed to talk to us."

"Understood. I want it on record that I'm cooperating," Sawyer curtly responded before signing the document.

After announcing everyone's name and position on the record, Garrison read the legal warning and had Sawyer sign it before he looked over the list of questions he'd prepared and the stack of photographs he'd brought. Then he lifted his gaze and noticed Sawyer's eyes fixated on the table's edge. Garrison saw what had captured the prisoner's attention. A small ant was slowly making its way along the edge of Sawyer's side of the table.

"There's a lot to talk about here, but I guess I'll start at the beginning," Garrison muttered.

"Your beginning, or mine?" Sawyer asked in a low, monotone voice without looking up from the ant.

Garrison and Mitchell exchanged glances, but neither spoke a word. Garrison let the silence hang in the room.

"You know what kind of a cutthroat business oil exploration is?" Sawyer began. "There are people out there who would punch a hole in every square inch of dirt that sits on top of that goddamned Permian basin. Environmentalists and tree huggers think fracking is the be-all, end-all problem. I know people who'd blow up the whole damn place if they thought it would squeeze another drop of oil out of the ground. If a company doesn't think you have what it takes to produce, they toss you out with the garbage. After Single Star fired me, I decided to up my game."

"Does ramping up your game include murder and fraud?" Mitchell shot back.

Sawyer ignored Mitchell's remark and kept his gaze on the ant.

"We all knew that Hank Dawson's ranch was the largest privately owned patch of dirt around, so every company took turns offering the old man a shit-ton of money, including me. The son of a bitch wouldn't sell. Then I heard that Dawson was considering selling to Clayton Walker's group. Jordan started putting pressure on me to produce, so I looked up Dawson's family tree and found out he didn't have one. That's when I talked to Rockland's director of security. He was driving the Escalade you chased. Anyway, Dustin said he knew a guy in El Paso that specialized in problem-solving. I told him I wanted the problem solved but didn't want to know anything about it."

"Did you put up the money to solve the problem?" Garrison asked.

"Everything costs money," Sawyer flatly stated. "The next thing I know, Dawson's dead, and I have the deed to his property."

"How much of this did Frank Jordan know?" Garrison asked.

"All Frank knew was what I told him. I told him I'd secured the sale of Dawson's ranch—before he was found dead. Jordan knew better than to ask any questions," Sawyer explained.

"How did you account for the money Rockland allegedly paid for the Dawson ranch?"

"That was easy. I just added a false accounts-payable disbursement to the money Dustin used to solve the problem."

"What about the dummy Sutton Land Company?" Garrison asked.

"That was easy. You know how that shit goes. All I needed was a burner phone and a fake email address created with a public computer," Sawyer quipped.

"What was the alleged disbursement?" Garrison demanded, scribbling notes as fast as he could.

"The cost for the ranch was entered as 25 million. Another 200 thousand went to Dustin and Hanlund."

"Who's Hanlund?" Mitchell asked, even though he already knew.

"He was Dustin's buddy, the passenger in the Escalade," Sawyer advised.

Garrison placed a photo of Richard Hardin's body on the table in front of Sawyer.

"Did you hire Richard Hardin?" Garrison asked.

"Hardin was a meth-head burglar. Hanlund knew him from El Paso. I didn't know anything about him until I read about it in the paper," Sawyer mumbled.

Garrison shifted in his chair and paused. He slid a photo of Colleen Trask's body lying in her driveway. "What about Colleen Trask?"

Sawyer paused for a long time. Garrison again let the silence overwhelm the room. The prisoner's demeanor altered from cold and callous to anxious and uncomfortable. His face flushed red, and he squirmed in his chair. He looked away from the Trask photo.

"Dustin told me there was a possible witness that could identify Dawson's signature and blow up the whole damn thing. I told him how he handled that problem was his own business," Sawyer confessed.

"What did you know about the hit on my officer and the drive-by shooting at the sheriff's Department?" Garrison asked.

Sawyer shook his head. "Look, I had nothing to do with that. Those two decided that on their own."

"And my detective?"

"I told you; I knew nothing about that."

Garrison leaned back in his chair and took a deep

breath. He set his pen down on his notepad and looked straight into Sawyer's face. The man refused to look Garrison in the eye.

"All right, I'll just make this simple. Did you hire Dustin, Hanlund, or anyone else to kill Richard Hardin, Hank Dawson, and Colleen Trask?" Garrison asked.

"I told you, I didn't kill anyone," Sawyer rebutted.

"That's not what I asked. I asked if you hired anyone to kill Richard Hardin, Hank Dawson, and Colleen Trask?"

"No, I didn't! I told you I wanted the problems solved! That's all!" Sawyer voice rose with an emotional ping.

"Sawyer, you're no idiot! You knew that 'solving the problem' meant those people would be killed! Didn't you?" Garrison shouted.

"Yes! You're damn right I knew! Killing a meth-head thief and an old stubborn drunk didn't mean anything to me! I needed that ranch!" Sawyer squealed.

"But Colleen Trask was neither of those, was she?"

Sawyer sat back in his chair and stared at the table. "I'm done talking! I'll take my lawyer now!"

Garrison paused to catch his breath. He caught Mitchell looking at him out of the corner of his eye. He nodded, letting Mitchell know he was finished. Mitchell opened the door and stepped into the hallway.

"We're finished here, deputy," Mitchell announced.

CHAPTER 61

MONDAY
(SEVEN DAYS AFTER SAWYER'S CONFESSION)

Under Amanda's supervision, Walker set a super-sized tray of coffee and pastries in the middle of an oval conference table, which Dan Barber had brought over from the town hall.

"Compliments of Ms. Callie Johnson," Amanda announced before taking a seat opposite Garrison. Dan Barber flanked him on his right, and Billy Mitchell on his left.

Walker took a seat next to Fernandez and Cooper. On the table in front of Garrison sat two thick, white binders.

"Please, y'all, help yourselves. We wouldn't want to tarnish the public image of cops and donuts," Garrison said, reaching for a cup of coffee and a glazed pastry. "I understand the last member of this group ran into traffic and will be here soon?" he added, looking at Fernandez.

"Jason just called. He'll be here in a moment," she confirmed.

Moments later, the front door rattled, then opened slowly with the help of an aluminum crutch, and Jason Lee limped into the room.

"I don't believe this entrance is ADA compliant," Lee snickered, prompting a boisterous round of laughs from the group.

"Don't make me laugh! These busted ribs are ruthless!" Garrison said, clutching his left side.

Lee leaned his crutches against the wall and sat in the last available chair. Amanda handed him a steaming cup of coffee before sliding the tray of assorted pastries toward him.

Now all accounted for; Garrison began the meeting. "Even though we're a small department, and with every television, radio station, and newspaper produced west of San Angelo reporting on it, I felt it was necessary to hold this debriefing and cover the efforts of everyone here regarding the solving of three homicides, multiple attempted capital murders of police officers, burglary and a multi-million-dollar land fraud."

"I thought you said this would be a great retirement job," Fernandez chimed in.

"The mayor told me the same thing," he answered with a grin and sharp glace at Dan Barber.

Barber shrugged and shook his head.

"Anyway, our mayor wanted to say a few words before I jump into this," Garrison stated, nodding at the binders.

"As most of you know, I was a Houston cop for thirty years, eventually becoming a captain in the Homicide division," Barber said. "I can honestly say I thought I had seen just about everything in my time at HPD. That said, I never thought I'd see a series of events like we had here, and I am incredibly thankful for the skill, experience, and tenacity of all of you here today."

He paused and looked around before adding, "I did tell John I thought this would be a great retirement job, and I still believe that. Let's hope we've got this bad one out of the way, and we get back to normal around here."

Garrison opened one of the binders and removed a case summary document.

"After the hospital released Sawyer, he surprisingly allowed the Rangers and then Billy and I to interview him. We believe Sawyer thought cooperating would keep him from getting the death penalty. After about an hour and a half, he stopped and asked for his lawyer, but not before we secured his confession. After admitting he unsuccessfully attempted to purchase Dawson's ranch legally, Sawyer confessed to paying his director of security and a hit man from El Paso to, as he called it "solve the problem," which led to the burglary at the county building, the forged documents regarding the Dawson ranch, and the murder of Ricky Hardin, Hank Dawson, and Colleen Trask. We also know those two suspects shot Cooper, the sheriff's building, and wanted to kill Fernandez before they died in the Escalade crash. Sawyer told us Frank Jordan was not involved in his plan, although Jordan's pressure on Sawyer to obtain more land for drilling had started the whole land scheme.

"On a side note, I received a call from the president of Rockland Oil yesterday. He apologized on behalf of his company and, believe it or not, offered me the position of director of security." Garrison laughed.

"Oh? I didn't hear about this?" Barber stammered.

"Well, despite the egregious amount of money he offered, I respectfully declined," Garrison assured his boss with a wry grin.

"Darn right he did!" Amanda chimed in.

"On a positive note, Dr. Finley declared Travis Cooper fit for duty, and we're damn glad he chose to return to us."

The group broke out with loud applause and whistles of approval.

"I also want to thank Sheriff Mitchell and his department for handling our calls for service while we were cracking this case," Garrison added.

"That's quite all right. We were glad to do it, and the bill I gave Mayor Barber for our mutual aid made it all worthwhile!" Mitchell said, laughing.

"I'm sure it did!" Barber exclaimed.

"I've also confirmed with our mayor that based on our recent success and the pending construction project on the south side of town," Garrison said, "I can add another officer to the department. This is especially good news because Dr. Ackerman said since I kept running around on this knee, I now need surgery to repair it. Correct, sir?" Garrison bobbed his head toward the mayor.

"Yes, Chief, that's correct, you can add another officer," Barber confirmed.

"And I also understand Detective Fernandez has been recruiting Detective Lee for that opening. Is that accurate, Detective Lee?" Garrison asked.

Lee swallowed a bite of donut and smiled. "Yes, sir. She has mentioned it, but I don't know if I could handle the pay cut." He chuckled at his own joke.

"We can discuss that at a later time," Garrison advised, trying to hold back a smirk.

Amanda's desk phone rang, interrupting the jovial gathering. Amanda quickly answered the call, jotted down a few notes, then hung up.

"That was Milt from the bait shop. He says he found a body floating in the lake near the boat dock," she announced.

Walker and Cooper jumped up from the table and headed for the door.

"On it, Chief!" Cooper yelled as the two officers ran out of the station to their waiting Interceptors.

"Son of a bitch! You've got to be kidding me!" Fernandez muttered as she pushed her chair back from the table.

"Billy, can you cover our calls until I find out what we have?" Garrison asked the sheriff.

Mitchell waved his hand and smiled at the mayor, who looked up at the ceiling in exasperation.

ACKNOWLEDGMENTS

While this is my fourth novel, it is my first in the crime fiction genre. I'm forever grateful for the inspiration that permits me to continue to write and explore new adventures in the literary world. I wish to thank the people and organizations that have helped me continue to improve my storytelling.

To my wife, Elizabeth, who continues to support and inspire me, offering important feedback throughout the creative process.

To my daughter and biggest fan, Rachel, who has elevated my public relations and marketing footprint in the industry.

To Janet Fix, whose literary production and editing expertise have guided me toward a new path in my writing voyage.

To everyone affiliated with *thewordverve* for their expert participation in the creation of this book

To Christine Baker, to whom this book is dedicated. I would not be where I am today without her encouragement and confidence in my abilities.

To my family, friends, and supporters who continue to motivate me.

And, of course, to the ever-expanding membership in the John Layne posse.

ABOUT THE AUTHOR

John Layne is an international, award-winning Historical Western and Contemporary Mystery Fiction author, screenwriter, and actor. A screenplay adaptation of his second novel, *Red River Reunion,* is currently under consideration for production. He is a member of The Authors Guild, Western Writers of America, Writers League of Texas, Wyoming Writers Inc., and the Oklahoma Writers Federation.

Stay current with news about John's books, movies, and events at www.johnlaynefiction.com as well as these sites:

Instagram: https://www.instagram.com/johnlayne.entertainment

Facebook: https://www.facebook.com/johnlaynefictionbooks

IMDb: https://www.imdb.com/name/nm13445965/

BOOKS BY JOHN LAYNE

John Garrison Mysteries

A Rude Reception, book 1

Luxton Danner Western Series

Gunslingers: A Story of the Old West, book 1
Red River Reunion, book 2
Return to Canyon Creek, book 3

www.ingramcontent.com/pod-product-compliance
Lightning Source LLC
Chambersburg PA
CBHW051429190726
48289CB00001B/119